**Praise for Annelise Ryan and her
Irresistible Mysteries**

DEAD OF WINTER

"Rich and multilayered . . . [Ryan] has a real gift
for creating memorable characters and storylines,
and not letting the several satellite stories
overwhelm her central one. I also found
following a death investigator, a job I'd never
heard of, to be interesting. There's plenty to
enjoy in this novel, and I imagine, plenty to
enjoy in this long series."
—*Mystery Scene Magazine*

"The freezing weather and the ominous scenarios
Mattie encounters make this a chilling tale of
twists and unforeseen happenings, as well as the
unrelenting duties Mattie faces while dealing with
a normal life. An independent, stubborn, yet
feisty protagonist, Maggie is a character others
can relate to and acknowledge a kinship with."
—*New York Journal of Books*

"Fast-paced . . . Series fans won't be
disappointed."
—*Publishers Weekly*

"The indomitable heroine overcomes a crazy quilt
of stories and threads to tackle the problems of
everyday practical living along with the high-
profile crimes she's trying to solve."
—*Kirkus*

Books by Annelise Ryan

The Helping Hands Mystery Series:
Needled to Death

The Mattie Winston Mystery Series:
Working Stiff
Scared Stiff
Frozen Stiff
Lucky Stiff
Board Stiff
Stiff Penalty
Stiff Competition
Dead in the Water
Dead Calm
Dead of Winter
Dead Ringer

Books by Allyson K. Abbott (who also writes as Annelise Ryan):
A Mack's Bar Mystery
Murder on the Rocks
Murder with a Twist
In the Drink
Shots in the Dark
A Toast to Murder
Last Call

Night Shift

A Helping Hands Mystery

Annelise Ryan

KENSINGTON BOOKS
www.kensingtonbooks.com

KENSINGTON BOOKS are published by

Kensington Publishing Corp.
119 West 40th Street
New York, NY 10018

All Kensington titles, imprints, and distributed lines are available at special quantity discounts for bulk purchases for sales promotion, premiums, fund-raising, educational, or institutional use.

Special book excerpts or customized printings can also be created to fit specific needs. For details, write or phone the office of the Kensington Sales Manager: Attn.: Sales Department. Kensington Publishing Corp., 119 West 40th Street, New York, NY 10018. Phone: 1-800-221-2647.

Kensington and the K logo Reg. U.S. Pat. & TM Off.

First Printing: August 2020
ISBN-13: 978-1-4967-1944-7
ISBN-10: 1-4967-1944-1

ISBN-13: 978-1-4967-1946-1 (ebook)
ISBN-10: 1-4967-1946-8 (ebook)

10 9 8 7 6 5 4 3 2 1

Printed in the United States of America

For Joyce and Bill

Chapter 1

"He's coming. He's mad and he's coming for me! Help me! Please!"

The man before me, his huge, blue eyes ablaze with fear and panic, is pacing back and forth, wearing a path through dingy shag carpeting. His hands hang at his sides, one opening and closing into a fist with each step, the other clutching a triangular box from the local Quik-E-Mart. The shape of the box is a dead giveaway, but the tangy smell of tomatoes, oregano, and melted cheese leave little doubt that there's a slice of pizza in that box. It's almost midnight, and the Quik-E-Mart is the only place in town to get any food at this hour. Despite their small size, the stores make very tasty breakfast sandwiches, hot dogs, brats, pizza, and soups. The aroma of the pizza makes my stomach growl loudly, and I hope no one can hear it over the rants of the pacing man, because this is neither the time nor the place.

The man's dark hair stands out from his head in what looks like a cartoonish testament to the fear he's displaying, though this is often what his curly, unkempt hair looks like. I know this because I know him. His name is Danny Hildebrand and he knows me, too, though you might be hard put to prove it right now. If eyes truly are the windows to the soul, one look at Danny's makes it clear that reason and sanity have left that particular building. At least for now.

I take a step closer and the police officer standing next to me, grabs my arm. "Hold back, Hildy," he warns. "This guy is twice your size."

This is a bit of an exaggeration, though not much of one. I barely hit the five-foot mark and Danny is around six-four. He's a big guy, no doubt about that.

"It's okay, Devo," I say in a side whisper, using Officer Patrick Devonshire's nickname. "I know the guy. He's never been violent."

"Still," Devo says, "stay a safe distance back."

I see Devo unholster his Taser and I give him a chastising look. "Please, give me a few minutes before you resort to that."

Devo frowns at me, but he keeps the Taser down at his side.

"Danny," I say, turning my attention back to the pacing man. "It's Hildy Schneider, remember? You and I have met before at the hospital. I'm the social worker there who always works with you. I helped you figure out a problem with your medications just a few months ago."

Danny doesn't acknowledge me with any words

or even a look my way, but his pacing slows almost imperceptibly. I count it as progress. I look over at the woman standing off in one corner, watching Danny with a heartbroken expression, chewing on her stubby fingernails. Her eyes are the mirror image of Danny's, and I idly wonder which parent they inherited them from.

"He lives with you now, Allie, doesn't he?" I ask.

She briefly shifts her gaze to me, nods spastically, and then goes back to watching her brother.

"Is he off his meds again?"

"No," she says with a hitch in her voice. "I help him with them every day to make sure he takes them like he's supposed to."

The man standing next to Allie, a tall, slender fellow, thirtyish, with thinning blond hair, lets out a loud sigh. "He's been doing really well lately," he says, looking at Allie with a sympathetic expression. "We don't know what's set him off, but whatever it is, I don't think he can stay here tonight. His behavior is too erratic. He's clearly unstable and as much as I love the guy, I love you more, Allie. I'm worried for your safety."

"I'm fine, Joel," Allie insists with a look of annoyance.

Joel gives us an imploring look. I don't know who he is, but he is clearly worried about both Allie and Danny, though his allegiance appears to lean more toward Allie. A boyfriend, perhaps? Could that be what's set Danny off this time? I know he and his sister are very close. Could jealousy be playing a role here?

I'm guessing, grasping at straws, and Devo

weighs in with his opinion in a whispered aside to me that is louder than I like. "This guy's off his rocker. A total nutcase."

Danny stops pacing and whirls on Devo, his hands clenched, his eyes wide with desperation. "I'm not crazy!" he yells, spittle flying off his lips. Then, in a quieter but still panicked tone, he looks at me and says, "I . . . I saw his ghost. It . . . it . . ." He squeezes his eyes closed, and his face contorts into a grimace, as if he's trying to crush the memory into oblivion. "It came out of the tree," he blurts out in a panicked tone, half sobbing. "Right out of the trunk!" He slaps his free hand on his forehead several times and stands there, taking huge gulping breaths. His eyes widen. "I saw him get killed and didn't do anything. Now he's haunting me!"

Danny suffers from schizophrenia, so bizarre claims and actions aren't too far outside his wheelhouse when things flair up. He's had these kinds of episodes before and I've seen and cared for him in the hospital ER during several of them, including one that happened just a few months ago. Though in the past he's always been haunted by voices, never actual ghosts.

"You know," I say to Devo, "I think this is a situation where Roscoe might be able to help. He's been effective with Danny in the past."

Devo stares at Danny for a few seconds, indecision stamped on his face. Then he looks at me and nods. "Yeah, okay. Go get him."

I hurry out of the living room and through the front door of the house we are in. Outside, parked at the curb, is the police cruiser Devo and I came in. It's an SUV, and my golden retriever, Roscoe, a trained therapy dog, is in the back. The hatch opens as I approach, no doubt from Devo hitting a button on the remote he has on him. Roscoe, contained inside a large carrier, thumps his tail with excitement when he sees me.

I open the carrier and hook him up to a leash that is kept in the back. Together we head inside and reenter the house without knocking. The tableau I left hasn't changed much. Danny is now squatting on the floor, one hand still palm-slapping his forehead, the other clutching that triangular box. His body trembles and I hear periodic sobs emanating from him. The slapping speeds up and it's almost as if he's trying to knock the demons that are haunting him right out of his head.

I realize the pizza box will need to be dealt with lest it provide too much of a distraction for Roscoe. He's trained to ignore food—or any other items he may encounter—and not eat anything unless he's told it's okay, an important bit of training for a hospital-visiting therapy dog who may come across food or pills in the course of his visits. But that smell is bound to be a distractor if he's too close to it. When I reach Devo, I tell Roscoe to sit and stay, and he does both. Then I walk up to Danny, take the box from his hand—he offers no resistance, which shows me just how out of his mind he must be because I'd die before letting go of a box that smelled that good—and carry it over to a side table.

With that done, I return to Roscoe, who whimpers a little, his head cocked to one side as he watches Danny sobbing on the floor. I undo his leash and quietly say, "Go to him."

Roscoe drops down and does a belly crawl toward Danny, nuzzling his nose against Danny's feet. Danny drops the slapping hand and looks at Roscoe with his tear-stained face. A hint of a smile forms on one side of his mouth. Roscoe sees it, too, and he gets up and sniffs around Danny's face for a few seconds before gently licking one salty tear that's about to drop from his jawline.

I'm not sure how Danny will react to this and my muscles tense. I'm ready to call Roscoe back if need be, but a moment later I see it won't be necessary. Danny reaches up and strokes Roscoe's furry head, eyeing him with affection. With one long, shuddering breath all the tension leaks out of Danny's body. Roscoe thumps his tail, lies down, and rests his chin on one of Danny's knees.

Devo holsters his Taser, and everyone breathes a sigh of relief. As Danny strokes Roscoe's head, I can see that his eyes look calmer and his muscles are more relaxed. After a minute or two, Danny lies down on the floor, stretching his body out alongside Roscoe's.

I look past Danny to Allie and Joel and, with a sideways motion of my head, gesture toward the kitchen, which is just off the living room. I say to Devo, "Let's talk to his sister. He'll be fine, and we can keep an eye on him from the other room."

Devo nods and we all make our way into the kitchen. Allie gestures toward a small table, the surface of which is nearly covered by a large bowl filled with fresh fruit—oranges, kiwis, apples, bananas, and grapes—and says, "Have a seat. Can I get you something to drink?"

"I'm fine here," I say. There are only two chairs around the table, and I figure Allie and Joel might need to sit in them. "I want to stay where I can keep an eye on Danny."

"Me, too," Devo says, positioning himself directly across from me on the other side of the doorway.

Joel walks over to the fridge and says, "I'm going to have a beer. Allie?"

Allie shakes her head. "I'm on call. I'll take a cream soda, though."

As Joel removes the drinks from the fridge, I gesture toward him with a nod and give Allie a questioning look.

"Oh, sorry," she says with an apologetic grin. "I should have introduced you." She gestures toward Joel. "This is Joel Niedermeyer. He's my fiancé." She proffers her left hand and shows me the small diamond on her ring finger, smiling at it for a few seconds before continuing. "And this is Hildy Schneider, the social worker I told you about."

"Congratulations," I say to the two of them. "You are a lucky guy, Joel."

Joel walks over and hands Allie her soda, then comes over to me and extends his free hand for a shake. "Don't I know it," he says with a smile. I take the offered hand, trying not to wince at the clammy wetness of his palm from holding the cold can of soda. "Allie has mentioned you. She says you've been a big help to her and Danny in the past. We really appreciate that."

"Well, that's what we social workers do," I say,

using all my willpower to not yank my hand away from him. When he finally releases me, I quickly wipe my palm on my pants as surreptitiously as I can. What I want to do is run over to the sink and stick my hand beneath a full-running faucet with water as hot as I can stand and then scrub it with soap. It's my OCD kicking in and I work at subduing the urge. I'm so focused, in fact, that I don't hear any of the introductory exchange between Devo and Joel until Joel says, "Hell of a way to meet you folks."

I try to keep my attention on the topic at hand, focusing on Allie's hand instead of mine. "So, when's the big day?" I ask her.

"Oh, I don't know," she says, popping the tab on her drink can. "I need to get Danny straight before I can even begin to think about planning something like that." She looks at Joel and smiles. "Joel is living here with us now, to help out."

Joel reaches over and massages one of her shoulders, then he leans in and kisses her on the temple. "She doesn't accept my help as much as I wish she would," he says, looking at Allie with an adoring smile.

"Tell us what happened," I say to Allie. "What led to you calling us tonight?"

Allie leans back against the counter in front of the sink and takes a drink of her soda, squeezing her eyes closed as she swallows. Joel walks over to the table and settles sideways into a chair, his long legs extended out and crossed at the ankle. Holding his beer in one hand, he raises it toward Allie and says, "Go ahead, hon, tell these people what happened. I would, but I'm not sure I fully understand it." He looks at me and adds, "I didn't hear or see the start of all this. I'm a nurse and I work the evening shift at the Sunrise Nursing Home. I got home right before you guys showed up."

Allie takes another gulp of her soda, and then, with a deep, bracing breath, begins. "Danny came home from a walk about ten minutes before I called you. He takes long strolls nearly every night now, and for a while it seemed like it was helping him, you know?" She gives me a look as if she's appealing for my understanding, so I nod. "Anyway, something clearly happened tonight that set him off, though to be honest he's been off for the past two nights. I could tell something was bothering him and I asked him yesterday, but all he said was that he was tired and thought maybe he was coming down with a cold or something."

"Was he displaying the usual behaviors that precede one of his episodes?"

Allie frowns and shakes her head. "Not really, no. He's been oddly sullen and withdrawn, and he seems to be unusually scatterbrained. That's not like him. Then tonight he came in from his walk and he was all wild and panicky. He was as pale as a ghost, which is ironic I suppose, because he started ranting about seeing one, saying that this ghost was after him, that it wanted him dead."

She pauses, taking another drink of her soda. Then she sets the can down on the counter and crosses her arms in front of her. "He kept saying that he saw someone get killed and didn't do anything about it. And now the ghost of the man who was killed is haunting him." She sighs and shakes her head, a mirthless smile on her face. "I tried to calm him down, telling him there was no such thing as ghosts, reminding him that I should know given my line of work."

Devo looks at me, eyebrows raised in question.

"She works at the Olson Funeral Home," I explain.

"I mostly do funeral planning," Allie tells him. "You know, meeting with families to help them figure out the specifics. Sometimes it's preplanning, older folks who come in and want to make arrangements ahead of time, so their family won't have to deal with it. There's a lot to it from choosing between burial and cremation, picking out a casket, deciding what clothes the deceased will wear, choosing the burial plot location, and of course, the fees associated with all of that. It can get intense at times."

"I can imagine," Devo says.

"Anyway," Allie goes on, "I kept trying to convince Danny that whatever he had seen, it wasn't a ghost. But he kept escalating, and then he started talking about needing to run and hide. The last time he said something like that he ran off and lived in the woods on the north side of town for two weeks. By the time we found him he'd been half-eaten alive by bugs, lost thirty pounds, and his illness was way out of control because he hadn't been taking his meds. We had to have him admitted to a psychiatric hospital for three months to get him back on track, and I don't want to have to go through anything like that again."

"I remember that episode," I say. "It was my first encounter with Danny. And Allie is right. He was in really rough shape that time."

"Maybe he should have stayed in the psych hospital," Devo says, sotto voce, glancing back into the living room. "At the very least he should be in a halfway house where he can be monitored and cared for by people who know what they're doing."

"I know what I'm doing," Allie snaps at him. "I promised my parents that I would look after my brother if anything happened to them. *That's* what I'm doing. Nobody knows him better than I do."

I lean toward Devo and say, "Their parents died in that plane crash in Montana five years ago."

"Oh, sorry," Devo says.

Allie gives him a wan smile. "It's been an adjustment, that's for sure. I swear I've been on top of his meds. I set them out for him and check each day to make sure he's taken them. I use one of those calendar pill dispensers with the days of the week on it to make sure he takes them all. He's usually fine when he's on his meds."

"I remember him saying he didn't like the meds the last time I saw him in the ER," I say. "He said they made him too lethargic. I talked with his physician and asked if there was something different he could try that might lessen that effect. His meds were changed then, weren't they?"

"They were," Allie says. "And Danny was really happy with the new meds. I saw a difference in him. He was perkier and more animated."

"It's possible that the meds aren't working any longer, or that his dose needs adjusting," I say. "I think it would be wise to take him to the ER tonight and get him checked over. Maybe there's something else going on. Physical illnesses can interfere with certain medications and you said he felt like he was coming down with something."

Allie nods, looking concerned. "Think he'll go without a fuss?" she asks.

I glance into the other room and see Danny and Roscoe stretched out on the floor together, Danny slowly petting the dog from head to tail repeatedly, Roscoe on his side, tongue lolling. Both look relaxed, happy, and serene.

"I think he'll go along if Roscoe goes with him. Let's give it a try and see what happens. Will you come with us?"

"Of course," Allie says.

"Do you want me to come?" Joel asks Allie.

She hesitates a moment, and then says, "Why don't you hold down the fort here at home for now. If I need you, I'll call."

"Okay," Joel says, sounding dejected. He punctuates his comment with a long slug of beer.

I turn to Devo. "There isn't room in your car for all of us to ride, so why don't I ride to the ER with Allie in her car and Roscoe can ride in the back seat with Danny. You follow us and meet us there, okay?"

Devo looks unsure of this arrangement. "What if the guy goes off again?"

"He won't. Look at him." Devo does, and I can tell from his expression that he's relenting. "It's what, a five-minute drive at most? We'll be fine, but you can stay right behind us just in case, okay?"

"Fine," Devo says with lingering reluctance. "But you better be right about this. The chief said your safety is our responsibility, so if anything happens to you, my butt is in a sling."

I see Allie give me a curious look. "Yeah, so why are you here with the cops?" she asks. "I mean, I'm glad you are but we don't usually see you outside of the hospital."

"I'm here because it's part of my new job, a second job really, because I still work at the hospital. It's a new program that the police department is launching called Helping Hands and it involves me and Roscoe riding around with them and offering up whatever services might be useful to the community at large, at least the parts of it that are dealing with the police. We can provide counseling, referrals, resources . . . that sort of thing." I pause and glance into the other room at my dog, still stretched out alongside Danny. "And, of course, Roscoe provides his own unique service."

"And a valuable service it is," Allie says, walking over and looking through the doorway at her brother. She studies the tableau for a few seconds and then says, "I think the program is a great idea. And I think you're the perfect woman for the job."

"Yeah, if she doesn't get herself killed," Devo grumbles.

"My brother is not a violent person, at least not intentionally," Allie protests, her hackles rising.

"It's the unintentional that worries me," Devo says.

"I'll be fine, Devo," I insist. "I took that self-defense class, and I have my pepper spray if I need it. But I won't." I've spent the past two weeks going through training for the new job: learning police procedures, taking self-defense classes, and getting taught basic safety measures.

Devo gives me his best skeptical look, one that

says he's smelling cow dung and lots of it. "I know you," he says. "You won't use that pepper spray with your dog in the car, so, don't imply that you will."

"If it's a matter of life and death, I most certainly will," I tell him in my most convincing voice. "But trust me, everything will be fine."

Famous last words.

Chapter 2

Danny is subdued as we walk him out to the car and settle him in the back seat with Roscoe. I strap Danny in, and Roscoe stretches out on the seat beside him, his head in Danny's lap. I don't have the means to strap Roscoe in but given the short drive and the fact that we won't be going much over twenty-five miles an hour, I think it will be okay. Hopefully, Allie is a good driver.

As soon as Allie and I are strapped into our respective seats in the front, she starts the car, backs out of her driveway, and pulls out at a nice, leisurely pace.

"How often do you ride around with the cops?" she says, once we're on the street.

"For now, I'm doing four shifts a week, Thursday through Sunday, from eleven at night until seven in the morning. My hospital hours got cut back some, so I don't work Fridays there now. Overall, the two jobs mesh well. It's going to be a little dicey on Thursdays because I have to work my regular hospital hours and then in the evening, when I could potentially sleep before the cop gig, I have my grief support group. By the time I get done with everything on Friday mornings, I will have been up for over twenty-four hours."

"Yuck," Allie says. "That must be hard to do."

"I'm hoping it will get easier," I say with a chuckle. "Last night was my first Thursday into Friday shift and I managed okay, but I was also excited about starting the new job and I think that gave me a bit of extra oomph. Once the newness wears off, I might have to rethink things. Maybe my grief support group will be willing to change the night we meet to Tuesday or Wednesday."

"Well, I'll say it again. I think it's a great idea to have you riding around with the cops. I know they mean well, but they just don't get Danny and his illness. There have been some difficult and scary confrontations in the past." She flips on her turn indicator—something I'm starting to think is a rarity among drivers these days—and takes a shortcut down a road that backs along the river and skirts along the length of the city cemetery.

I hear a whine from the back seat and I'm not sure if it came from Danny or Roscoe. When I turn to look, I see Danny's eyes widen with fear as he stares out his side window at the cemetery. Crap! Clearly the drive past the cemetery wasn't a good choice given Danny's issues, but it didn't register with me at first, and obviously it didn't register with Allie either.

Danny starts breathing faster, and shallower, moaning slightly.

"Danny, it's okay. There's nothing there," I say, twisting my body around so I can see him.

Roscoe pushes his head higher onto Danny's lap, but there's no comforting him at this point.

"Look!" Danny whispers, pointing toward the cemetery. "There he is." His voice breaks and he is practically whimpering. One hand reaches for the door handle. I sense he's ready to whip that door open and jump out of the car, an insane and illogical move if he thinks the ghost is here. His chances of escape are far better in a car, but logic isn't putting in much of an appearance for Danny right now.

I reach back and take hold of the wrist closest to me, knowing that if Danny makes up his mind to bolt, I won't be able to stop him. But I'm hoping my touch will have a steadying, grounding effect. "Danny, look at me," I say in my best commanding voice. "Right now! Look . . . at . . . me."

He doesn't. His eyes are glued to the cemetery. Allie has slowed the car down to nearly a crawl and I fear she's about to pull over. Part of me thinks that's a smart move in case Danny does try to jump out, but another part of me realizes that we need to get as far away from the cemetery as we can, as soon as we can.

Behind us, Devo turns on his lights.

"Danny, look at me!" I say again, more sternly this time. I squeeze his hand hard to try to break his concentration on the cemetery. This works. He turns and looks at me, his eyes wide with fear.

Beads of sweat have broken out on his forehead, and his color is so pale he looks like a ghost himself.

"Allie, drive." I say. "Get us past this cemetery."

She does what I tell her, hitting the gas and making the car lurch forward. To an outsider watching all of this, it would look like Devo is trying to do a traffic stop, and we, the culprits, have just decided to run. Fortunately, Devo doesn't make any other maneuvers to stop us, though he does keep his lights on. At least he isn't using the siren. Not only might it attract unwanted attention, I have a feeling the sound of it would escalate Danny's panic.

"It's okay, Danny," I say in my best soothing voice. "You're completely safe here. Roscoe is with you and he'll protect you."

Danny stares at me but I don't think he sees me. All he sees are the frightening images playing out in his head. But at least the hand that was on the door moves away from the handle.

"You're safe and you're okay," I repeat. "We'll be at the hospital in another minute or two and then we can get you checked out, look at your meds and make sure everything is the way it needs to be, okay?"

Danny doesn't answer, but his breathing slows and a hand settles on Roscoe's head and begins stroking the soft fur there.

I glance off to the side and see that Allie is turning into the parking lot of the hospital. She pulls up to the entrance to the ER and shifts the car into park.

"We're here," I tell Danny. He seems calm, so I

undo the latch on my seatbelt and turn around to face front. I'm out of the car in seconds and opening the back door beside Danny. Devo has pulled up behind us and he's already out of his car standing next to me. I take Danny's hand and give Roscoe a sideways head nod. Roscoe backs off Danny's lap, rising to a sitting position beside him. I tug gently at Danny's hand and he climbs out of the car.

"What happened back there?" Devo asks.

"Just a moment of panic. We got through it fine. Can you put Roscoe back in your car?"

Devo hesitates, frowning. I'm not sure if he's put out by the fact that I'm giving him directions and not filling him in on exactly what happened, or if he's worried about not accompanying me when I take Danny inside.

"Everything is under control," I tell Devo. I look up at Danny, who is standing beside the car's back door, staring off into space, chewing on the side of his thumbnail. "Ready to get things straightened out, Danny?" I say.

He nods, still chewing, his eyes scanning the surrounding area.

Devo hesitates a few seconds longer, his scowl deepening, but then he sighs and turns to the inside of Allie's car. "Come on, Roscoe," he says, and my dog obediently hops out of the back seat and follows Devo to his car.

I breathe a sigh of relief, whisper "good dog," under my breath, and then Allie and I steer Danny inside to the registration area of the ER.

* * *

An hour later, Danny is lying on a stretcher in a glass-walled room, sound asleep. The curtains to the room are open so the ER staff and anyone else in the area can see him clearly. He's been given a shot of medication to relax him and it's working like a charm. Allie and I are seated in the hallway outside his room and the doctor on duty, Susan Finnegan, is listening to a brief history of Danny's mental health issues provided by both me and Allie. She is new to the doctor's group on staff here and doesn't know Danny the way some of the other doctors and the nurses do. The way I do.

"Typically, when he starts hallucinating and behaving like he did tonight it's because he's off his meds," I explain. "Though his reaction tonight is a little different from his usual. Danny typically has auditory hallucinations, the classic schizophrenic voices in his head. To my knowledge he's never had a visual hallucination before, so that's new. Right Allie?"

She nods, looking worried, and chewing on the side of her thumb the same way her brother had earlier.

"Allie has assured me that she's been checking his pill dispenser every day to make sure the meds are being taken," I go on. "And ever since they changed Danny's meds a few months ago, he's been good about taking them. He tended to stop them before because they made him feel so dead and leaden, but he says the new ones don't do that."

"Just because the pills are no longer in the slots in the pill dispenser doesn't mean he's actually taking them," Dr. Finnegan says. "He might be removing them from the dispenser and flushing them down the toilet. Do you watch him swallow the pills?" she asks Allie.

Allie is staring off into space, her mind clearly elsewhere, and she doesn't answer. Dr. Finnegan looks at me over Allie's head and arches her brows.

"Allie," I say, nudging her with my arm. "Dr. Finnegan asked you if you watch Danny actually swallow the pills each day."

Allie blinks several times rapidly and stares at first me, then the doctor. "Sorry," she says. "And no, I don't watch him swallow them. I leave for work earlier than him so I'm not there to supervise him. Besides, he doesn't like it when I treat him like a child. I do ask him every day and he's said he has. He's not a very good liar and I can usually tell when he's trying to put one over on me."

"Maybe he isn't lying," Dr. Finnegan suggests. "Maybe he thinks he has taken the pills. If he's imagining ghosts and people getting murdered, it's not much of a leap to think that he might be imagining that he takes his pills."

Allie frowns and looks like she's about to say something, but then she bites it back. Her eyes go to the floor.

Dr. Finnegan watches her with a concerned expression. "Do we need to look at placement somewhere for Danny?" she asks softly. "Even if it's only temporary. Perhaps it's not wise for him to be at your house right now."

Allie bristles. "No, I want him home with me. Joel is there to help now and I'll be extra vigilant about his medications and make sure—" Music fills the air, and Allie pulls her cell phone out of her purse. I realize it's a ring tone and recognize the tune as Queen's "Another One Bites the Dust." Allie says, "Sorry, I have to take this call. It's the funeral home and I'm on call tonight."

She hops up and hurries off down an adjacent hallway, her phone to her ear. Dr. Finnegan and I look at one another for a second, and then we both burst out laughing. Once we have ourselves under control again, she says, "Let me know what she finally decides to do. We can let him sleep here for now and reassess in a little while if she needs to leave for a call."

I thank her and wait for Allie's return. Standing at one end of the desk, I shove my hands into the pockets of my bomber-style jacket—a special police-issue item that Chief Hanson gifted me with on my first day—and feel something round and fuzzy. Puzzled, I pull it out and see that it's a kiwi. I must have grabbed one from the bowl on the table at Allie's house, though I have no memory of doing so.

This isn't the first time this has happened to me. Throughout my adult years I've discovered odd pocketed food items from time to time with no memory of how they got in there. My shrinks have said it's a manifestation of my obsessive-compulsive disorder brought about by the lack of control I felt over my own life while growing up. That's because I grew up in the foster system after my mother was murdered, and in several of the homes I stayed in there were certain items and privileges that were reserved for the "natural" kids only and not allowed to us fosters. Food treats often fell into that category. If a foster kid did manage to secure a special food treat, it might get stolen by one of the other kids or confiscated by the adults in the home. As a result, I developed a habit of hoarding and hiding food to protect and preserve it.

I can't blame the foster system for all my quirks. My mother raised me for my first seven years, what the experts consider to be the formative years, but given the fact that my mother was a prostitute and my father was a mystery man who remains unidentified—assuming my mother even knew who he was—I'm guessing my chances at any normal development were slim to none.

I see Allie approaching and shove the fruit back into my pocket, embarrassed and ashamed. Allie has a chagrined look on her face and for a moment I'm afraid she knows I've copped a piece of her fruit.

"That was a work call," she says, and I breathe a sigh of relief. "I need to pick up a body. But the good news is it's a patient here at the hospital up on the floor."

"Then you don't have far to go."

"Except I can't very well pick her up in my personal car. I need to go to the funeral home and grab one of the hearses." She sighs, frowns, and stares at Danny, who looks quite peaceful in his sleep—for now.

"Dr. Finnegan said he can stay here and sleep off the medication they gave him," I tell her. "Why don't you go take care of your work detail and then check back with Dr. Finnegan when you're done. I think she'd be amenable to letting Danny go home with you if he seems okay when he wakes up."

She gives me a meager smile, and her phone, which she is holding in her hand, goes off again, a different ring tone this time. Allie's smile falters and I see hesitation in her expression as she stares at the face of the phone. Finally, with a look of resolve, she answers it.

"Hey, Joel," she says, turning away from me, her voice low.

I listen as she explains to Joel what is going on, stating simply that Danny is doing better with some medication the ER doctor has given him. After telling him she needs to go out on a call, she listens for a long time, then says, "I love you, too," and disconnects the call.

"Everything okay?" I ask her.

She nods. "Joel is learning . . . and adapting. He's been a lifesaver, so eager to help and all, but I don't think he fully realized how difficult things can get. That's why I agreed to let him move in with us. I figured if we're ever going to tie the knot, he needs to know exactly what he's getting into. He's embraced it all without hesitation, but I'm reluctant to let him take on too much too soon. I don't want to scare him off. Having him here has been such a help and relief for me."

"I didn't realize you were dating anyone. How long have you known him?"

"About a year. We hit it off right away and he proposed just a few weeks ago."

I see Devo standing over by the nurse's desk, and he gives me a questioning look as he points at his watch. "I need to go back out with the police officer," I tell Allie. "Danny will be fine here. The ER staff knows him well, and they'll take care of him until you get back. Are you okay with that?"

She nods without hesitation. "We've been down this road before." She pauses and frowns. "Though the fact that Danny's having visual hallucinations, and not just hearing his usual voices, worries me. They've been quite bizarre, more than just the ghost thing." She shoots me a worried look and I know she wants me to ask for specifics, so she can use me as her sounding board.

"How so?"

"Before you and the police officer got to my place, he was saying how he'd watched a man get killed and did nothing to stop it."

"Yes, I heard him say that, too. He seems to think that's why this ghost is appearing to him."

"But you didn't hear all of it. He was very specific about the details of how this man died. He said they put a gun under his chin and blew the top of his head off." She shivers and gives me a worried look. "There haven't been any deaths like that in the area, have there?"

I shake my head. "None that I know of. I'll check with Officer Devonshire to make sure, but I think I would have heard about it if there had been. Heck, in a town this size we all would have heard about it. Gossip goes through Sorenson at lightning-quick speeds."

Another meager smile graces Allie's lips. "You're right." She looks away, then back at me, her smile faltering. "Danny also said that a spotted purple and pink dinosaur watched the murder."

I take a second to digest this. I can tell Allie is scared for her brother and worried about what these bizarre and very specific visual hallucinations might mean in terms of his mental stability.

"A spotted purple and pink dinosaur?" I echo, both amused and bemused. "That's a good one. And you're right, it's a bit different from Danny's usual auditory hallucinations."

In the past, whenever Danny went off his meds, he'd hear voices telling him to do things. Some of the voices were kindly and suggested he do silly things, but others were more frightening, both in how they came across to him and in what they told him to do, things like taking off his clothes and running into the lake in the dead of winter.

"I'll mention the dinosaur thing to Dr. Finnegan," I tell Allie. "Maybe the new meds Danny's on have visual hallucinations as a side effect." This suggestion wins me a hopeful look from Allie.

"Oh, if only it's something that simple." She reaches over and gives my arm a squeeze. "Thank you, Hildy. You've always been so good with Danny and me. We appreciate all your help."

"My pleasure," I tell her, and I mean it. I don't like all my patients, and some I like more than others. Regardless of how I feel about them, I always strive to give them my best. But Allie and her brother have always been high on my list of favorites. I love Allie's dogged determination and the fierce love she has for her brother. And Danny, while cursed with some nasty mental illness challenges, has a big heart.

I'm expecting Allie to leave, but she's still standing there looking at her brother, chewing on one side of her thumbnail the same way Danny had earlier.

"What is it Allie?"

"I have to admit, that ghost thing has me a little freaked."

I dismiss her concern with a *pfft* and a wave of my hand. "The ghost part of Danny's hallucination doesn't worry me nearly as much as the dinosaur. It would be easy for him to misinterpret something like a bit of fog he saw during a period when his emotions were heightened, and his mental status was out of balance."

Allie is staring at me in a most disconcerting way and I can tell she's holding back.

"What aren't you telling me?" I ask her after a few seconds.

Allie looks around us to see if anyone is nearby or listening in on our conversation. Satisfied that we are alone, she leans in close to me and says, "When we were driving by the cemetery on the way here, Danny said he saw the ghost."

"Yes, he did. I'm sure seeing the cemetery triggered it. I don't know what he saw . . . maybe it was something he cooked up in his imagination."

"I don't think so," Allie says just above a whisper. "Unless I'm as crazy as my brother. I saw it, too."

I look at her, my brow furrowed. "You saw what?" I say, thinking I must have misunderstood or misheard her.

"I saw the ghost," she says softly. "It was exactly

like Danny said earlier. An older man's face and body, all wispy and white, easy to see yet with no real substance. And it appeared right out of the trunk of a big old tree in the cemetery when we drove by."

Chapter 3

Allie's revelation is disturbing on more than one
level. While I still favor the idea that she saw something—fog or mist—and her mind simply inter-
preted things the way her brother had described
them, I also wonder if Allie might have inherited
some of her brother's mental illness. She confided
in me some time back that an aunt had had schizophrenia and had killed herself as a result, and
these things can run in families. Granted, at thirty-
something, Allie is a bit old only now to be mani-
festing signs of the illness, which typically present
in the late teens and early twenties. That's when it
first appeared with Danny, and the guy's been
struggling with it for more than a decade now.

I reassure Allie with some verbal gobbledygook
about how our minds can play tricks and make us
see things that are suggested to us when we're
under high emotional stress. It's not complete

nonsense; this can and does happen to people all the time and might have happened to Allie. But something in my gut says this isn't the case.

It looks like further contemplation will have to wait because Devo is telling me that he just got a call from the sheriff's department asking Sorenson for an assist on a call for a welfare check.

"The daughter of a farmer who lives not too far outside our city limits said she hasn't been able to reach her father all day and that's not like him," Devo explains.

"Maybe he took a trip," I suggest.

"Daughter claims the guy is a homebody who never goes anywhere, especially since his wife died four years ago. She says she has a standing call time with him every Friday evening. And since today is her birthday, she's certain her father wouldn't miss the call tonight unless something was wrong. The girls—he has two daughters, both living in Minnesota—are thinking he might be ill or injured."

"Or maybe he has a new relationship in his life," I counter.

"Maybe," Devo says with a shrug. "Either way, this is the kind of call your position is designed to help with. If the guy is hurt, or if he's depressed, or having a mental breakdown of some sort, you can step in. If it turns out to be nothing, I think your presence will help minimize our intrusion to some degree."

"Okay, give me a minute. I'll meet you outside." I check in with Dr. Finnegan and leave my number in case I'm needed for anything more with Danny, though the plan for now is to reassess him when the medication wears off and determine if he's safe to be sent home with his sister.

Five minutes later, Devo and I are back in the cruiser, Roscoe inside his carrier, heading out of town.

"Do you get a lot of assist calls for stuff outside the city limits?" I ask Devo.

"Depends. The sheriff's office shares a lot of duties with us and they assist us here in town when we need extra manpower. We often share investigations, too. Right now, the sheriff's office is short-staffed, so they utilize us when they can for help with things. Something like a welfare check isn't likely to involve any jurisdictional issues unless a crime has been committed. If we find that's the case, then the sheriff's department will need to come out to the site and take charge, though we can continue to assist."

"It's nice that you guys all work together," I observe. "No competition issues between you then?"

"I didn't say that," Devo says with a roll of his eyes. "Things can get territorial at times, especially when there's fun stuff like a big drug bust or a murder. But for the penny-ante stuff, like traffic accidents and welfare checks, it's not a problem."

"Murder is fun then?" I say, giving him an arch look.

"No, that's not what I meant," he says. He squirms in his seat and gives me an annoyed look.

I chuckle at his discomfort. "I get it. You guys are all a bunch of adrenaline junkies. You're like the ER staff and the EMS folks."

"I suppose," Devo says. "Nights like last night drive me a little crazy."

My first night on the new job was a quiet one. The only calls that came in were for a nuisance noise complaint from a man whose neighbor was having a party that lasted well into the wee hours of the morning with lots of loud revelers and pounding music, and a call from a lady who lives along the river and found a huge snapping turtle on her back deck when her dogs started barking and wouldn't stop. Devo informed me that the cops serve as animal control during off hours, so we had to figure out a way to dispatch the critter, as the lady was afraid to let her dogs out into the yard to do their business. Devo picked the turtle up by its tail and carried it down to the river, where he then let it go. The turtle was none too happy about this ignominious dispatch and it tried its darnedest to snake its long neck over its shell and bite Devo's hand while it was being carried, but Devo never flinched. I admit, I was impressed.

Since those two calls were the only ones we had, the rest of our eight-hour shift was spent with Devo driving and me yakking at him about everything under the sun. I downed several high-octane coffees before and during the shift so I could stay awake, and I was wired. I suspect this is why Devo didn't look happy to see me at the start of our shift tonight, though so far we are keeping ourselves well occupied.

He turns off the highway onto a rutted dirt and gravel drive and shifts into park. His headlights had briefly illuminated a newspaper tube and a mailbox with the name Fletcher applied to the side of it in reflective, sticky letters mounted on a post at the base of the driveway. Devo gets out to check them and finds two newspapers in the tube and several pieces of mail in the mailbox.

He leaves them and gets back in the car, steering it up the drive, which takes us toward a weathered old barn with a fieldstone foundation, a common site in these parts. But before we reach the barn, the drive veers to the left and splits off, with one portion leading to the resident farmhouse and another leg going off toward a silo, some other outbuildings, and, eventually, the barn.

The farmhouse is typical for the area: white, two-story, a large propane tank positioned beside it, the exterior of the house showing its age and in bad need of a paint job. I'm betting it's not much better on the inside. All the windows in the house are dark and it appears as if no one is home. Then again, it's nearly two in the morning, so the occupants may simply be asleep.

"Isn't this an odd time to be doing a welfare check?" I ask Devo. "Anyone who is home will likely be sleeping."

"It would be for most people," he says. "but the daughter told the sheriff's department that her father typically gets up around two-thirty or three in the morning, a habit born out of all his years of farming. So, if we wake him at two, it's not that far outside his normal hours. If no one answers we can take a cursory look around, but unless we find something alarming, we'll likely come back later and try again."

The drive forms a circle in front of the house, making its way around a giant old oak tree that I'd bet is a hundred years old or more. Devo pulls up by the front porch and shifts the car into park. He updates our location via his radio and then the two of us get out and make our way up the wooden steps to the front door. There is a screen door that creaks as Devo opens it. The main door has glass in the upper half of it, a lace curtain hanging on the inside. Devo looks for a doorbell but there is simply a hole in the wall where one might have been. With a sigh, Devo knocks hard on the door's glass.

We wait, and I listen to the gentle soughing of the warm night breeze through the branches of the oak tree. After a minute or so, Devo knocks again, harder this time, and he announces that we are the Sorenson Police Department. Still no answer.

I reach down and try to give the doorknob a turn. It doesn't move and Devo chastises me with a "Hey, don't do that."

"Should we go around back?" I suggest. "I'll bet there's another door."

Frowning, Devo agrees, and he leads the way off the front porch and heads around the far side of the house, the part we haven't put eyes on yet. He scans the windows as we go—they are all dark, just like the front windows and those on the other side of the house—and we find one near the back that is open. We round the corner to the backyard, past an older model, rust-scarred pickup parked on the grass, and a sudden gust of wind rises up and lifts the hair off my neck. With it comes a smell that seems to be coming from inside the house, a disturbing, carnal smell with underlying hints of urine and feces. It makes the tiny hairs growing out of my neck rise to attention.

I'm about to ask Devo if he caught the same whiff but I know the answer when he says, "Oh, hell."

There is a back door, a simple, two-step, concrete stoop leading up to it. Like the front door, this one has glass in the upper half of it, but unlike the front one there is no curtain and the glass here is divided into small panes. Devo pulls on a pair of latex gloves that he takes from his pocket, and then he hands me a pair. I pull them on—they are too big for me, but they'll do for now—and clasp my hands in front of me. I know from the training I was required to go through before starting this job that the gloves are as much for my protection as they are for ensuring that I don't contaminate any possible crime scenes.

Devo mounts the steps and shines his flashlight through the glass to the interior of the house. He reaches down and tries the doorknob, but it doesn't turn. With a sigh, he turns his flashlight around and uses the butt end of it to break the lower left pane of the glass window in the door. Then he carefully clears away enough shards so that he can reach his hand inside and undo the lock without cutting himself.

"You should wait out here," he says to me, opening the door.

"I'm okay," I say.

He shakes his head. "Wait out here until I see what's inside."

"I'm fairly certain you have a dead body inside," I say.

Devo shoots me a look that is part curiosity, part perturbation. "How—"

"I smell old blood—lots of it—and excreta. That's not a smell one easily forgets or confuses with anything else. So, the only real question at this point is whether the death is by natural causes, suicide, or suspicious circumstances."

"Right," Devo says, drawing the word out and continuing to look at me with wary curiosity. "And until I determine which it is, you need to stay out here. If this turns out to be a crime scene, I don't need you traipsing about contaminating evidence."

"I have never traipsed once in my entire life," I assure him. "And I was required to go through those police procedure classes before starting this job, remember? I know how to handle myself at a scene."

Devo glares at me, but apparently my look of determination convinces him. "Fine. Just don't touch anything. And stay behind me."

I walk up the steps and follow Devo inside. The smell of death and old blood grows stronger and as soon as we pass through a mudroom, Devo reaches along the wall and finds a light switch. When he flips it, the scene it reveals is a stark one, the kind most people only see in their nightmares.

We are at the threshold of a kitchen and there is a large, oval wooden table in the center of the room. To my right is a big, double porcelain sink and cabinetry that looks like it was built in place about a half century ago. The countertops are blue tile, several of them broken or missing in spots. Dirty dishes are stacked in the sink and there is a dishrack on the counter with a red and white striped kitchen towel beneath it. To my immediate left are more cabinets going to the corner, and against the next wall is an old-fashioned wooden hutch with several drawers and doors in the bottom, a flat work area in the middle, and two cabinet storage areas at the top.

I take all of this in in a split second and then focus my attention on the elephant in the room: the dead man seated at the table. His head is lolled back, and I can see a dark hole in the soft spot under his chin. Tufts of dark hair protrude from his head around his ears, and the top of his head is a bloody mess that appears oddly misshapen, too flat. He looks like the old Dick Tracy villain Flattop. Both of his arms are hanging at his sides and beneath the hand of the right one, the one closest to me, I see a handgun resting on the floor. He is dressed in pajamas. The only sounds I can hear are that of Devo's heavy breathing and the low buzz of flies, several of which are darting in and around the man's gaping mouth and bloodied scalp.

Devo mutters, "Aw crap," and then grabs for his radio to call for backup. Except he doesn't. He hesitates, and when I look over at him, I see that his eyes are focused on the ceiling. He grimaces, swallowing so hard that his Adam's apple bounces spastically for a second. I follow his gaze and see something dark on the ceiling. At first, I can't figure out what it is because despite what appears to be a solid center a couple of inches wide, the sides are very irregular and thready looking. It resembles a paramecium I remember seeing through a microscope in a biology class once. Was it in high school? Or college? *Like it matters.* The mind takes some weird side trips at times like these.

I let my eyes drift back to the dead man, to the odd shape of his head. And then, with a sickening start, I realize what's on the ceiling. It's the top of his head.

I look over at Devo, worried. Rumors run through the police department like rats in a catacomb and one of the ones I've heard repeated several times is that Devo has a weak stomach. It's said to be even odds whether he'll toss his cookies at a grim crime scene and this one certainly qualifies as grim. I feel my own stomach lurch a bit and try to distract myself.

"Think it's a suicide?" I say, hoping to maybe distract Devo some, too.

He doesn't answer.

I divert my eyes away from the ceiling and look back at the hutch. Doing my best to focus on something, anything other than the dead man and that paramecium on the ceiling, I zero in on a whimsical cookie jar sitting at the back of the hutch's middle work area. My gut does another flip-flop, but for a different reason this time.

"Uh, we have a problem, Devo," I say, and I hear the tremor in my voice.

He glances over at me and makes a face. He licks his lips and exhales through pursed lips.

"You okay?" I say. "You're not going to barf, are you?"

"No, of course not," he shoots back irritably. "Are you? If that's the problem, go back outside."

"That's not the problem." I take a few careful

steps toward the hutch, making sure I don't step on any blood or other material, and point to the cookie jar. "This is."

Devo looks at the cookie jar, then at me, his expression suggesting that he thinks I've lost my mind. "I'm not following you, Hildy."

"Remember what Danny kept saying at the house when we first got there?"

"Yeah, he was babbling some nonsense about seeing ghosts. The guy's a nutter. So what?"

"So, when I was talking with Allie some more about it later, she told me about the stuff Danny was saying before we got there, stuff that made no sense and led us to believe that in addition to his usual auditory hallucinations, he might be having visual ones, too. One of the things he said was that he saw a man get killed and a spotted purple and pink dinosaur watched the whole thing."

Devo snorts a quick laugh, but the humor quickly fades from his expression as he looks again at the cookie jar. I'd bet it's an antique, probably dating back to the forties or fifties. The main body of the jar is purple with little pink spots on it, and it has four feet at the bottom. Attached to one end is a green plate and protruding from that plate are three pink horns. Two eyes are painted on the green plate below and between two of the horns. It looks like a cartoonish triceratops.

"I think our gentleman here might have been murdered," I tell Devo. "And what's more, I think Danny Hildebrand saw it happen."

Chapter 4

The little dinosaur cookie jar distracts Devo enough to get him back on track. He radios dispatch and asks to have the sheriff's department send someone out to the site. He also requests the medical examiner's office, at least one more uniformed police officer, and an evidence technician.

When he's done with that, Devo tells me to stay put so he can do a quick check of the rest of the house to make sure it's empty. I do as I'm told, resisting an urge to go back outside where the air is fresh. After Devo returns and declares the house secure, the two of us stand there at the entry to the kitchen, staring at the scene.

"I'm not convinced it's a homicide," Devo says after a moment. "It looks like a suicide."

"It does," I agree.

"Maybe Danny saw the guy shoot himself," Devo suggests. "With as twisted as his thought processes are, he could segue that into a murder in his mind, couldn't he?"

I shrug. It's possible, except I don't think that's what happened here, though I can't support my theory. Yet.

"I suppose that could be the case," I admit reluctantly. "I'll have to talk to his sister and see if Danny had anything to do with this man, or this farm. Why would he even be here?"

"Maybe he's the one who killed him," Devo tosses out in a slightly mocking tone that tells me he doesn't favor this theory. He looks at the victim for a moment and his color pales. Wanting to distract him, I glance around the room.

"What's that?" I say, pointing toward the counter on the far right.

Devo dutifully looks where I've pointed and then the two of us venture slowly around the perimeter of the room, taking care not to step in any blood spatter. The thing I pointed to is on the counter between the stove and the sink. It's a torn square of paper towel with a spoon on top of it, and there is a carton of milk and a half-full bottle of Jack Daniels behind it. There is a microwave mounted above the stove, and when I stand on tiptoe, I see through the glass that there is something inside.

"Hey, Devo," I say. "There's a mug in this microwave and judging from the spoon and paper towel, it looks like our victim was preparing himself a hot toddy. Maybe some warm milk to help him sleep? He *is* in his pajamas. That seems like odd behavior for someone who's about to kill themselves, doesn't it?"

Devo looks down at me with a hint of annoyance. "You probably shouldn't be in here," he says, avoiding my question. "You could be contaminating evidence."

"No more than you are," I counter. "I didn't touch anything and even if I had, I'm wearing gloves. I'm thinking we should probably be wearing booties though, too, don't you?"

Devo glances at his feet, then mine, clearly annoyed now. He gifts me with an eye roll, and says, "Let's both get out of here until the others show up." One arm raises and he points toward the back door wearing a stern expression. "Go."

I go. When I get outside, I take a moment to study the star-studded sky above us. Out here in the country, without any light pollution to speak of, there are hundreds, maybe thousands more stars visible than I typically can see in town. It's beautiful, and a stark contrast to the ugliness inside. There is a light breeze and the mid-May temperature is in the mid-fifties—jacket weather, though many Wisconsinites find these temps more in the range of sweatshirt or sweater weather. Or even just a long-sleeved shirt. Cold tends to be a relative term around here.

"Did you see a suicide note in there anywhere?" I ask Devo after a minute or two of silence goes by.

He shoots me a look and shakes his head. "Didn't look hard for one, though."

I give half a nod, letting him have the point for now, but also making it clear that I don't think he'll find one. Danny's words had been very explicit. He didn't just say he saw the man die, he said he saw *them* kill him. Thoughts of Danny make me want to see how he's doing. "I'm going to check in with the hospital," I tell Devo.

He nods, and I step off the stoop and walk a few feet away as I take out my cell phone and dial the hospital ER. It takes a minute or so to get Dr. Finnegan on the phone, and when I finally ask her how Danny is doing, she informs me that he's still sleeping off the medication she gave him earlier.

"Is his sister there by any chance?" I ask.

"No, she hasn't come back yet," Dr. Finnegan says.

"When she does come back, would you have her call me?"

"Sure." I give the doctor my number even though I'm certain Allie has it.

By the time I hang up, there are headlights coming up the drive. The first people to arrive, one right behind the other, are a county sheriff—a fireplug of a man with a name badge that says P. Carson—and Christopher Malone, the medicolegal death investigator for the ME's office.

Sheriff Pete Carson doesn't look happy to be here and he has a deep scowl on his face as he climbs out of his police cruiser and marches over to Devo.

"What the heck," he says, looking accusingly at Devo, as if he thinks he's the one who killed the man in the house. "I for sure could have done without something like this. Our department is stretched thinner than a tanning deer skin right now."

"Sorry," Devo says. "We'll help as much as we can."

Christopher Malone stands by holding a giant tackle box and listening to this exchange before he says, "Exactly what is this?"

Devo sets about explaining why we're here, what we found, and what we've surmised so far. As he's doing so, two more vehicles come up the drive, a car containing Dr. Otto Morton, the medical examiner on duty, and a white evidence van driven by Laura Kingston, a part-time evidence technician who splits her hours between the police department and the ME's office. I realize things could get interesting if the rumors I've heard can be believed, because I heard one that has Laura Kingston dating Devo.

A minute later, a cop car from Sorenson arrives with not one but two uniformed officers: Brenda Joiner and Al Whitman, a twelve-year veteran of the Sorenson PD and, if the PD rumor mill can be believed, something of an enigma. Al has been a uniformed officer since his first day on the job and has never shown any interest in advancing his career. He seems content doing what he does, and he is well known in town as a reasonable, kind, and friendly officer. He and his wife, Karen, who is a stay-at-home mom, have five kids ranging in age from eleven to two. This makes it even more puzzling that Al has never tried to advance his career and, presumably, his paycheck, but their income is augmented by Karen operating a day care out of their home—five kids apparently isn't enough to have underfoot. Between the two of them they seem to manage nicely. It helps that they live in a house they own free and clear, a huge old Victorian that Karen inherited from her grandmother.

I know all this about the Whitmans in part because of town and PD gossips, and in part because Karen's kids have been in the ER lots of times with the usual litany of childhood illnesses and accidents. I got involved a couple of years ago when one of the nurses in the ER was worried that an injury incurred by one of the Whitman kids didn't fit the story the kid told. The nurse was concerned about potential child abuse and called me after reporting the case to Child Protective Services.

It turned out that the kid's injury— a spiral fracture of the bones in his forearm, a classic abuse injury —really didn't fit the story, but his parents weren't the guilty parties. A neighborhood kid who was known to be a bully was the culprit and his victim made up a story about his arm injury out of fear that the bully in question would come after him again if he told the truth.

The investigation conducted by both me and CPS was a thorough one, though it took a while to get to the truth. In the process, Karen nearly lost her childcare business, Al was put on probation and nearly lost his job, and I made friends with the family because I sensed all along that the injured kid was lying not out of fear of his parents, but of someone else. Thanks to my years in the foster system, I understand the dynamics of childhood better than most adults, particularly those who had privileged, protected upbringings. I'm also good at sniffing out lies.

Both Al and Brenda acknowledge me as they join the group at the base of the back stairs, all of them gloving and suiting up in preparation for going inside. In a matter of minutes, the scene has gone from one of quiet isolation to one of controlled chaos. I want to go inside and watch, so I don one of the paper biohazard suits that Laura has in her van—suits designed to protect the investigators as well as the integrity of the crime scene—surprised that she has one that fits me reasonably well.

"Your build is similar to that of Dr. Rybarceski's," she tells me as she hands me a packaged suit. "So, we have a lot of these in that size."

I take my jacket off and put my suit on, suspecting that I now resemble the Poppin' Fresh Doughboy. No one pays me much attention as we all head inside the house, and I feel a little trill of excitement, knowing that I'm about to see my first official processing of a death scene. It's not exactly what I was hired to do, but I'm sure it will be interesting and educational. One of these days, I'm hoping to be able to solve my mother's murder, and this scenario should be good practice for honing my investigative skills.

If there were family members here, someone grieving, or someone who perhaps might have been involved in the death, then my area of expertise would get called into action. But there doesn't seem to be anyone else living in the farmhouse other than the farmer who owns it and he is, presumably, the dead man. For the moment, I'm little more than an observer.

There is a wallet in the man's overalls that Devo pulls out and, when he opens it, he finds a driver's license. The name on it is Arthur Fletcher, though it's impossible at this point to tell if the picture matches the dead man at the table. However, there is one telling characteristic: a large mole on the right cheek just below the eye. It is present in both the license picture and on the man before us. Another distinguishing mark is a scar, a white gash that traces the arc of the eye socket on the left side of the man's face. This, too, is present in the license picture.

"I don't suppose we can call it official until you guys do your thing and get fingerprints or dental records," Devo says to Dr Morton. Then he looks at the dead man and grimaces. "Though I don't suppose dental records are going to be of much use here. It looks like he shot out half his teeth."

"You mean *they* shot out," I say, and everyone in the room turns to look at me. "There's no suicide note, and he had a toddy heating in the microwave," I explain. I nod my head toward the appliance, and everyone looks there instead.

After a moment, Otto looks at Devo. "Is she right? There's no suicide note?"

"Not that I found," Devo admits. "But I haven't done an extensive search. I think it's too early to be jumping to conclusions." He shoots me a warning look, but I shrug it off. "Maybe it would be best if you waited outside," he says then. "We don't want to risk contaminating the scene if you happen to be right."

I have to give the guy credit. He's come up with a way to punish me while also acknowledging that my powers of observation might well be spot on. Not wanting to ruffle too many feathers this early in my job, I decide to let it go. I need to let Roscoe out for a walk and a pee anyway.

Outside, I strip off my bio-suit and toss it over a barrel by the back door for now. Roscoe is delighted to be released from his pen, though being a good-natured pup, he tolerates it without complaint when he's confined. He makes it clear that it isn't his favorite place to be, however, by skulking into and bolting out of the cage. I'm hoping that in time he'll get more used to it and find it less of an onus.

I decide to let him off leash so he can run off some energy. We are far enough away from the road that it poses no danger, and to keep him from going near the house I walk toward the barn and the other outbuildings, knowing Roscoe will stay close to me. He sniffs happily, wagging his tail, occasionally snorting some dust when he smells something interesting. But as I close in on the barn, he stops dead in his tracks, staring at the building. A low, rumbling growl emanates from him and it makes the hair on both of our necks rise.

"What is it, boy?" I reach down and run a hand over his neck, feeling the tension in his fur. He raises his nose in the air and sniffs several times; then moves forward again. I'm a.bit reluctant to follow him, but he no longer seems to be on alert, so I trail a few feet behind him.

A minute later we are standing at the entrance to the barn, a large, sliding wooden door that is open wide enough for at least two side-by-side cars to fit through. I peer inside, making out odd-shaped shadows in the dark. After a moment my eyes settle on an odd glow of light about fifty feet away that seems to be coming from the floor.

Roscoe looks up at me as if to ask if it's okay to go inside. I glance back toward the house and see light emanating from several windows. The others are clearly busy doing their thing and I can see little to gain in disrupting that process to have them come and check out some unknown bit of light that might be nothing at all. I don't want them to start thinking I'm a scaredy-cat, or that I have an overactive imagination, though the latter is likely a reasonable descriptor for me.

I wish I had a flashlight, and then realize that I do. After digging into my jacket pocket, I take out my cell phone and activate the flashlight app on it. It's not as powerful as a real flashlight, but it's strong enough that it creates a five- or six-foot circle of light around me. Holding it aloft, I cross the threshold, Roscoe at my side. The first thing I look for is a light switch. I turn and shine the light on the wall around the door and find a bank of six switches connected to a web of conduit to the left. I walk over to it and flip the first three switches. A bank of long, fluorescent lights suspended from the ceiling come to life with a few random, sizzling blinks.

The shadows I saw before now take on form. There are hay bales stacked along the wall to my left, tucked beneath a second-floor loft that is accessed by a ladder about twenty feet away. I venture forward several feet and to my right I see four small stalls, each one empty except for a smattering of straw on the floor. Straight ahead is a combine with an attachment that has rows of big, circular blades. Something about it bothers me, but I can't quite put a finger on what it is.

Up beyond the combine the barn extends a good distance and more shadows loom. I go back and flip the other three wall switches, lighting up the rest of the building. I see more machinery, more stalls, and more equipment. And then there's that thin crack of light just beneath that attachment on the first combine that appears to be coming up from below. I approach it, but the crack is too far under those circular blades for me to examine it up close. Still, it's easy to see that there is a cellar beneath the barn, apparently with the lights on. Could someone be down there? I look around for a way to access it but don't see anything.

I listen for sounds of movement or life beneath me, but the cavernous barn is utterly quiet except for the rustle of some small critter in the hay bales that piques Roscoe's interest. I do a slow revolution, taking in the sights and smells, idly wondering what the various tractor and combine attachments are meant to do, and that's when I realize what's bothering me about the equipment. It's clean. Every surface I can see is polished, shining, and lacking so much as a speck of a dirt. They are showroom ready. It's May, prime planting time, and there are fields all around us. I would think there'd be some evidence of this stuff being used.

Roscoe, tail wagging, nose sniffing, is staring at the hay bales and whimpering.

"Leave it," I tell him. "It's probably a mouse, or maybe a barn cat and they can be mean. You don't want to tangle with one of those." Roscoe looks back at me as I speak but he stays put.

I hear a loud *thud* then from the other end of the barn, a noise like a door closing, followed by the sound of running feet pounding on the barn's wood floor. Frightened and ready to bolt back the way I came, I'm about to slap a hand on my thigh in a come-on gesture to Roscoe when the world goes dark. I stand frozen to the spot, waiting for my eyes to adjust, thinking the lights must be on a timer, or maybe a motion sensor. There is a period of silence and then I hear a car door slam and an engine come to life. All of this seems to be coming from the far end of the barn, though it's hard to be sure because of the weird acoustics. The hairs on my arms and along the back of my neck rise to attention and, showing he is in sync with my emotions, Roscoe lets out a low, menacing growl, a ruff of fur rising along the back of his neck.

I turn around and squint, trying to see out the open barn door. There is a pole light down by the house and I can see all the vehicles parked there, none of them running, none of them moving. My eyes have adjusted enough to the dark that I can now see the vague outline of the barn door and I walk toward it as fast as I can, eager to escape the building's confines. As soon as I step outside, I breathe a sigh of relief. That's when I hear the crunch of tires on gravel coming from somewhere behind me. I scurry around to the back side of the barn and look toward the sound in time to see the red glow of taillights disappearing across what appears to be a field.

Somebody was out here, I realize, and it might be the someone who killed the farmer.

Time to interrupt the others.

Chapter 5

I make my way to the back door of the house as fast as I can, looking over my shoulder several times. I hesitate at the back stoop, unsure if I should put Roscoe in the car or let him follow me into the house. Neither answer seems right, so I tell him to sit and stay, and I enter the house alone.

The kitchen is brightly lit and filled with people, little groups of two or three, each one carrying on a conversation. I can't see the victim because both Laura and Doc Morton are standing between him and me, and for a moment the tableau looks as if there's a party going on at the house with several of the guests hanging out in the kitchen having a chat. It's a bizarrely disorienting moment, and I quickly shake it off.

"There was someone here on the property," I say to no one in particular.

Nobody acknowledges me. In fact, no one has bothered to so much as look at me since I entered the room. That overactive imagination kicks in and for a moment I wonder if I'm dead, if I ran into the killer out there in the barn and now I'm nothing more than a ghost, a spirit, the thing of Danny's nightmare, since none of these people seem to be able to hear or see me. I hold my hands out in front of me and stare at them. They look solid and real enough, so I try again, more affirmative with my declaration and a little louder this time.

"Someone was here on the property. Just now. What if it was the killer?"

This time I get the attention I want. They all pause with what they are doing and turn to look at me. It's Brenda Joiner who first seems to get the importance of my words.

"There's someone here on the property?" she says, her hand reflexively feeling for her gun, which is currently hidden beneath her white Tyvek body suit. She hurries across the room toward me with Devo and Sheriff Carson on her heels.

"There was," I say. "It was out by the barn. I heard someone running and then heard a car door close. And I saw a car driving across the fields beyond the barn."

"What did this person look like?" Sheriff Carson asks.

"I don't know," I say with an apologetic shrug. "The lights in the barn went out on me all of a sudden and I couldn't see my own hand in front of my face, much less anything else."

Brenda, Devo, and Sheriff Carson push past me, and I follow them. Outside they shed their body suits like a second skin and then quick march toward the barn. After telling Roscoe to come and heel, I trot after them, struggling to keep up. The three cops stop at the open entrance to the barn and look inside, staring into the darkness and giving me time to catch up.

I show them where the light switches are but, before flipping them on, I also point out the spot of light coming up through the floor beneath the combine. "Look at that," I say, panting slightly. I'm embarrassed by how out of breath I am. "It looks like it's coming up through the floor. I think there's a cellar beneath this barn."

There are grunts of acknowledgment, and then Sheriff Carson walks over and flips the switches for the lights. As the fluorescents sizzle and crackle to life, I'm forced to close my eyes temporarily against the brightness.

"I'll scout the perimeter," Carson says. "You guys check out the interior." With that, Carson goes outside and makes his way around to the front side of the barn.

Devo and Brenda both undo the snaps on their holsters, though neither one pulls their gun. They step inside and without a word they split so that Devo is checking out the left side of the barn where the hay bales are stacked and Brenda is scouting out the empty stalls. They both disappear as they work their ways past the combine toward the other end of the barn. They are amazingly quiet at their task, and the silence feels suddenly ominous. I realize I'm alone and standing in bright light—an easy target. I swallow hard and reach down to touch Roscoe's head for a little reassurance.

Seconds tick by and the night is utterly silent again, the cops stealthy in their work. Then I hear Pete Carson holler from the back side of the building. "Found an entrance."

Roscoe and I hurry out of the barn and around the corner to the back side of the building. There I see Sheriff Carson shining his flashlight on a bulkhead-style cellar door located about halfway down the length of the building. I start toward him and see Brenda and Devo come around the far end of the building. We all meet in the middle.

"Hildy was right," Devo says. "There are fresh tire tracks out there. Looks like there's an old dirt road that runs between two fields. It probably connects to County Road D. And there is a matching set of switches for the lights at the other end of the barn." He looks at me with a sympathetic smile. "I'm guessing that's how you got plunged into darkness."

"There's also a trapdoor in the floor of the barn near that end," Brenda says. "That might be where the person Hildy heard came from. It has a keypad padlock on it, so it can't be opened from inside the barn unless you know the combination."

Carson looks at the bulkhead doors. "These are padlocked, too, but with a more traditional lock. I'm guessing the key is around here somewhere. Though I suppose we could saw the lock off."

"I saw a ring of keys hanging by the backdoor of the house," Brenda says. "Might be worth a try. I'll run and get them."

Brenda takes off at a trot toward the house, leaving the three of us and Roscoe standing by awkwardly, waiting. I feel Pete Carson's eyes on me and after trying to ignore it for a bit, I finally cave and look at him.

"You're the new social worker," he says. I nod. He shifts his gaze to Devo. "How's it going so far?"

"It's going great," I say quickly before Devo has a chance to answer. He shoots me a sidelong look while Carson clucks his tongue.

"She's right," Devo says. "It's her second night and she's already proven herself with a mental health situation. The dog, too."

Carson looks down at Roscoe, who thumps his tail at the attention. "What's his name?" Carson asks.

"Roscoe." At the sound of his name, Roscoe's tail picks up the beat and he grins at Devo, tongue lolling out one side of his mouth.

Carson walks over and puts a tentative hand on Roscoe's head. Roscoe butts his head up into Carson's palm, and then leans against Carson's leg. The effect of this simple encounter is rapid and amazing. I watch as all the tension dissipates from Carson's body. His posture eases, his facial muscles relax, and a hint of a smile forms. The awesome and mighty power of dog love at work.

Brenda's return breaks the moment, and she hands the key ring to Carson, who hits pay dirt with the second key he tries. Roscoe and I back away from the bulkhead doors and both Carson and Brenda take their guns out while Devo grabs ahold of the right bulkhead door in preparation for opening it. He counts down from three with his fingers—the use of silence at this point seems

unnecessary to me, but what do I know—and then
he lifts the door and lets it fall to the side.

Light spills out from below, but no sound emanates from within. After waiting several seconds
to make sure no one and nothing is coming out of
the basement, Devo hurries around and opens the
other door. He then tells me to stay put until he
announces it clear, and then the three of them
make their way down the stairs, guns at the ready.

Roscoe and I wait, tensed, for several minutes.
Then Devo yells, "All clear."

I venture down the stairs, Roscoe at my side,
and enter a large room that, at first, appears to be
separated into two sections. The largest area, in
front of me and off to my right, is filled with
wooden planters sporting hundreds of healthy
plants, fed and watered by an overhead irrigation
system of hoses. Lights in the ceiling mimic day-
light. I realize as I scan the area that there is a
third section down at the end to my right. It appears to be a greenhouse of sorts with plastic
sheeting, grow lights, and heaters.

At the far end to my left, beyond the rows of
plants, there is a small closed-off area with large
glass windows and its own door. At first, I think it
must be a kitchen because I can see a sink and a
stove in the room, but then I notice Bunsen burners, flasks, glass tubing, and other items that suggest it's a lab of some kind.

Most of the plants I see are instantly recogniz-
able by the unique shape and serrated edges of
the leaves. "Wow. It looks like our farmer has quite
the little marijuana farm going," I observe.

"I suppose that's one way to keep the farm afloat," Brenda says. "Make a little extra cash on the side."

"I'm not sure it's for extra cash," I say. "It may be the primary source of income. That equipment upstairs doesn't look very used, and there's no livestock on this farm."

Sheriff Carson gives me an approving look. "That's an excellent observation."

"Thanks," I say, feeling a blush of pleasure. "Do you think this marijuana is the reason he was killed?"

"Illegal drugs and murder?" Sheriff Carson says. "They go together like a hand and glove."

Brenda has wandered down a row of plants that look different from the others. There is a long line of them, bushy plants with red stalks and large maroon leaves.

"These aren't marijuana plants," she says with a frown. "Not sure what they are. And who knows what that stuff is growing behind curtain number one," she adds, nodding toward the plastic sheeted area. "I'm going to get Laura up here to get some pictures and take some samples. She knows plants."

Brenda takes out her cell phone, frowns at it, and then waves it around in the air. "No signal here," she says. She pockets the phone and uses her radio instead to contact Al and request that Laura be sent up to the barn.

While Brenda is doing that, Devo says, "If Mr. Fletcher was killed for this stuff, why is it still here? You'd think whoever killed him would have taken the plants, or at least tried to hide it and his death better."

"Maybe they haven't had time yet," I say. "Do we have an estimate on how long Mr. Fletcher has been dead?"

Carson answers this one. "Doc Morton said the guy is in full rigor. He gave a rough estimate between eighteen and thirty-six hours based on that."

"I don't think our victim was killed because of the marijuana," Brenda says, staring at the red-stalked plants with a frown. "I think there's more to this,"

"Such as?" Sheriff Carson asks, eyebrows arched questioningly.

"Let's wait and let's see what Laura says," Brenda demurs. "She has a degree in forensic botany, and I think she'll be able to shed some light for us."

As if on cue, we hear a "Yoo-hoo" from the area of the bulkhead stairs and then Laura Kingston descends into the marijuana pit. "Okay, I'm here. Oh, boy, it looks like we have quite the pot den down here, don't we? What was our farmer man cooking? Oh, look, a stove! We really could be cooking something, couldn't we? Though I suppose smoking would be more accurate, wouldn't it? I wonder why there's a stove in a barn cellar. Maybe the farmer was processing the plants for the oil? The pot plants are illegal, but the oil can be harvested and sold, particularly if the THC is removed. But you need special permits for that and—" She stops midsentence, staring at the bush beside Brenda. Slowly, her eyes move down the row. She stares at the makeshift greenhouse area and takes off toward it. Finding a gap in the plastic sheeting, she pushes it aside and looks at what's growing behind it. There is a long silence, something that rarely happens when Laura is in the room because she's a total motormouth. Her silence now is telling. And scary. Those hairs on my arms and neck start to rise again.

Finally, she lets the plastic fall back into place and turns toward the rest of us. "Oh my," she says, her eyes big.

"What?" Devo says.

"These," Laura says, pointing to the row of red-stalked plants, "are castor bean bushes. And this," she pulls back the plastic and points to a plant inside the greenhouse area, some sort of tree, "is a nux vomica." She points to other plants behind the plastic. "And these are jequirity bean plants." She turns and looks at all of us, a worried expression on her face. "These plants can be interesting ornamentals, but only one of them, the castor bush, would typically be grown in our area. The nux vomica and the jequirity are tropicals." She makes an equivocal face and shrugs. "Maybe they're being grown here to sell to a garden center of some sort but . . ." Her tone makes it clear this is not what she thinks.

Brenda and Laura exchange a look that makes me nervous.

"But what?" Devo says, clearly impatient.

"Yeah, get to the point," Sheriff Carson says irritably.

"Well, they're also the source for some of the strongest and deadliest poisons known to man: strychnine, ricin, and abrin."

I take a couple of steps back from the plants, tugging on Roscoe's leash.

Laura points to the glass-walled room at the opposite end of the barn. "Given the presence of what appears to be a chem lab along with these plants, I'm guessing the reason for growing them is a nefarious one. I think we have a potential bioterrorism situation in the making here. The marijuana plants are likely a form of financing."

I don't like the sound of this at all and suddenly I'm afraid to even breathe the air in here. Worried for myself and Roscoe, I say, "I'm going to step outside and call the hospital, check on Danny." Devo nods distractedly and I make a hasty retreat.

Walking toward Devo's cruiser, I take out my cell phone to call the hospital, but I can't get a signal. I keep walking, holding the phone toward the sky and waving it from one side to the other, watching for some bars. I'm almost at the house when I finally get two bars. I dial the number for the ER and a nurse answers.

"Hi, it's Hildy. I'm calling to see how Danny is doing."

"He's gone," the nurse says. "Just left, in fact. He went home with his sister about ten minutes ago."

"How was he?"

"Better. He still insists he saw a ghost, but other than that he was alert and oriented and seemed to be living in the real world."

"Okay, thanks." I disconnect the call, put Roscoe in the carrier in the back of Devo's cruiser, and then venture inside the house. I find Doc Morton and Christopher there, working the scene along with Al Whitman. Al and Christopher are busy swabbing blood spatter on the wall and ceiling, and I suspect they will be at it for a while because there's plenty of it. A quick glance tells me the paramecium has been removed, most likely bagged to take along to the morgue with the body. Doc Morton is laying out a special bag on the kitchen floor in preparation for removing the body from the scene.

"Find anything interesting?" I ask.

"Well, you were right about this not being a suicide," Doc Morton says. "There are only scant traces of gunshot residue on the victim's hands. If he'd been holding the gun when it fired, there should be a lot more, but instead, there are void patterns that indicate someone else might have been holding the victim's hands and the gun when it was fired." He pauses and frowns, and I can tell there's something else. I'm about to prompt him when he adds, "And it's possible our Mr. Fletcher was already dead when the shot was fired."

"Really? How can you tell?"

"I won't be sure until I do a full postmortem," he says. "But there are some things that don't add up, like a lack of bleeding in the gunshot wound, the lack of any putrefaction, which should have started by now, and livor mortis—that's the settling of blood—along his back, which implies he died in a supine position and was later moved. Something is off here, but I'm not sure yet what it is."

"Why did you guys steal Laura?" Christopher asks. "I hope Devo isn't playing favorites."

"Playing favorites?" I say, acting dumb even though I know what Christopher is implying. While I'm not averse to listening to gossip—knowledge in this town can be valuable—I try not to participate in its spread if I can help it.

Al chuckles. "Rumor has it he and Laura are an item."

"Oh, right. Well, I don't think that's why they called her up to the barn. They needed her expertise in botany." As I fill them in on what we found, all three men stop what they're doing, and I have their full, undivided attention.

"Potential bioterrorism," Doc Morton says, shaking his head woefully. "That's some scary stuff. I'm betting those plants have something to do with why our Mr. Fletcher here was murdered." He gives the room a wary once-over.

I can't help it. I look over my shoulder toward the back door. At first all I see is the moonlit landscape behind the house. But then a large shadow fills the doorway and starts to move toward me.

Chapter 6

My heart skips a beat before the looming shadow takes on the features of Detective Bob Richmond. I let my breath out in an explosive sigh of relief.

"Hildy, what's going on?" Bob says. "You look like you've just seen a ghost."

I'd say the man has a knack for irony except I don't think he knows about what's gone on so far this evening. "You did frighten me there for a second," I tell him. "And while I haven't seen a ghost, others have."

As Bob steps past me into the kitchen and surveys the scene, I fill him in on my experience with Danny earlier in the evening, our assumption that he was having a schizophrenic episode, and then the realization that the death he said he witnessed might have been all too real.

"He told us he saw it happen," I explain. "And that a spotted purple and pink dinosaur watched the whole thing." Richmond shoots me an amused, skeptical look. "Yeah, yeah, I know what you're thinking, big guy," I say with a wink, and I'm tickled to see Richmond's ears turn bright red. "But don't rush to any conclusions. Look over there." I point toward the cabinet behind our victim where the dinosaur cookie jar still sits in all its purple and pink polka-dotted glory.

Richmond's smile fades and his brow furrows. "So, you think this guy Danny saw our victim commit suicide?"

Doc Morton rises from his bent over position, grunting a little. "Pretty sure it's not a suicide," he says. "There isn't enough GSR on his hands for him to have been the one who pulled the trigger. And while I can't say for sure yet—I need to do the autopsy first—it appears that our victim might have been dead before he was shot."

"Plus, there's no suicide note," I toss out. "And there's a toddy in the microwave. Who fixes a nighttime toddy right before they kill themselves?"

Bob shrugs. "Stranger things have happened. Do we have any ideas about motive?"

"Oh, yeah," I say before anyone else can speak. Bob looks at me with amusement. "You need to go out to the barn," I tell him. "There's a crop out there you'll find very interesting. And a bit terrifying."

Bob arches his brows in curiosity. "Do say. Want to lead the way?"

I don't. Part of me doesn't want to go anywhere near those plants again. Not the marijuana; it's harmless enough. But the others unnerve me.

Knowing how poisonous they can be makes me not want to be near them in any way. But I suck it up, nod, and turn to head back to the barn.

Outside the house, Bob says, "You've certainly started off with a bang. How's the job going so far?"

"Was that a pun?" I say, giving Bob a sly smile. "A bit of dark cop humor?"

Bob frowns, looking deep in thought for a second before I see enlightenment—and a hint of a smile—on his face. "Unintentional," he says.

"Too bad. It was a good one. As for how the job is going, it's only my second shift. Too soon to pass judgment. Though I will say it's nice having Roscoe with me and I think the two of us have made a difference in several people's lives already."

"That's great."

"Thanks again for putting in a word for me with the chief."

"You're welcome."

"Have you heard any, um, feedback about what people think about the program?"

"Can't say that I have." I frown at this and Bob sees it. "Don't be disappointed by that. As you pointed out, it's only your second night. I suspect most folks are going to wait a while to see how things play out before deciding if they're in favor of it or not."

He has a point. I'm desperate for this program to be a success because the position is my dream job. Chief Hanson applied for and received a grant to launch the program as a trial, so I need to make it successful if I want it to continue. Having a social worker ride around with the officers on duty has its risks, but hopefully the benefits will outweigh them. The availability of on-site counseling services alone should prove helpful, to the department staff as well as the community at large.

As soon as I heard about the program, which has been dubbed Helping Hands, I knew I wanted to be a part of it. I used all my powers of persuasion on Detective Richmond to get him to recommend me, and I figured I had a leg up in the qualifications department because I'm not only an experienced social worker with a nicely varied work history, I'm a victim myself. I hoped that level of empathy and understanding would help move me to the top of the list of candidates. Plus, I pitched the idea of having Roscoe, a certified therapy dog, be part of the package. That idea isn't a new one. There are a few other police departments in the country that have started using therapy dogs with the beat cops, though I think our program, with the combined canine and human components, is unique so far.

Because of the tenuous nature of the program, I haven't resigned from my hospital position. As luck would have it, my hours there were cut just before I got the offer from the PD, so it's possible, though not easy, to balance the two jobs. Complicating things is the fact that my boss at the hospital, Crystal Hoffheimer, also applied for the police job. She was interviewed right away—before I was, in fact—and I thought for sure she would get it.

My winning out over my boss had the potential to make things uncomfortable or awkward at the hospital, but so far Crystal has handled it all with good-natured aplomb. I intend to be very careful to make sure the new job doesn't interfere with or affect my old one.

"It's not going to be too much, working both places?" Richmond asks as we walk.

"I'll manage," I tell him. "It will keep me busy and out of trouble."

Bob arches a brow at that comment but says nothing. We walk in silence until we're only feet from the barn. Then Bob stops and puts a hand on my arm, stopping me as well. "There's something I want to ask you," he says. "I know this isn't the best time, but I've been hesitant to call you. I knew your schedule was crazy with the training you had to do and your regular job, and I didn't want to risk interrupting your sleep. Figured I'd see you eventually, anyway, and here you are."

"Here I am," I say with a smile, wondering what this is all about.

He shuffles his feet, looking at everything but me. This is easy for him given that he's a little over six feet tall. He mutters a couple of "ums" and then finally manages to get his words out. "When you and I went out to dinner that one time a few weeks ago, did you invite me simply because you wanted my help with that boy's case?"

"No. I told you I was interested in you on a . . . nonwork level."

He nods, shuffling some more and licking his lips. "I know that's what you said, but I also know that women sometimes say things they think we men want to hear. In order to get what they want."

"Then let me clarify things for you," I say. "Bob Richmond, I would love to go out on a date with you. More than one, in fact. It's going to be hard for me to fit it into my schedule now that I'm balancing two jobs, but let's figure out a way to make it happen. Okay?"

He looks at me finally, smiling in a way that is oddly boyish. It makes my heart do an extra pittypat. "Okay," he says. With that, he turns and continues toward the barn, leaving me to catch up with his long-legged stride.

"Head to the left, toward the back side," I tell him. "There's a cellar door there that will take you where the others are. And that's where your possible motive is, as well."

Though I'm none too eager to go back into that cellar with its dangerous and potentially poisonous payload, my curiosity gives me courage. I follow Bob down the cellar stairs and into the Garden of Evil. There are some brief greetings exchanged, and then I listen as Devo brings Bob up to speed with the entire case, starting with Mr Fletcher and how we found him, and finishing with how Roscoe and I discovered the basement area. At that point, he turns things over to Laura, who is busy snapping pictures and cutting samples from the many plants.

"There are some interesting specimens down here," she tells Bob. "Of course, the marijuana isn't particularly harmful, though it is illegal to be growing it like this without a special dispensation. It's good stuff, too. The guy who grew it has a green thumb, I'd wager, because the plants are healthy and robust. I'm guessing there's enough down here to produce a thousand pounds of pot. He stood to make a good amount of money selling the stuff. Not now, of course. He's dead, and I suppose all the plants will have to be confiscated." She says this with a tinge of remorse in her voice.

"The more interesting thing is the other plants he was growing," she continues without pause. "This is a castor plant," she says, pointing to the red-stalked bush with the maroon leaves. "Its beans contain ricin. Behind that plastic curtain down there you'll find jequirity bean plants, which contain something called abrin that is even more toxic than ricin, and a little tree called a nux vomica, which contains strychnine and brucine, both of which are deadly. I also found some aconite, sometimes referred to as wolfsbane or monkshood . . . also deadly. And several cassava plants, which can be used to make cyanide. So aside from the recreational pot plants, this area is a biological warfare factory. There's enough potential poison in this room to kill a small country's population."

The list of poisons has grown since I was last down here and it's all I can do not to turn and run out of the cellar as fast as my stubby, unfit legs will carry me.

"Now one might argue that our farmer was growing these plants to sell to a gardening center as ornamentals, but the fact that some of them aren't native to and won't grow in this area suggests otherwise. As does that." She raises an arm and points accusingly at the enclosed laboratory area.

Laura pauses in her diatribe then—a rare event for her—but no one tries to jump in. They are all rendered speechless. Laura stares at Bob for a few seconds, then she goes back to snipping cuttings and placing them in evidence bags, resuming her work as if she hadn't just scared the hell out of all of us with her visions of a bioterrorist Armageddon.

"Mother of God," Richmond says. "What the hell was this guy up to?"

"I'm guessing he did it for money," I say. "That is one of the oldest motives in the books, right? Though I suppose we can't rule out the possibility that he's an anarchist."

Bob turns around and looks at me with astonishment, as if he either forgot I'm here and is shocked that I'm still present or is simply surprised that I would say anything.

"You should take a close look at his finances," I go on. "Based on the lack of livestock and how clean the combine, tractor, and all their various attachments are upstairs, I'd wager this place hasn't seen any legitimate farming action for some time."

"Except there are crops planted in some of the surrounding fields," Laura tosses out.

Bob looks thoughtful. The others all return to whatever they were doing before Laura listed off the ingredients for world annihilation, though everyone seems to be eyeing the plants with a new wariness.

"Laura, can you see what you can dig up on the guy's finances when you get done with what you're doing here?" Bob asks.

Laura also has an MBA and is an expert in forensic finance. She had a hard time deciding what she wanted to be when she grew up and entertained career changes several times while working as a teaching assistant for a university professor. As a result, she has acquired an amazing level of knowledge and expertise in a number of areas despite being shy of thirty. Her energy, determination, and intelligence amaze me.

Bob says to me, "You think this Danny fellow witnessed our victim's murder?"

"It sure sounded like it," I say with a nod.

"What connection does he have to this place?"

"I have no idea. I suppose we'll have to ask him. Or I can call his sister and ask her, if you want." I take out my cell phone.

"Kind of late to be calling anyone now, isn't it?" Bob says, glancing at his watch.

"Normally, I'd say yes, but Allie is most likely awake and up. She just took her brother home from the ER a bit ago and she's on call tonight for the funeral home where she works."

"Okay, do it," Bob says. "But put it on speaker. I want to hear."

I look at my phone and see it has no service here. "I'm going to have to go back toward the house to get reception," I tell him. He nods and waves a hand toward the stairs. I climb up, grateful to be back in the fresh air. As I walk back toward the house with Bob following me, I once again wave my phone around in the air, searching for a signal. We are nearly to the back porch before I manage to get a couple of bars. I dial Allie's number and put the call on speaker as Bob requested. After it rings five times, I'm preparing to leave a voice mail when Allie answers with a breathless, "Hello?"

"Allie, it's Hildy. Did I catch you at a bad time?"

"No, I just wasn't by my phone. What's up?"

"How's Danny?"

"He's sleeping right now. He seemed better when I brought him home. Fingers crossed. Sorry I didn't call you."

"That's okay. Do you know if Danny has any connections to a man by the name of Arthur Fletcher who lives out on a farm located between County Roads B and D?"

"Not that I'm aware of. Why?"

Bob shakes his head and puts a finger to his lips, letting me know I'm not to tell Allie anything about what's going on yet.

"I'll tell you more later," I say. "I have an idea about something that might help explain Danny's state of mind, but I can't talk about it yet. I'll call you later this morning to see how he's doing. If anything happens in the meantime, you call me, okay?"

"I will. Thanks, Hildy."

As I disconnect the call Bob says, "Mum's the word on what we found out here, at least with the poisonous plants. I don't want it getting out and starting a panic."

"Got it. And it seems I might have been wrong when I assumed Danny's rants about seeing someone get killed were schizophrenic hallucinations. I'm glad he managed to get away without getting killed himself."

Bob makes a face and cocks his head to one side, looking at me.

"What?" I say.

"You think Danny saw someone kill Mr. Fletcher?"

"It certainly sounds possible. Maybe he was looking in through one of the kitchen windows. Or he could have been in the house somewhere." My mind is racing with possible scenarios until Bob hits on the one I haven't embraced yet, because I don't want to believe it.

"Or maybe," he says, pausing for effect, "Danny is the one who killed him."

Chapter 7

Since it's Saturday, I don't have to worry about getting to my other job on time. It turns out this is a good thing, because we are at the farm well into the morning.

The site became a very busy place after Bob's arrival because he called both the FBI and Homeland Security, and both agencies sent out men of their own. There were guys in hazmat suits, and a series of vans that drove in and parked behind the barn. I couldn't see what they were doing and didn't want to. For now, I preferred to keep my distance from that barn and its evil contents.

I kept myself near Devo's car and Roscoe, letting him out of the vehicle again, but keeping him on leash and as far away from the barn as possible. When Devo finally emerged from the barn to tell me he would take me back to the station as soon as he checked with Bob, who was currently in the house, I was relieved and ready to go. I was dead tired and eager to be away from this place, so I happily loaded Roscoe into his pen and then climbed into the front seat of the squad car to wait for Devo.

Now, ten minutes have gone by, and I'm growing impatient. Relief fills me when I see both Bob and Devo finally emerge from the house, but my enthusiasm flags when I see Bob walk over to my side of the squad car and indicate that I should roll my window down.

"Hildy, I'm wondering if you might be willing to help me out with something this morning."

"What?" I ask with mixed feelings. I'm enjoying this police stuff quite a bit, but my bed is calling to me.

"I need to pick up Danny Hildebrand and bring him into the station for questioning. I understand that his current situation is a bit, um, delicate, and I know you've worked with him and have something of a rapport with both him and his sister."

"I suppose I do," I say, wondering where this is going.

"Would you be willing to sit in when I question him? I think he might be more forthcoming with you. And if you think Roscoe will help calm the guy, we can include him, too."

Every inch of my body is telling me to say no, that bed and sleep is more of a priority right now. But this is what I was hired to do by the police department and since the job approval is only temporary, a trial run so to speak, I figure anything I can do to make it seem more viable, useful, and indispensable is to my advantage. So, against my weary body's better judgment, I say yes. Besides, I do know Danny and his sister quite well and I've invested a lot of time and effort into their lives already. Now is not the time to give up on that.

Two cups of coffee, a bad case of reflux, and a little over an hour later, I am seated in the police station conference room, Roscoe sitting on my right, but faced away from me. Bob Richmond calls this an interrogation room but I have a hard time seeing it as such. I'm in a cushy chair situated at the head of an oblong, faux wood table in a room that looks like it was decorated by someone who did too much LSD back in the sixties. The colors are mostly blues and browns, but the shades within these color families don't match well. The blue in the carpet is a rich royal color but the blue in the fabric on the chairs is more of a turquoise. This might not be so bad if it wasn't for the orange and yellow in the chairs, and the chartreuse and purple in the carpet. Someone's color wheel ran far off the road.

Bob Richmond is seated beside me to my left, his back to the door of the room, and across from him are Danny and Allie, Danny to my direct right and his sister on his right. My seat at the head of the table doesn't signify any type of position or authority. It's simply designed to be a buffer position that puts me between Bob and Danny.

For now, the room is silent. No one is saying anything because we are waiting on one other person to arrive: Danny's lawyer. Bob isn't happy about this. That's obvious from the expression on his face, and the impatient way he's tapping his pen on the tabletop. Allie is leaning back in her chair, her arms folded defensively over her chest, frowning at Bob. Danny is sitting calmly, his only movement that of his left hand as he strokes the top of Roscoe's head, which is currently resting in Danny's lap. No one seems compelled to fill the awkward silence—a surprising situation in and of itself. Most people find such lulls painfully awkward and uncomfortable.

I suppose the current situation is my fault to some degree. Based on the look Bob gave me a while ago, I know he believes that. But I only did what I felt I had to do to protect my patient. Granted, my relationship with Danny in this new role is somewhat murkily defined, but I feel certain it couldn't and shouldn't negate my previous professional relationship with him. It's a topic that will have to be clarified at some point because in a town the size of Sorenson, the odds of me encountering someone I've worked with at the hospital while doing my job for the PD are high.

Devo had driven me to Allie's place when we left the farm so we could ask Danny to come to the police station for a chat. Clearly Danny was a key person of interest in the dead farmer's case, if not a suspect, and it was urgent that Bob talk with him on the matter. Allie had answered the door, and when Devo explained that we wanted to take Danny down to the station to talk about the killing he claimed to have seen, Allie immediately got defensive.

"No one believed him about that earlier," she said, narrowing her eyes at Devo. She then looked at me. "You said you thought it was a manifestation of his schizophrenia. What's different now?"

Before I could answer, Devo said, "We have reason to believe he might have actually seen something. It's important that we talk to him."

Allie, being no dummy, immediately made the connection. "You found someone dead," she said bluntly.

"Yes," I said quickly.

Joel, looking sleepy-eyed and with his hair ruffled from bed, appeared over Allie's shoulder. "Who's dead?" he asked.

No one answered him.

Allie's eyes narrowed as she looked back at Devo. "Do you want to talk to Danny because you think he witnessed something or because you think he may be involved?"

Devo, in an impressive bit of evasive cop-speak said, "It's imperative that we speak to him as soon as possible. Time is always of the essence in these cases. If your brother saw something he shouldn't have, he might be in danger."

I had to hand it to Devo; it was a brilliant response. He'd handily avoided answering the question Allie had asked while simultaneously making her feel the urgent need of the situation. But Allie isn't your average person and she'd been dealing with her brother for too long and under too many circumstances to be so easily manipulated.

"He just got home from the ER, after a supposed breakdown," she said. "I don't think now is the time to be asking him anything." She jutted her chin at Devo in a manner that clearly communicated her commitment. "I wouldn't want anything he might say to be taken out of context," she concluded, arching one eyebrow.

Joel agreed. "Give the guy a break. He's not even sure what's real at this point. It's not fair to be questioning him now."

Devo again stressed the urgent nature of our request. "I know it's not ideal, but as I said before, time is of the essence here. A crime may have been committed and your brother is the best lead we have right now."

I gave mental kudos to Devo once again for referring to Danny as a lead rather than a potential suspect, even though I knew the latter label was likely a better fit, at least in the eyes of the cops.

Knowing that Allie suspected the cops' interest in her brother was more than as a witness, I said, "Allie, would you feel better about Danny talking to the cops if he had someone there to watch out for his interests?" In asking this, I was referring to myself since we hadn't let Allie know that the plan was for me and Roscoe to be present. But my wording put a different idea into Allie's head.

"Yes, Hildy, it would," she said, her face lighting up. "That's a great idea. Let me see if I can get my lawyer on the phone." With that, she spun on her heel and headed off to another room with Joel tailing behind her, leaving me and Devo standing just inside the front door.

Devo looked down at me, shaking his head. "Richmond isn't going to be happy that you did that," he said in a fatalistic tone.

"She misunderstood what I was saying. I was referring to me as the person who would be looking out for Danny, not a lawyer."

"Still, when Richmond hears about it. . . ." He moves his finger across his throat in a slashing motion.

Feeling irritated, I fired back. "Though in hindsight, I think it's a good idea that Danny have a lawyer there. Clearly you guys think he might be a suspect." I kept my voice low, not wanting Allie to hear.

"Well, now we'll never know," Devo whispered back. "Lawyers never let anyone say anything."

I figured that I'd not only mucked things up with my unclear suggestion to Allie, but that I likely had also delayed the talk with Danny. Keeping my mouth shut might have meant getting to my bed sooner rather than later, an appealing thought. But it wasn't to be.

Allie returned to us and said, "Danny and I will be at the station shortly. Our lawyer will meet us there and we will talk to you only after that happens. Okay?"

It wasn't like we had a choice, and so Devo had driven me to the station, where I had to stand before Bob Richmond's withering stare while it was explained how I'd managed to mess everything up. I was tempted to try to defend myself by telling Bob that I felt certain Danny hadn't killed anyone, that his schizoid breaks had never before been violent, but I kept my mouth shut and took my punishment, which was simply Bob's disapproving expression and periodic sighs of frustration. Not so bad, really. And if truth be told, I couldn't swear one hundred percent that Danny hadn't done something bad. I truly didn't think he had killed anyone, but clearly he'd been on that farm and had seen something bad happen, so who was to say how involved he was?

So it is that the four of us—five if you counted Roscoe—came to be sitting in the ugliest conference room I've ever seen, patiently awaiting the arrival of Danny's lawyer. When the door behind Bob finally opens, it's as if everyone in the room breathes a sigh of relief. Even Bob looks glad for the lawyer's presence, at least initially.

The man of relief who breezes into the room has wavy, greasy-looking, strawberry-blond hair, and he's wearing a pale blue suit with a wide collar like the leisure suits that were so popular back in the seventies, making me wonder if he bought it off the rack at the local Goodwill or St. Vinnie's stores. He sidles past Bob, tosses a battered briefcase onto the tabletop, and settles into the chair to Bob's immediate left, looking across the table at Danny and Allie.

"They didn't try to talk to you yet, did they?" he asks.

Allie shakes her head. Danny just stares at the man. He has a glassy-eyed, sleepy look that worries me. I suspect he is still under the influence of some powerful medications.

"Okay, then," the newcomer says. "Let the record show that Danny Hildebrand's attorney of record, Lucien Colter, has arrived. Have you Mirandized my client yet?" he looks expectantly at Bob, who I notice has his eyes closed, his head shaking ever so slightly.

With a very weighty sigh, Bob says, "I haven't said or done a thing, Lucien. Per Allie's instructions, which I gather came from you, we have simply brought them here and let them have a seat. I've had the recorder running the whole time in case you want to question my word on that. I do have a lot of questions to ask Mr. Hildebrand however, so if you're ready, I'd like to begin."

"What are you questioning Danny about?" Lucien asks, reaching forward and undoing the latches on his briefcase. They snap open and he lifts the lid, reaching inside. I expect to see him remove a sheaf of papers, or perhaps a pad and pen, but instead he pulls out a paper-wrapped sandwich from a local restaurant. "You don't mind?" he asks Bob, showing him the sandwich. "I haven't had breakfast yet and I'm ravenous. Have you tried these breakfast sandwiches from Eddies?" he asks, naming a local café. "They're the bomb. I'm fond of the egg, cheese, and bacon on a bagel combo myself. Great way to start the day. Speaking of starting the day, is there any coffee to be had here?"

Bob looks like he wants to hit the man, but instead he mutters, "Of course," through tight, thinned lips. He rises from his chair and exits the room, leaving the door open behind him. I suspect he could have called out to someone else to get the coffee and bring it in, but I gather that he wants and probably needs the break to collect his patience.

Lucien starts unwrapping his sandwich, and the aroma gets Roscoe's interest. The dog lifts his head from Danny's lap and peers across the table, nose sniffing.

"Good lord, is that a dog?" Lucien says in a loud voice. Then he hollers, "What the devil, Richmond? Are you trying to sneak in an illegal search here?" Without waiting for an answer, he takes a huge bite of his sandwich. Bits of cheesy egg fall out of the bagel, landing on his shirt. He looks down at his chest, plucks a morsel from the fabric, and plops it in his mouth. Chewing so hard that the muscles in his jaw are popping like Mexican jumping beans, he smiles at Allie and Danny, then turns his head toward me. "Who the devil are you?" he asks around a mouthful of half-chewed food.

"Hildy Schneider. I'm a social worker at the hospital, and I also work for the police department, assisting them as needed."

Bob walks back into the room carrying a Styrofoam cup of coffee that he sets down in front of Lucien. I wonder if he was tempted to slip in a bit of something from one of those plants we found out at the Fletcher farm.

"What the heck have you got going here today, Richmond?" Lucien asks. "Why is there a dog sniffing around my client? And why is this woman in here?" He nods toward me, then rips another bite off his sandwich. He stares at Bob while he chews, and after a few seconds says, around a mouthful of sandwich, "Oh, sorry, didn't mean to be rude. Want some?" He thrusts the partially eaten sandwich toward Bob.

"No, thank you," Bob says through gritted teeth. "The dog and Ms. Schneider are here to make your client more comfortable. Hildy knows him and has worked with him before."

"And the drug-sniffing dog?" Lucien says.

"He isn't a drug-sniffing dog, he's a therapy dog," I explain. "Danny knows him and has found him to be comforting in the past."

Lucien chomps away, considering this.

"Your client has already talked about the murder scene," Bob says. "He seemed upset about it."

"You spoke to my client without me present?" Lucien says, rearing back and straightening with righteous indignation.

"We thought it was one of his schizophrenic breaks at the time," I explain. "It happened last night, and he ended up in the ER. He was sedated and later sent home."

Bob nods. "What Hildy said is correct. At the time, we didn't know there had been a murder, or a death of any sort for that matter. I didn't hear what your client said, but one of my officers did. It was something about a polka-dotted dinosaur."

"A polka-dotted dinosaur," Lucien scoffs. "Do tell." Bob opens his mouth to say something more, but Lucien interrupts him before he can get a word out. "But first, let's do the Miranda thing since we don't know where this is going. And I want everything recorded."

"As I mentioned before, I started recording as soon as we all entered the room and before you got here," Bob says. "I didn't want there to be any question about us asking Danny anything before you arrived, so I made sure everything was on the record."

Lucien frowns, apparently disappointed by this, though I'm not sure why.

Roscoe, tired of staring longingly at Lucien's

sandwich and realizing he isn't going to get anything, sighs and drops his head back onto Danny's leg.

"Well then," Lucien says, setting his sandwich down on the paper wrapper and taking up his coffee. "Let's Mirandize and get on with it."

Bob reads Danny the Miranda warning while Lucien loudly slurps at his coffee. Then Bob says, "Danny, I want to begin by asking you about what you do during the day. Do you have a job?"

Danny stares at the tabletop, giving no indication he has heard the question.

Allie says, "Danny works at the food processing plant out at the industrial park."

Bob stares at Danny, who is still fixated on the tabletop. "What days do you usually work?" Bob asks.

Still no answer from Danny and once again Allie fills in the blanks. "He goes in Monday through Friday from nine-ish in the morning until around one or two in the afternoon."

"Nine-ish?" Bob asks.

"His hours are flexible to some degree," Allie explains.

Bob, clearly becoming frustrated with Danny's inability or unwillingness to answer says, "Danny, I need you to talk to me. Stop letting your sister speak for you."

Danny's eyes finally shift from the tabletop to Bob.

"I want you to tell me about the man who got killed," Bob says quickly, taking advantage of Danny's apparent attention. "You told Hildy you saw the man get killed."

Danny squeezes his eyes closed, his forehead wrinkling in concentration. The hand stroking Roscoe's head freezes in place at the back of the dog's neck. A second later, Danny snatches his hand away from the dog and starts rubbing both hands together on top of the table. "Artie's dead," Danny says. He starts to rock in his seat. "He's dead. And the purple and pink polka-dot dinosaur saw the whole thing happen."

Bob frowns.

"May I?" I say, placing a hand on Bob's arm. He nods. I turn the other way and say, "Danny, can you tell me what the purple and pink polka dot dinosaur saw?"

Danny opens his eyes and looks across the table at Bob. Then he looks at me. His rocking motion speeds up and his expression turns panicked. "He's dead," he says. "They shot him because he wouldn't do it. And now he's a ghost." He pauses and looks at me, wide-eyed and clearly afraid. "He's mad at me because I didn't help him. I didn't stop them." His voice is rising and Roscoe inches closer to him, nuzzling his nose on Danny's belly. This contact has an immediate and startling effect, though I suppose I shouldn't be surprised at what Roscoe can do anymore. I've seen him work his magic too many times.

Danny's hand drifts to the dog's head and he starts stroking again, though with a degree of urgency. Still, he seems calmer. Roscoe rolls his eyes upward, looking at Danny, and snuggles his face in harder. Danny's petting slows, his body visibly relaxes, and he looks down at Roscoe with a smile. "Good boy," Danny murmurs.

Roscoe thumps his tail a couple of times in response.

"Danny," I say, "can you tell me what it is that the man . . . Artie wouldn't do?"

At first, I think he hasn't heard me, or that he's going to ignore me. There is little to no reaction from him and he keeps petting Roscoe, smiling beatifically at the dog. Just as I'm about to nudge him again, he finally provides an answer . . . a chilling one.

"Artie said he wouldn't kill them all."

Chapter 8

I look at Bob with a wary expression but neither of us says anything. Even Lucien appears nonplussed, and I get the sense that this man is rarely at a loss for words. Danny has also fallen silent, though he continues to stroke Roscoe's head.

"Danny, do you know who killed Artie?"

Danny looks at me, his expression neutral. Then his gaze takes on that glassy-eyed, unfocused quality again as he stares off into space. "Artie killed Artie. Do you understand?" he says, with a mimicking tone to his voice. Then, in his normal voice he says, "I understand. Artie killed Artie."

"He knows the victim's name well enough, even uses a nickname," Bob says. "If we find his prints out at that farmhouse, or in the barn—"

"I think my client needs to stop answering your questions," Lucien says with a worried expression.

"Don't stop him," I say. "I think he's echoing

what someone else told him to say. Don't you hear it in his voice?"

Lucien chews on his lower lip, looking indecisive. Before he can say anything, Bob leans forward and says, "Danny, did someone tell you to say that Arthur . . . Artie killed himself?"

I half expect Lucien to object to this, but he stays silent.

Danny frowns, still staring off into space, seeing who knew what—nothing pleasant judging from the terrified look on his face. Finally, tears welling in his eyes, he says, "Artie *has* to kill Artie, or the others will die. The others can't die." He breaks into sobs, his whole body shaking. Roscoe snuggles in again.

Allie reaches over and rubs her brother's shoulder. "It's okay, Danny," she says. She looks at me with a pleading expression that speaks volumes without her saying another word.

I nod at her. "I don't think Danny is going to be able to help us much today," I say to Bob. "He isn't thinking clearly yet, and this ghost thing has too strong a hold on him. We need to give him more time for his meds to get better balanced."

Clearly, Bob isn't happy about this and he makes one last desperate attempt to get a clear answer. "Danny, did you kill Arthur?" he says.

"Danny, don't answer that!" Lucien says. "My client is done answering questions for today." Lucien pushes back his chair and stands.

"I'm going to have to hold him," Bob says. "He may be a killer."

"My brother didn't kill anyone," Allie says, clearly upset. "Please don't lock him up. It won't go well if you do. He doesn't like restraints of any sort."

"I have to agree with Allie," I say. "And Danny isn't going anywhere. He's not a flight risk."

Bob shakes his head and makes a face of disapproval, but I can tell he's going to cave.

"What proof do you have that my client was even near your victim at the time of his death?" Lucien asks.

"We know he knew the victim based on his use of a nickname for him," Bob says. "And we can also place him at the scene. He saw something there, something unusual that one wouldn't normally know or mention."

"What?" Lucien snaps. "That ridiculous polka-dotted dinosaur you mentioned?" His tone is heavy with skepticism.

"I know it sounds farfetched," I say, "but there was a pink and purple polka-dotted dinosaur cookie jar on the counter right behind Mr. Fletcher's body."

"Which means my client could have seen it at any time," Lucien points out. "Perhaps he incorporated the image of that cookie jar into whatever schizoid hallucination he is experiencing with this current break from reality. It proves nothing. Do you have anything else? His prints on the weapon, perhaps? Or blood spatter evidence on him or his clothing?"

Bob sighs irritably. "When your client first started spouting off the stuff about someone getting killed, we had no idea there was any truth behind it. There was no reason to examine him or his clothing for blood spatter. We do have his fingerprints on file now. We obtained those upon his arrival here at the station, but I don't know yet if they match any found on the gun or at the house."

"So, is that your long-winded way of saying no?" Lucien asks.

Rather than answer Lucien's obviously mocking question, Bob looks at Allie and says, "Has your brother changed his clothes since he came home last night and started talking about death and ghosts?"

Allie looks at her brother and nods.

"There was no obvious blood spatter on his clothes when I saw him," I say.

"Doesn't mean it wasn't there," Bob says. "It could be microscopic." He looks at Lucien. "I would like to search your client's house for the clothing he was wearing last night."

"And I'd like to visit the moon," Lucien says with a sardonic smile. "Get a warrant." With that, he closes his briefcase and says to Allie, "Take your brother home. And if anyone shows up at your house wanting to come inside and look around, don't let them in. Call me first."

Allie nods, gets up from her chair, and nudges her brother's arm. "Come on, Danny. Let's go home."

"Roscoe, come," I say, and my dog dutifully backs up several steps, though he doesn't take his eyes off Danny's face.

Danny pushes back his chair and stands, smiling briefly at Roscoe before walking around the end of the table behind me and to the door that Lucien is now holding open. Allie mutters, "Thanks, Hildy," as she follows him, and she gives Roscoe a good-boy pat on the head. Lucien is the last one out and he shuts the door firmly behind him, not quite a slam, but something of a statement nonetheless, it seems to me.

Bob looks over at me with a tired, frustrated expression. "Your thoughts?" he says.

"I think that lawyer is a piece of work. Rude and crude."

"And today was nothing. I've seen him much worse. Did you know that he's Mattie Winston's brother-in-law? He's married to her sister, Desi."

"Really?" I'm a little surprised to hear this and it makes me wonder what this sister is like. I've met Mattie a few times and she seems very down-to-earth, a no-nonsense person. She doesn't strike me as someone who would tolerate Lucien Colter very well. Her sister must be nothing like her. "Do you know the sister?" I ask Bob.

"Can't say I know her, but I've met her a few times. She's very nice. I don't quite get how she ended up with Lucien."

I shrug and smile. "The heart wants what the heart wants."

This creates an awkward silence between us. Despite a mutual attraction, Bob and I have been out on only one date. And that was only sort of a date. I had to hijack some potential evidence in a case and essentially bribe him with it to get him to eat dinner with me. I did make it clear that I was interested in pursuing him on a nonwork level, however, and after today's inquiry, it's clear that the two of us are on a potential romantic path together. Complicating this—as if a sixteen-year age difference and the fact that Bob is practically a fifty-year-old virgin aren't complications enough— I've also been on one dinner date with Jonas Kriedeman, the police department evidence tech and single father to an adorable and somewhat precocious little girl named Sofie. That date consisted of dinner at Jonas's house with him and Sofie.

Each man knew I'd seen the other, and in the three weeks since, neither one of them has seen fit to ask me out again. I figure if I sit around waiting for these men to take the initiative, I'll grow old and moldy all alone.

Bob rousts me from my thoughts and snaps me back to the here and now. "Give me your thoughts on Danny."

"I've known him for two years now and I've worked with him and his sister through several of his mental breaks."

"Breaks?" Bob says with a scoffing chuckle. "You make it sound like he's taking a mental health vacation or something."

"Well, in essence, he is," I say. "Danny functions completely normally when his meds are in balance and his schizophrenia is in check. You wouldn't know he has a mental health problem. But the medications have some horrible side effects, like impotence, sedation, clouded thinking, and taste alterations. If they're severe enough they can lead some people to stop taking the meds. They typically do okay at first because it takes a while for the levels to wear off, but eventually their illness takes hold again and you're back to square one, trying to balance the effects of the meds with the desired quality of life."

"Danny doesn't always take his meds?" Bob asks.

"That's been an issue for him in the past, for the very reasons I just gave you. But the last time I saw him he was on a new mix of meds and they seemed to be working well and not giving him the kinds of side effects that he hates."

"In the past, when he stopped taking his meds, did he ever get violent?"

I shake my head. "No, never. Danny often hears voices, but I've never known him to be violent. That's not to say that he couldn't be. The voices one hears during a schizophrenic break can be quite convincing and determined. Danny wouldn't be the first person to act on them, but his voices have never been provocative on a violent level."

"There's a first time for everything," Bob says.

"I suppose. Last night's episode wasn't quite his typical break," I admit. I summarize the events that led to our trip to the ER. "Danny had the auditory hallucinations as usual, but last night he apparently had some visual ones, as well. He claims he saw a ghost, though I suppose that might have been the work of an overstressed imagination."

"Do you think he killed Arthur Fletcher?"

"I don't," I say without hesitation, talking through a yawn. "Do I think he knows what happened out there at that farm? Yes, I do. Lucien is right about the possibility of Danny incorporating the cookie jar into whatever fantasy scenario his mind cooked up, so I don't know if he witnessed it happening, or simply saw the dead man afterward. Clearly, he was there, however. That cookie jar matched his description too closely for any other explanation. We just have to figure out how, why, and when he was there." I pause for another yawn and my jaw cracks loudly.

Bob smiles at me. "You've been up all night. You should go home and get some sleep."

"It is a bit past my bedtime," I say, shifting in my chair to relieve some body kinks. "I'm supposed to ride again tonight with Brenda Joiner."

"Are you looking forward to it?"

"Never a dull moment," I say archly. "But I like it that way. It's been both fun and educational so far. And I like to think it's been helpful, too."

Bob pushes his chair back and starts to get up. I realize it's now or never if I'm going to take the plunge.

"Today is Saturday and that means I can sleep during the day and have my evening free before I go out to ride with Brenda at eleven. Any chance I can interest you in having dinner with me again?"

Bob cocks his head to one side and eyes me for a moment. I try to read his expression but can't guess what he's thinking. Finally, he says, "What about Jonas?"

"I haven't heard anything from him since my initial dinner with him and his daughter. But if you're asking me if I've ruled him out as a suitor, then my answer would be no. I like you both. I need more data before I can come to any conclusions."

"You sound very methodical and scientific about it," Bob observes.

"Does that bother you?"

"On the contrary. I kind of like it. And yes, we can have dinner tonight. Though it will have to be a quick one. The sheriff's department has a detective assigned to this case, but they've asked us to help. They have tasked me with a lot of the groundwork, and I need to be working the case until I can make some headway. So, there is a possibility I might have to cancel on you. I've also got the FBI and Homeland Security directing and giving me work to do, so I'm not sure just how involved I'll need to be. Plus, I think the DEA is in the mix now, too."

"Quite the alphabet soup," I say. "Who's ultimately in charge?"

"The county guys, technically," Bob says with a frown. "But they're operating on a skeleton crew. They're stretched too thin just with the car accidents and overdoses they get calls for." He sighs wearily. "I can tell you how it will go because I've dealt with these multi-jurisdictional situations before. The federal agencies will argue over who gets to be in charge and just when you think they're about to kill one another, they'll all step back, see me as someone they can boss around, and then slap an investigation coordinator title on me. Basically, it means I get to do all the dirty work, report back to each of them, and then they'll take most of the credit." He pauses, sighs, and shakes his head. "It's like working with the Hydra, except I'm not Heracles."

I give him a surprised look. "You're up on your Greek and Roman mythology, I see," I say, admittedly impressed.

He shrugs. "Yeah, I read a lot when I was younger. Still do, for that matter. I was a fat kid who didn't participate in sports and didn't have a lot of friends, so I spent my time with books exploring alternate worlds."

"We have less than stellar childhoods in common, it seems," I say. We share an awkward moment of gazing at one another with half smiles before Bob clears his throat and looks away. "With regards to dinner," I say, "tell you what. I make a mean sausage sandwich with onions, peppers, and provolone cheese. How about we plan to meet at my place and if something comes up and you can't get away, I'll bring the sandwich to you."

Bob frowns. "That doesn't sound like much of a date."

"Sometimes you have to take what you can get. I'm nothing if not adaptable. Growing up in the foster system teaches you that."

He smiles. "You're an interesting woman, Hildy Schneider."

"Yeah, you've said that before. Makes me think you might need to get out in the world a little more. How does six sound for dinner?" This question triggers another in my mind.

"Sounds just fine. I'll see you then. If I can't make it or think I'll be late, I'll text you." He pauses and I realize after a second that he's staring at me. "Is that okay?" he says.

"Sorry, I was thinking about something. Is what okay?"

"If I text you to cancel or say I'll be late. Is that an acceptable thing to do these days? I have a hard time keeping up with all this new technology and the etiquette that goes with it."

"That's fine. Or if you're more comfortable calling, do so."

Bob tilts his head to one side, studying me. "What were you thinking about just now?"

"The timeline. Doc Morton said the time of death was eighteen to thirty-six hours earlier, but that there were things that didn't quite add up. If he's right, it sounds like Arthur Fletcher was killed earlier in the day yesterday, or maybe even the day before. When we got to Allie's house last night, Danny was pacing, ranting, and holding a slice of pizza from Quik-E-Mart. I took it away from him and set it aside when I was trying to talk to him. The pizza was warm, so he had to have been there right before he got home. That makes sense, because the city cemetery is nearby and that's where Danny said he saw the ghost. Maybe there's video of him there. And we should have asked him, or Allie, if he worked at the food processing plant yesterday. He might have an alibi for the time of death if we can nail down when it was."

Bob assumes a wistful expression for a moment. "That's good to know," he says. "I'll look into it." He jots down some notes on the pad in front of him, identical to one he gave me at the start of the session, which remains on the table in front of me, blank, but exquisitely aligned with the table's edge and the pen that is resting beside it.

I get up then and, on cue, Roscoe rises at my side. I try unsuccessfully to stifle a big yawn, and Bob smiles at me.

"Go home and get some sleep."

"Will do."

"And thank you for helping out with this. I might need to use you two again down the road if I get another chance to talk to Danny."

"Happy to help." Another yawn threatens and I manage to strike this one down. But I can hear my bed calling to me, and I hurry toward its siren song.

Chapter 9

As soon as Roscoe and I are in my car, I realize I'll need to go to the grocery store sometime before this evening to get the necessary ingredients for the sausage sandwiches. Knowing how unmotivated I typically am when I first wake up, I make the decision to do my shopping now and get it out of the way. Plus, the forecast is calling for rain later in the day, so better to get it done before the clouds move in.

I tell Roscoe to stay in the car and I crack the windows for him. With the temperature in the fifties, he should be fine. The grocery store isn't very busy, and the shelves appear fully stocked, making me realize that this is an ideal time to shop. I grab a hand basket and head for each of the items I need based on the mental list in my head. I'm too tired to dawdle and impulse shop, which is probably a good thing since that's when I typically buy the fattening stuff.

It takes me all of ten minutes to gather everything I need, and I'm headed for the checkout area when I hear someone say, "Hildy!"

I recognize the voice, but it takes me a moment to find the face that goes with it. After a quick scan, I spot Miranda Knopf in a checkout line two registers over. Miranda is a new evening and night weekend dispatcher at the police station. She moved here a couple of months ago from Seattle. I've chatted with her a couple of times and we get along easily and well. She, like me, isn't very tall, though she has me by an inch or two, but aside from that her physique couldn't be more different from mine. Whereas I tend to be soft and round, she is hard and wiry, with an athletic, boyish build. We do both have blond hair, though hers is cut very short and I wear mine in a longer pageboy style.

Miranda motions toward the front of the store, indicating she'll chat with me once we both get through checkout, and I nod my understanding. She takes longer to get there than I do since she has a cart of groceries and I have only a few items.

"Thanks for waiting," she says. "I wanted to ask how it went with your first couple of shifts on the job."

"It's been interesting," I say. "And last night was a doozy." There are too many people around for me to tell her much of what happened, so I simply say, "I'm sure you'll be hearing about it later today when you get to work."

"Ooh . . . sounds intriguing. You go out again tonight, right?"

"I do. I'm on my way home now to get some

sleep. Bob Richmond asked me to stick around this morning for a suspect interview, so my shift ran a little long."

"Well then, you best get home and get some sleep so you're ready for tonight." She smiles broadly and does a gleeful lift of her shoulders. "It will be our first shift working together," she says. "How fun! I'll see you then." She practically skips away, pushing her cart before her, a cart that I notice has a lot of frozen meals in it. Miranda also volunteers with the local EMS group, running on the ambulance during the week when she's not working dispatch. And she's going to college, working toward becoming a physician's assistant. With a schedule like that, it's a good thing she has all that youthful energy.

I do not have that level of energy, however. I'm not sure of Miranda's age, though I'm willing to bet I have at least a decade on her, maybe more. It might be easier if I was in better physical shape, a reminder of my two-week commitment to Bob Richmond to go to the gym with him in the mornings. While I stuck to my original promise, with mixed results, now that I have the second job in place, I don't see it happening often.

I carry my groceries home, eager to climb into the softness of my bed, and I'm in the middle of putting the food away when Roscoe thumps his tail and makes a sudden mad dash to the front door. I know this means P.J. is about to descend upon me and I sigh wearily.

P.J. is my neighbor's eleven-year-old daughter, a red-headed, freckle-faced dynamo of a kid who's socially awkward, highly inquisitive, and a huge help to me most of the time. Her parents, who were surprised when P.J. came along since their only other child was a fifteen-year-old boy and they didn't think they could have any more kids, are busy and involved in their respective careers. Her mother is a highly successful real estate broker, and her father is the manager of the largest grocery store in town. They don't neglect P.J., but they don't spend a lot of time with her either, and P.J.'s brother has been out on his own for years now.

Hence, P.J. has adopted me as something of a surrogate family member, the exact nature of our relationship something that is fluid and not always definable. The relationship between P.J. and Roscoe, however, is easily defined. It's a mutual admiration society. Those two adore one another, at least as much as P.J. is capable of experiencing an emotion like adoration. I suspect the child fits somewhere on the autism spectrum, albeit at the high-functioning end. My unproven diagnosis is Asperger's, but I'm not an expert. All I know is that the kid is whip-smart and has no filters; her words often bite like the crack of a whip.

P.J. has been walking Roscoe for me ever since the day I first brought him home, which wasn't long after I moved in. Roscoe was a fifteen-week-old puppy then, the lone survivor in a car accident that killed his owner. I ended up adopting Roscoe during my first month on the job at the hospital, and when I brought him home, P.J. happened to be outside her house trying to fix her bicycle. Prior to this day, P.J. had watched me, though *stared* might be a better word choice, but hadn't otherwise acknowledged me in any way. The minute Roscoe descended from the seat of my car and waggled his furry little butt in my driveway, P.J. was hooked. She got up immediately, abandoning her bicycle project, and hurried over to Roscoe, who just as quickly abandoned his attentiveness to me, transferring it to P.J. The two of them have been practically inseparable since.

My friendship with P.J. took a bit longer, but eventually she started talking to me more. When I asked her if she'd be willing to walk Roscoe regularly if I paid her and gave her a key to my house, it was the beginning of a comfortable if still occasionally awkward relationship.

My arrangement with P.J. requires her to knock before using the key in the mornings but this morning she doesn't do this since she most likely just saw me enter the house with the groceries and knows I'm up and about.

"You're late," I hear behind me. This is typical P.J.: no greeting, no subtle segue into the topic, just the facts, ma'am. "Did the cops shoot anyone?"

"Good morning, P.J.," I say, smiling at her as I put the sausages in the fridge.

"Oh, right," she says with a frown, recalling my previous attempts to teach her some basic social standards. "Good morning, Hildy. How did your shift go?"

"It went well. And yes, I'm later than expected. Things came up."

"Uh-huh."

"I'm very tired," I reply. I start to say something more but P.J. can't stand it any longer.

"Did the cops shoot anyone?" she asks again.

I can't help but chuckle. "No, they didn't shoot anyone."

"What did they do?"

"Well, the cop I was with got a call to check on someone that hadn't been seen for a while and when we did that, we discovered that the man was dead."

P.J.'s eyes grow wide with interest. "You saw a dead person?" she says.

I nod.

P.J. cocks her head to one side and assumes a thoughtful expression. "I've never seen a dead person. I've seen dead animals. There was a squirrel that someone ran over in the street, and I found a dead baby bird in my backyard once." She says this in a dispassionate, clinical way. "Do dead people look like dead animals?"

Not your typical question, and one that isn't all that easy to field.

"It depends," I say. "There are a lot of ways to die. I'm guessing the squirrel you saw in the road looked a lot different from the baby bird."

"Oh, sure," she says. "The squirrel was squashed and its insides were on the outside."

"Yes, well," I say, swallowing as I try to wipe that image from my mind, "people die in different ways, too."

"Have you ever seen a squashed person?" P.J. asks, her eyes wide with . . . curiosity, awe, fear? I'm not sure.

"No, and I hope I never do," I answer honestly. "Sometimes people die a peaceful death and sometimes they die a violent death."

"How did the person last night die?"

I'm starting to feel a little uncomfortable with P.J.'s level of morbid fascination on this topic, and despite my belief that it's best to answer questions as honestly as one can with kids, I decide to take a detour on this one. "I can't tell you that, P.J. I've explained to you that I can't talk about the people I take care of at the hospital because I have to protect their privacy, right?"

P.J. nods, pouting because she can sense the disappointment coming.

"Well, police work uses the same rules. I have to follow the rules of confidentiality."

P.J. looks crestfallen, but not for long.

"However," I add, "if you listen to the news or read the paper, you'll probably get an answer in the next day or so."

Her expression brightens and she says, "Okay." With that she turns and walks over to the coat tree by the front door and grabs Roscoe's leash. "Come on, boy," she says, and Roscoe dutifully hurries over to her, tail wagging.

"I'm going to bed," I tell P.J. "I'm exhausted. Do you mind just letting Roscoe back in and locking the front door behind you when you go?"

"Okay."

Five seconds later, she and Roscoe are out the door.

Five minutes after that, I'm in bed, sound asleep.

Chapter 10

It takes several attempts to get the bleariness out of my eyes when I awaken sometime later. I aim toward the clock on my bedside stand and blink hard, rub my eyes, and blink again until I can make out the numbers. It's three-fifty-eight, two minutes before my alarm is set to go off. I probe the top of the clock, feeling for the button that will turn off the alarm, and manage to slide it into the off position. Then I sit up on the side of the bed and stare at the wall for a minute or two. The cobwebs in my head are thick and resilient. My mind doesn't want to let go of its dream state, but eventually it caves.

I shuffle into the bathroom, look in the mirror, and wish my vision was all fuzzy again. Going to bed with makeup on is never a good thing. Priority one is a shower, and I turn the water on as hot as I can stand it.

Ten minutes later I step out of the shower feeling somewhat refreshed. I towel off, wrap my wet hair in another towel, and slip on my robe. Then I shuffle out to the kitchen and turn on the coffee pot. Roscoe is lying on the floor at one end of my kitchen island—he likes that spot for some reason—and he opens his eyes and thumps his tail a few times when he sees me. On top of the island I see one of my notepads and a pen, and peer closer at it. P.J. has left me a note stating that she will be back to walk Roscoe again around four-thirty. I grab my cell phone, which I left sitting on the island, and curse when I see that the battery charge is at five percent. I hope it is enough and make a quick phone call to Allie Hildebrand.

"Hello?"

"Allie, it's Hildy. I was calling to see how you guys are doing. The battery in my phone is almost dead, so if we get cut off, I apologize. How's Danny? And how are you?"

"We've been better," she says, and her voice sounds as weary as I feel right now. "I think Danny is okay. He went out for a walk a little while ago. I wasn't sure if I should let him, but he seemed okay at the time. He's been gone for over an hour now. Do you think I should be worried?"

"Didn't you say that Danny usually goes out for walks?"

"Yeah, in the evenings, but he also goes out a lot when he's hearing his voices. And we all know how his last walk turned out."

"Was he hearing voices before he left?"

"I don't know. I don't think so."

"Does he have a cell phone?"

"He does, but he didn't take it with him. He

couldn't find it." She sighs again, and then says, "I'm going to go out and look. . . ." She pauses, and then says, "Someone just came in. Oh, it's Joel, home from work. He picked up part of an extra shift today."

In the background I hear Joel ask Allie who she's talking to. She tells him it's me and then says she's worried about Danny because he's been gone so long.

Joel mutters something I can't make out because Allie coughs a few times. Then she comes back on and says, "Joel is going to go look for him while I stay here in case he comes home."

"While I have you, can you tell me if Danny worked his regular job yesterday?"

Allie hesitates for a moment. "Hildy, how closely are you working with the police? My lawyer said I needed to be careful around you because you were a way for the cops to sidestep justice and the proper processes."

"If you tell me something that you don't want me to share with the police, I won't," I tell her, thinking that I really need to get someone to clarify exactly what my obligations are and where my allegiances should lie. It could be tricky navigating this new landscape, particularly if I'm still working at the hospital.

"I don't suppose it hurts to tell you that Danny went to work yesterday since other people will be able to vouch for him in that regard," Allie says. "Joel told me he left in the morning around nine, and when I got home from my job at the funeral home at five-thirty, Danny had left a voice mail on the phone saying that he was working late on a special project."

"When did you see him again?"

"He came home around eight or so. He seemed agitated. He gets that way when he's tired, or if something happens at work. He said he wanted to go for a walk and left. I didn't see him again until he came home from the Quik-E-Mart. That was right before I called the police."

"So, as far as you know, he was gone all day?"

She hesitates, no doubt parsing the implications of my question and her answer to it. "Yes, at work. In fact, now that I think about it, that should give him an alibi for most of yesterday, right?"

If he really was at work. I have my doubts. "Yes, I suppose it would," I say.

"I wish he would come home," she says. "I'm worried about him."

"If you want, I can put in a word at the police station and see if the patrol officers on duty can keep an eye out for him."

"Oh God, no," Allie whines. "No more police."

"They won't need to pick him up or anything, unless he acts out in a dangerous way. I'll ask them to call me if they spot him but not approach him, and then I'll pass the information on to you, okay?"

Allie sighs. "I suppose. Thanks, Hildy. Gotta go." Before I can say anymore, the call is disconnected. I place another call to the police station and ask for Bob Richmond. I half expect to be told I need to leave a message, but the dispatcher puts me through without question.

"Detective Richmond."

"Hi, Bob, it's Hildy. Just checking in to see if we're still on for tonight?"

"Tonight?" he says, sounding confused. "Oh, right. Dinner. Sorry. I was momentarily distracted. Yes, I believe we are on unless something else comes up at the last minute."

"Great. Can you come by at six?"

"Should be able to. See you then."

"Wait, I have one more thing I need to talk to you about. It's regarding Danny Hildebrand."

"What's he done now?"

"Nothing, that I know of. But he's taken off from his home and his sister is worried about him. Her fiancé has gone out to look for him. I was wondering if the cops who are on duty might keep an eye out for him and let me know if they see him anywhere, so I can pass the information along to his sister."

"I don't see why not," Bob says. "I'll have the dispatcher put out a page."

"Thanks. And I also got Allie to tell me that as far as she knows, Danny went to work yesterday, and he called at some point and left her a message saying that he was going to be working late. That gives you something to check for an alibi. Any word yet on the exact time of death?"

"No, last time I checked in with him, Doc Morton said he's still looking into some things. And your information about Danny's work hours yesterday is interesting because I already followed up with his employer to try and verify his whereabouts. Danny's boss, a guy named Brett Kvalheim, said Danny has been edgy and off for the past few

weeks and has been hit and miss with his shifts.
Brett knows about his mental health problems and
apparently this isn't the first time Danny has had
issues. Brett said he cuts Danny a lot of slack because he has a brother with similar issues."

"That's nice."

"Yeah, I guess. But here's the thing. Danny
sometimes comes and goes when he pleases. He's
salaried and gets the same paycheck every week as
long as he does his job, and Brett said that when
he's focused and functioning at his peak, he can
crank stuff out like nobody's business."

"Okay," I say, not seeing where this is going yet.

"Danny did go in to work yesterday," Bob goes
on. "But nobody saw him after lunch time."

"Oh."

"Yeah," Bob says, no doubt thinking the same
thing. "I'd love to ask the guy where he was, but
Lucien Colter is keeping him strictly off limits.
And Judge McCallister denied the search warrant." He lets out a grunt of disgust and frustration. "I'd really like to get a look at the clothes he
was wearing that night."

"Well, I wasn't looking for anything minute, but
I can tell you there was no obvious blood spatter
on his clothes when I saw him. You could ask the
ER nurse who took care of him, and Dr. Finnegan,
see if they noticed anything."

"Yeah, I did that. Their answer was the same as
yours. They didn't notice anything, but they
weren't looking for it, either, and couldn't say for
sure one way or the other."

"Frustrating," I say.

"It is." There is a pregnant pause, and then Bob

gives birth to his thoughts. "If he turns up, maybe you could ask him where he was the rest of the day."

There's that line again, and I don't want to cross it. "I think we need to talk about this," I tell him. "Let's do it over dinner. See you at six."

"Yeah, okay. Should I bring anything?"

"Just your handsome self," I say, hoping to eliminate the tension I can feel stretching between us. My comment garners a nervous cough that I imagine is accompanied by a rapidly flushing face. Bob doesn't take compliments or flirting very well, but it has served its purpose and put him off topic. At least for now. "See you at six," I say again, and then I disconnect the call, plug the phone in to let it charge, and turn to go back to my bedroom to get dressed.

I've only managed a single step when I discover that P.J.'s arrival is imminent. I know this because Roscoe's head pops up and cocks to one side, and then he gets up and makes a mad scramble to the front door. Sure enough, as soon as he reaches the door, it opens and P.J. walks in.

"Hello there," I say.

"Hi." She walks over, studies me with an unnerving intensity for several seconds, and then says, "Maybe you should go back to bed. You still look tired."

Classic P.J. "I *am* tired, but I'll survive. It's going to take some time to get used to my new schedule."

P.J. considers this for a few seconds and then shrugs. "Come on, Roscoe," she says. She hitches up one strap on the backpack she is wearing, and with no further comment she spins around, grabs his leash from the coat tree by the door, and leads the dog outside.

The two of them are gone for half an hour, and by the time they return, I have settled on what to wear for my dinner date with Bob Richmond. The man strikes me as someone who is no-nonsense, down-to-earth, and not into fancy-schmancy stuff, which is fine by me. I don't mind getting glammed up once in a blue moon for a special occasion, but for the most part I prefer to keep things simple. Thus, I opt for a basic slacks and blouse combo, black for the slacks, baby blue for the blouse, a color I've been told looks good on me as it brings out the color of my eyes.

When P.J. returns, she gives my outfit a squinting, critical eye and I brace myself for another P.J.-ism. But to my surprise she says, "You look nice. Is that what you wear when you're working with the police?"

"No, I have a dinner date."

"With who?" She unhooks Roscoe's leash, hangs it up, and heads for the cupboard in the kitchen that contains the dog treats.

"Detective Richmond."

"He's the one that made you go to the gym, right?"

"He didn't make me go," I say, though in a way he kind of did. He basically blackmailed me into it. "And I enjoyed it."

This gets me an amused look from P.J.

"What?" I say.

"You did not enjoy it. You whined every single

time you went, you told me how much you hated it, and you compared the workout equipment to . . ." She rolls her eyes heavenward for a second, searching for the words, and then quotes me verbatim. "Torture equipment from Machiavelli's secret dungeon."

"I said that?" I ask, knowing full well that I did.

"You did. It made me go home and look up Machiavelli. Interesting guy and philosophy."

"You're eleven. You're not supposed to know about things like Machiavelli," I tell her. "I hope you didn't tell your parents where you heard it."

"They don't pay any attention to what I'm doing," she says dispassionately. If this bothers her, it doesn't show. "And if you think I'm too young to know about Machiavelli, you shouldn't have mentioned him in front of me."

"Touché," I say, making a mental note to be more careful in the future. P.J. is extremely bright and much older mentally than her physical age. Sometimes it's easy to forget that she's still a kid. "And just so you know, even though I complained a lot about the exercise, I didn't hate it. In fact, I feel better having done it and I even managed to drop five pounds." Even as I say this, I recall how tired and out of breath I was last night trying to keep up with the cops as they hurried out to the barn and how much I hated myself for it. *You were just tired*, I tell myself.

"That's good," P.J. observes. "You are overweight." This is said matter-of-factly and without judgment, though I still feel the sting of her blunt honesty for a few seconds. I turn away and open the fridge to hide any expression that might have leaked onto my face.

I'm expecting P.J. to return home now that she's done with Roscoe, but instead she slips her backpack off and sets it on the floor, takes a bottle of water out of it, and then climbs onto one of the barstools at my kitchen island.

"You're cooking?" she says, watching as I take the sausages out and set them on the stove.

"I am. Sausage sandwiches."

I grab the folding stool I keep tucked beside the fridge and use it to climb up and get an onion and a rainbow of peppers—green, red, orange, and yellow—from a hanging wire basket above the island. I wash the peppers and then set them and my best cutting knife on the island and pull out a cutting board from a lower cabinet.

"I can slice those up if you want," P.J. offers as I remove an apron from a drawer and put it on.

"I have time to do it, but thanks."

"When is Detective Richmond coming?"

"Six."

P.J. looks pointedly at the clock on the wall. "That means you only have about forty-five minutes," she says.

I sense she's trying to make a point that I'm clearly not seeing, so I give her a questioning look.

"You have to cook the sausages, the onion, and the peppers, and you still have to get yourself ready."

"I have myself ready," I say. "You even said my outfit looked nice."

"It does. But what about your makeup?"

"What about it?"

"Aren't you going to put any on?"

"I put on lipstick and some mascara."

P.J. gives me a look of disappointment that borders on disgust. "I thought you said you liked this guy."

"I do."

"Don't you want to impress him?"

"I don't want to do myself up like a hooker," I grumble.

"What does that mean?"

Recalling our previous discussion about Machiavelli, I say, "Never mind. What do you think I'm missing?"

"Well, my mom wears makeup, and she always looks nice." This is true. P.J.s mother always looks beautifully put together. "She's been giving me lessons on how to do makeup to enhance one's natural beauty," P.J. says in a sing-songy voice that makes me think she's mimicking her mother. "She says I'm too young to wear makeup yet, but that there's no harm in teaching me how to do it so I'll be ready when I'm older. I think the real reason she taught me is that her eyesight has gotten bad and she can't see well enough to do her own makeup anymore, especially her eyes. I do it for her all the time. I could do yours."

The idea of an eleven-year-old doing my makeup triggers visions of circus clown faces. "I think I'll be fine like I am," I say.

P.J.'s expression turns sad. It's such an unexpected sight that it makes my heart ache. "Okay, fine," I say with resignation. "I hope you can do it quickly."

"I can," she says, hopping off the stool and heading for my bedroom. As I follow her in there, it occurs to me that this is a kid who never displays emotion, and that I may have just been played by an eleven-year-old.

Chapter 11

It turns out that P.J.'s mother taught her quite well. The child manages to artfully apply shadow, concealer, highlighter, and rouge in a way that makes my eyes look bigger and brighter, contours my cheeks, and yet still looks reasonably natural. She convinces me to try a different lipstick that's more of a nude color and accuses me of wearing the brighter colors, which she claims make my lips look like the butt on a baboon, to try and draw attention away from my other features because I don't feel confident about them. The fact that this bit of insight might be spot on irritates me, but when I see the results of P.J.'s ministrations, all is forgiven and forgotten.

When P.J. has me looking as good as I can, she settles in at the island counter with a knife and the peppers and starts slicing them up for me while I go about cooking the sausages. I watch as she sneaks small tastes of each one, her judgment clear by the expression on her face. The yellow and orange peppers pass muster, but the green and red ones do not. Knowing P.J. as I do, I can't help but wonder how much her preferences are related to the color of the peppers as opposed to the taste.

"You better let me cut up the onion," she says when she's done. "If you do it, it will make your eyes water and ruin your makeup."

This makes perfect sense to me. "Okay, but be careful," I tell her. "I don't want to have to explain to your parents why you're in need of stitches or missing a finger."

P.J. is as adept with a knife as she is with a make-up brush. Her slices on the onion are thin and perfect, and though her eyes water a little, she doesn't look like she's been on an hours-long crying jag the way I usually do when I slice them up.

I melt some butter in a frying pan, and then add the peppers and onions, seasoning them with pepper and garlic salt.

"Smells good," P.J. says, hopping down from her stool. "I should go home now." She turns and heads for the door while I struggle with an impulse to invite her to join Bob and me for dinner. The kid is a loner, and that bothers me. It doesn't seem to bother her, however, and I keep reminding myself of that fact.

She opens the door and I hear her say, "Oh, hello."

"Hi," says Bob. "You're P.J., right?"

"I am. And you're Bob, Hildy's date, right?" P.J.'s inflection is identical to Bob's and I wonder if she's mimicking him as a way of mocking him, or if she's simply trying to pick up on his social cues.

"I am," Bob says, sounding amused.

P.J. then pushes past him and heads home without uttering another word.

"Come on in," I say to him, waving my utensil in the air.

He steps inside and closes the door. "That kid is different," he says, shrugging off his jacket, which he hangs on a hook of the coat tree.

I've turned my attention back to the sautéing veggies on the stove, so it takes me a moment to realize that Bob is still standing by the coat tree, hands in his pockets, looking around like a lost kid.

"Come over and grab a seat at the island," I tell him.

He does so as I open the fridge and remove two bottles of Michelob lite. I hold them up with a questioning look and Bob gives me a grudging nod.

"Bottle or glass?" I ask.

"I'm fine with the bottle."

I set both bottles in front of him and say, "Open mine, will you?"

He does so as I stir the peppers and onions some more. "Food will be ready in about five minutes. Would you like cheddar cheese or provolone on your sandwich?"

"Provolone, please." He takes a long swig of his beer as I get out the sliced cheese and the hoagie rolls. "It smells like heaven," Bob says.

"Good. Hope you're hungry."

"I'm always hungry. That's how I managed to get myself up to over four hundred pounds."

"I'm afraid the sausage isn't particularly healthy," I tell him, "but the cheese is a lower fat variety, if that helps."

"I'm fine with whatever you serve," he says. "I learned long ago that if I deprive myself too much it doesn't help my situation. So, I indulge now and again when I feel the need and compensate by working out a little longer and a little harder."

"You sound very disciplined," I say.

"I have to be, or I'll backslide." He takes another swig of his beer. "Speaking of discipline, what are your thoughts on continuing at the gym?"

I turn back to the stove and speak over my shoulder, not wanting to look him in the eye. "To be honest, I'm torn. I've seen a difference already in just two weeks, and that makes me feel good about it, but I hated nearly every moment I spent in that gym. I don't know. I've never much liked exercise for the sake of exercise and it took every ounce of motivation I had in me to make myself go each day." I finally turn around and look at him. "You made it kind of fun and interesting, but I won't be able to go with you in the early mornings anymore because of the new job. I'll be getting off work around the time you're supposed to be starting."

"I could change my times, if that helps."

"No, don't do that. I wouldn't want you to upset your routine for me because I can't promise I'm going to stick with it. With two jobs, it's going to be all I can do to find time to eat, sleep, and run my usual errands."

"You have a point," Bob says, frowning and taking another drink. "Working two jobs has to be hard."

His cell phone rings then, saving me from any further excuse making, so I turn my focus back to dinner making instead. I listen to Bob's end of the phone call, hoping it won't be anything that will force him to leave, but all he says is, "I see," "Okay," and, "Thanks for letting me know."

"Dinner's ready," I say with a smile, turning to face him. His apologetic expression makes my smile droop. "Don't tell me," I say, unable to hide my disappointment. "You have to leave."

"I should. Danny Hildebrand has turned up."

"Where? Is he okay?"

"He appears to be okay physically. Not sure about the mental part. Someone spotted him in the city cemetery, wandering around talking to various graves."

"Hm," I say, frowning. Had Danny had another break from reality? "Can I go with you?"

"Wouldn't have it any other way. You seem to have an in with the guy. Should we call his sister?"

"Not yet," I say, thinking. "Let me talk to him first."

Bob eyes the stovetop and licks his lips. "There's nothing that says we can't take our sandwiches on the go, eat them along the way."

My stomach rumbles at the suggestion. "Good idea. Come over here and fix yourself one."

We waste five minutes constructing our respective sandwiches and I dig out a roll of foil to wrap around them and catch drips. The sandwiches aren't ideal for eating on the go, but we'll have to make do. I rip off several squares of paper towel to bring along as well.

I tell Roscoe to stay and grab a jacket from the tree. Bob helps me put it on. "Ride with me?" he says.

"Sure."

He heads out the door and I follow. His car is parked at the curb, and he unlocks the passenger side door for me before going around to his own. As soon as we are settled, he says, "By the way, you look very nice tonight."

"Thank you," I say, beaming a smile that seems to bubble up from my chest. I have both sandwiches on my lap and I focus on positioning them just so, so I don't have to look at Bob. I love the compliment, but it's making my face flush hot and I don't want him to see it. "Do you think you can safely eat and drive at the same time? These sandwiches are best when they're hot."

"Wrap the foil around one end of it, leave the other end open, and hand it to me. Trust me, eating while driving is a favorite pastime of mine."

I do as he says and hand him the sandwich. He takes a big bite out of it, moaning with delight as he chews. I wrap my own sandwich in a similar manner and join him. For the first few minutes the only sounds in the car are the engine and the noise the two of us make as we chew. At one point I see a bit of juice leak out the side of Bob's mouth closest to me and I reach up with a paper towel.

"May I?" I ask.

He nods, his mouth too full to speak. I dab at the juice, and the intimacy of the action makes my face flush hot again. I turn away and look out my side window. We are almost at the cemetery already. While I enjoy living in a small town for many reasons, the fact that it doesn't take long to get from one place to another can be both a blessing and a curse. In this case it's a curse. Neither of us is close to finishing the sandwiches when we arrive at the entrance to the cemetery and I hear Bob sigh as he pulls into a parking spot.

"I'll have to eat the rest of it later," he says, looking at the remains of the sandwich in a way that I wish he would look at me. He wraps the foil around the eaten end and sets the sandwich on the seat beside him. I hand him a paper towel, and he wipes his face in a surprisingly dainty manner as I wrap up the remains of my own sandwich. I dab at my face, not wanting to undo any of P.J.'s magical ministrations. When we're both cleaned up and done mourning our sandwiches, we exchange a look and get out of the car.

The entrance to the cemetery is marked by a large wrought-iron gate connected to a fence that extends around the perimeter of the area. I've always found the fence to be something of a conundrum, particularly since the gate is never closed, much less locked. So why fence off the graves? Was it to keep people out or to keep the ghosts in? Either way, it wasn't going to be very effective. While the gate opening is large enough to drive through, there are no roads in the cemetery, only paved pathways that meander between the graves.

Most of the graves near the entrance are older ones dating back to the second half of the 1800s, when Sorenson was first founded. The headstones, which range in size from small plates recessed into the ground to two large mausoleums, are weathered but still readable. Several large oaks, including one majestic northern red oak that is rumored to date back to the late 1800s, are scattered across the ten-acre property, providing a pastoral setting, plenty of shade, and in the fall, an abundance of acorns.

There is a warm evening breeze blowing through the treetops, which are sporting new growths of leaves. The rustling sound, combined with the soft babble of the river that runs along the far south side of the cemetery, makes it a surprisingly peaceful setting. The property is on a hillside, and the entrance is on the high side. Bob and I meander along the pathways, making a gradual descent, and we have nearly traversed the length of the cemetery before we see Danny.

He is sitting at the base of a tree—a maple in this case—legs bent up, head bowed, arms crossed over the tops of his knees. As we approach him, I hear the faint murmur of his voice, though it's too soft to make out any words. I'm afraid we're going to startle him, so I put a hand on Bob's arm to stop our approach.

"Let me," I whisper.

Bob nods, and I take a few more steps, closing the distance between me and Danny. When I'm about ten feet away from him, I say, "Danny, it's Hildy." He lifts his head and looks at me with a tear-stained face. "What are you doing here?" I ask him, closing the remaining distance between us. He watches my every move and when I reach him, I sit down beside him, my back against the tree trunk. "Are you okay?"

Danny looks me up and down, a puzzled expression on his face, as if he has no idea who I am or how I got here. He looks shell-shocked, and tired.

"Talk to me, Danny," I say. I reach over and put a hand on the arm closest to me. "I'm worried about you. Allie is worried about you, too."

Danny looks away then and he spots Bob standing near a headstone about twenty feet away. "Are the cops after me?" he asks.

"No. He's here because I'm on a date with him and I've been looking for you. When I heard someone had seen you here, I came right away. Detective Richmond came with me."

Danny gives me a skeptical look.

"Hey, I don't go out on many dates, Danny. And while I am worried about you, I'm not going to let that ruin my social life, what little of it there is. I don't want to end up an old maid." I say this in a jocular, teasing tone and I'm relieved when Danny cracks a smile.

"So, help me out," I say. "Why are you here? What's going on inside that head of yours? Are you hearing voices?"

Danny shakes his head. "No, not really. Not like I do when I'm sick. It's different, a mix of voices with snippets of conversation. Nothing that makes sense to me, but I think it's more of a memory than any of my voices." He spits these words out in a frantic, hurried ramble, his eyes tearing up as he speaks. "And then I keep seeing Artie, his face staring at me with that purple and pink polka-dotted dinosaur behind him, and I can tell he's wondering why I'm just standing there, letting him die . . . letting them kill him, and doing nothing."

Since Danny seems to be having one of his more lucid moments, I ask him, "Who killed Artie?"

He closes his eyes, his face screwing into a grimace. "I don't know," he says with frustration. "I can't see or remember any faces. I just keep seeing an image of Artie looking afraid and then I see an image of Artie dead." He pauses and shudders.

"Could you have done something? Could you have stopped Artie's death?" From the corner of my eye I see Bob inch closer, his head turned sideways in an effort—I assume—to hear us better.

Danny squeezes his eyes closed and a tiny moan escapes his lips. "I don't know. I don't even know if the image of Artie and that dinosaur is a real one or something my stupid sick brain cooked up."

"Were there any voices talking to you when Artie died?"

He frowns, then nods.

"What were the voices saying?"

"That Artie had to kill Artie. It had to be that way."

"Did Artie kill himself?"

Danny shrugs, then shakes his head. "He didn't want to die. He didn't want all the people to die. But the voice in my head kept saying that was how it had to be."

"Did the voice in your head tell you to kill Artie?"

He looks at me then, his eyes wide open. "It did," he whispers. "But I said no. The dinosaur knows."

"What does the dinosaur know?"

"It knows Artie didn't want to die." He glances around, his expression wary. "That's why Artie's ghost is here. He's mad that he's dead."

I'm about to ask Danny if he's seen the ghost

today when I hear a female voice call out his name. I recognize the voice as Allie's, and sure enough I see her and Joel up near the top of the hill, hurrying down toward us. I curse their arrival and wonder how they knew to find Danny here. Bob fades into the long shadow of a tree, watching.

"Danny, thank goodness we found you," Joel says, arriving first. He squats down beside Danny, a hand on his shoulder. "Hey, bro, you okay?"

Allie reaches us then, frantic and a bit out of breath. "For heaven's sake, Danny, you had me worried half to death." She seems to realize what she's said and where she is then, because she looks around at the headstones and grimaces. "What are you doing here? Are you okay?"

"I'm okay," Danny says, and he sounds surprisingly calm and collected. "I came here because I needed to talk to the ghost."

Allie shoots me a worried look. Joel casts a glance at our surroundings and then looks back at Danny. "I don't see any ghost here," he says in a calm, reasoned voice. "Did one put in an appearance?"

"Not yet," Danny says. "I'm waiting for him."

"You don't need to be in a cemetery for a ghost to come to you," I say. "Besides, Artie isn't buried yet, so he isn't here in this cemetery."

"His ghost is," Danny says adamantly. "I saw him last night. He came out of that tree." He points directly to the tree where Bob is standing, partially obscured by the growing shadows cast by the setting sun. Allie and Joel both turn to look where Danny is pointing, an automatic reaction, their pending dismissals ready on their lips. But the sight of Bob standing beneath the tree makes them both gasp before they realize that the image they are seeing is made of real flesh, blood, and bone.

Allie clamps a hand over her heart. "Who is that?" she says breathlessly, squinting into the sunlight that is backlighting Bob and making it hard, if not impossible, to see his face.

"That's Hildy's date," Danny says.

"He's right, it is," I say. "It's Detective Richmond, the one who questioned you earlier."

Allie flares at that. "Are you questioning Danny without our attorney present?"

"Nothing official," I say. "And only me. Detective Richmond hasn't said a word to him."

"You should go and be with him," Danny says. "This isn't a very good date so far."

"No, it's not," I agree with a chuckle.

Danny pushes himself up to a standing position, brushing dirt from the seat of his jeans. Joel stands, too, and then Danny turns and offers me a hand. I take it, and he hauls me to my feet.

"I'm hungry," Danny says. "I'll look for Artie again after I eat." With this matter-of-fact comment, he walks to the path and starts trudging up the hill. Joel scurries after him.

Allie looks at me with lingering suspicion. "Are you really on a date?"

"Sadly, yes."

She takes a moment to digest this, then leans in closer to me and in a whisper says, "Do you want me to help you out of it?"

"No," I say with a smile. "But thanks."

"In that case, I'm sorry Danny interrupted things. How did you know he was here?"

"The cops told us. I asked them to keep an eye out for him and let me know if they saw him. I assume they called you as well?"

"They did," Allie says. She casts a look after her brother and Joel. "Do you think he's okay?"

I sigh, watching the two men walk up the hill. "I don't know," I say honestly. I hate to equivocate, but Danny is a bit of a puzzle to me at this point. "I don't think he's in a crisis state, if that helps. But that doesn't mean he won't go into one sometime soon."

Allie's head lolls back on her shoulders and she lets out a little whimper. "He's been doing so good for so long," she says. "What's sending him off the deep end?"

"I think it's Arthur Fletcher's death," I tell her. "For whatever reason, whether he saw the man killed, watched him commit suicide, or killed the man himself, Mr. Fletcher's death has been an emotional trigger for him."

"Danny didn't kill anyone," she insists.

"I'm inclined to agree with you," I tell her. "But he was involved in some manner. We have to figure out what it was and how it fits into the bigger picture."

"Allie, come on," Joel yells from the top of the hill.

Allie lets out an impatient sigh. "I should go," she says.

I nod. "Call me if . . . well . . . call me if you need anything, okay?"

"I will." With that she scurries off, huffing and puffing her way back up the hill.

Bob Richmond walks down to where I am and says, "I must say, Hildy Schneider, dates with you are never dull. What's next on the agenda?"

Chapter 12

After a brief discussion—brief, because I don't have any spare breath after climbing up the hill to the parking area and Bob's car—we decide to go to Bob's house. He offers, or rather asks if I'd be willing to go there, first stating that it's not far away, and then telling me that he's thinking of redecorating the place and after seeing what I've done with my house, he wants to get my ideas. He tops it off by saying we can reheat our sandwiches there and finish them off.

I realize this could be a ploy to get me somewhere where we can be more intimate without the threat of a dog's cold nose or a curious young neighbor appearing unexpectedly, but I kind of doubt it. Bob doesn't have a lot of experience when it comes to wooing the opposite sex and I doubt he's capable of being that conniving. Frankly, I'm not all that experienced myself, but after a mental debate of about two seconds, I decide to just go along and see what happens.

Bob's house is a Craftsman style circa 1920 located on a five-acre plot of land along one of the highways leading out of town. It's a bucolic country setting less than a mile beyond the city limits. The house is set back from the road several hundred feet and it looks every bit of its one hundred years. The outside is faded and chipped clapboard that might have been a colonial blue at one time but is now a dull beige with bits of blue clinging to the boards for dear life. The brick stairs leading up to the front porch are chipped and faded, with large chunks of brick missing. The wood columns on either side of the stairs and at the corners of the porch appear to have been white at one time, though now they are covered in a thin layer of green algae thanks to the house's north-facing location. There is no garage, and the driveway is rutted dirt and gravel.

Despite the relaxing, country setting, the house is utterly lacking in curb appeal. The yard is a mix of yellow, brown, and pale green with large bald spots, and there are no bushes or flowers to speak of, just several large trees: a beautiful red maple on one side of the house and three giant oaks standing sentinel around the rest of the building. The lattice board that is supposed to be covering the area under the porch is broken and weathered, and I see something scurry away under there as we approach the porch.

"I haven't done much with the place," Bob says as we stand at the base of the stairs.

"That's an understatement."

He looks at me with a grimace. "Is it that bad?"

"Let me put it this way. It's a good thing your house isn't part of a larger neighborhood or you would have been tarred and feathered by now."

"I was going to work on it when I was retired but by then I was so fat and lazy I couldn't muster up the motivation." He says this in a tone of remorseful grief, then adds, "Thank goodness I got shot."

"Now there's a line you don't hear every day," I say with a grin.

Bob surveys the front façade of the house and sighs. "Now there's so much . . . it's overwhelming. I don't know where to start."

"Just pick a project and start there. Figure out what you can do yourself, and what you need to hire out. If it were me, I'd hire someone to paint the outside and then I'd start on replacing that lattice around the porch. Maybe go to the gardening center and get some suggestions on landscaping and put in some plants. Trust me, once you start it's easy to keep going. Easy and expensive. But you have to start somewhere before the place falls down around you. Think of it as an investment and take proper care of it."

Bob nods. "You're blunt and to the point," he says, and for a moment I fear I've offended him. But then he adds, "I like that about you. Let's go inside and see what your thoughts are there."

We mount the porch stairs and Bob unlocks the front door and steps inside, holding the door for me. It's like walking into a cave. The first room I enter is big and being used as a living room, judging from the chairs, sofa, TV, and tables. There is a

lovely stone fireplace centered on the wall to the
left with a large-screen TV mounted above it. Two
windows flank the fireplace above built-in shelves
with glass doors and both built-ins are filled with
books. There are two more floor-to-ceiling book-
cases built into the wall shared with the dining
room, and these are also filled with books. The
windows on either side of the fireplace are small
but they face east and should let in some nice
morning sun. But any light entering this room is
likely to get sucked into the gloom. The walls and
the built-ins are painted a dark brown color. The
tray ceiling helps a little as it is, or used to be,
white, but it's bordered with heavy, dark wood trim
that further dampens the mood of the room.

The furnishings look comfortable if old: a dark
brown, stuffed sofa facing the fireplace, a brown
leather recliner perpendicular to the fireplace,
and across from the recliner is a love seat in the
same material as the sofa. Mismatched end tables
flank the love seat and recliner, and a huge, polished, irregularly shaped slab of crosscut tree on a
pedestal sits in front of the couch. There are lamps
on both end tables, and there is a small overhead
fixture in the ceiling above the couch. Only one of
the lamps is turned on and the light it emits is
meager at best.

The only other potential source for light is a
large picture window in the porch wall, but it's covered with drapes made from a brown textured material. It seems that everything in the room is
brown except for one bright yellow throw pillow
on the sofa that stands out amidst the drab like a
lighthouse beacon on a dark, foggy night.

Bob sees me eyeing the pillow. "I just got that," he says. "I noticed how you have colorful pillows in your living room and I kind of liked it, so I thought I'd try something like that here. It gives the room a touch of brightness, don't you think?"

Oh, dear. I don't have the heart to tell Bob that his living room has all the ambience of a medieval dungeon and one neon yellow pillow isn't going to fix that. That pillow is like a random piece of corn in the middle of a giant turd. Still, he's trying, and I find his effort, and his interest in it all, endearing.

"You've got the right idea," I tell him. "But I think it's going to take a little more than one pillow. Is that yellow a color you like?"

"I suppose," he says with a shrug. "I mainly picked it because it was on sale. Got it for a buck fifty." He is clearly quite proud of this fact and it's all I can do not to laugh.

"There is a ton of potential in this room," I say. "You have a good arrangement with the furniture and the focus on the fireplace. Your seating also creates a nice conversation area. I think the biggest negative is that it's awfully dark in here . . . dark and very brown. Do you keep the curtains closed all the time?"

He nods. "I like my privacy."

"You're quite isolated out here, so it isn't like you have people walking by your window all the time. You could open those curtains to let in some light and still have some degree of privacy."

"Yeah, but that window faces out toward the road, and people driving by can see in."

He sounds pretty committed to some sort of

drapery on that window, so I start thinking about alternative ways to lighten things up. I'm about to suggest a paint job when he says, "Why do I need to worry about a good conversation area? I live here by myself. It's not like I'm talking to anyone."

"Well, you might have guests out, like me," I say, smiling. "It's nice if you have seating that allows people to easily converse without having to sit at an awkward angle, or crane their necks around."

"Hmpf."

"Does this room feel dark to you?" I ask, trying to get a feel for how much change this lifelong bachelor might be up for.

He gives the room a quick scan. "It does," he admits. "And I'm thinking about getting some new furniture. I've had that couch for nearly twenty years, and it has some sagging issues." He looks away, clearly embarrassed. "I used to sleep on it a lot when I was heavier because I was too damned fat and out of shape to climb the stairs to my bedroom."

I glance over at the stairwell tucked into a far corner of the living room. It starts with three stairs that lead to a small landing and then it makes a ninety-degree turn for the rest of the steps. I wonder how many bedrooms there are upstairs and how they're being used, but figure we have our work cut out for us with just the first floor for now.

"I would love to help you buy some new furniture," I say, meaning it. "And I have some ideas for this room that I think will brighten it up for you but still keep it cozy. Show me the rest of this floor."

Bob gives me a tour, starting with the dining

room, which is right off the living room. Here the walls are covered with hideous wallpaper that has giant red and pink flowers on it, the only place to sit is at a picnic table located in the middle of the room, and there is a rusted metal and glass chandelier hanging from the ceiling that looks like a funhouse nightmare. The room's saving graces are the light oak hardwood floors, which are in surprisingly good shape, and two large windows, one facing east the other facing south, that will give the room plenty of light once the heavy drapes—the same ones that are in the living room—are removed.

"I've been meaning to buy a proper dining room set, but no one ever eats in here," Bob says, looking at the picnic table. "It's just me, and I either eat in the kitchen or in the living room. And frankly, that wallpaper gives me a headache."

Finally, something we agree on. "What about the woman you were dating a few months ago?" I ask. "Did you ever bring her out here?"

"You mean Rose?" Bob shakes his head, and his face flushes red. "Naw, I knew she'd hate it. Her house was heavily decorated, and she had all these designer names for things. All I know is that it was a lot of pink, frilly crap. Being inside that house felt like being inside a bottle of Pepto Bismol."

I can't help but laugh at this despite a determined effort not to. Fortunately, Bob not only doesn't appear offended by my laughter, he visibly relaxes and chuckles along with me. After a few seconds he says, "Yeah, our tastes were definitely not in sync. I like your place, your taste. It suits me."

There is an odd sense of intimacy in his words,

and for a few seconds we hold one another's gaze. Then I clear my throat and look away. "Again, lots of potential in this room," I say. "Show me the kitchen."

Finally, we enter a room with plenty of natural light and it's as if we took a ride in a time machine back to the fifties. Unlike the other rooms, this one is painted a sunny yellow color. The cabinets are painted a minty green, and the floor is covered in large, square, black-and-white tiles. In the center of the room is a table made with yellow Formica and chrome, with four matching chairs. The refrigerator is a standard, white model, and the only newer-looking thing in the room. The stove, which I instantly covet, is a gas, four-burner behemoth of white enamel with a griddle in the center, two side-by-side ovens, and two storage drawers. There is no dishwasher. Instead there is a large porcelain sink with two sections, one deeper than the other, and a built-on drainboard to one side, sporting a dish rack with several plates and glasses drying in it. The counters are covered with black-and-white tiles that are a smaller, mirror copy of the floor.

"This room is amazing!" I tell Bob. "I love the retro look of it."

Bob looks surprised. "Really? I thought it was kind of outdated."

"Oh, it is, but in a good way." Bob looks at me like I've lost my mind. "It's complicated," I say with a shrug and a smile.

"Apparently," Bob observes with a hint of sarcasm. Then he changes the subject. "I'll reheat our sandwiches in the oven. And I have some chocolate chip ice cream in the freezer for dessert, if you're up for it. It's low fat but it tastes decent enough."

"Sounds good to me."

Bob turns on the oven while I check out and use the first-floor bathroom, a simple half bath with a pedestal sink and a toilet located off the kitchen. The toilet seat is chipped and cracked, and the floor is covered with worn white linoleum, the underlying floorboard showing through in front of the sink. Over the sink is a mirrored medicine cabinet that is rusted on both sides. I check myself out in the mirror and see that P.J.'s makeup is holding up well. Then I try to decide if I should wash my hands with hot or cold water since there is no way to combine them—each one has its own faucet. I opt for cold, happy to see that the hand towel hanging from a hook in the wall is freshly laundered. Bob isn't a pig, at least. The house may have a little more dust than some places, but it's largely neat and clean. I know from experience that bachelor pads often aren't.

This gets me to wondering how Bob managed when he was over four hundred pounds and didn't want to climb the stairs. Had he used this tiny bathroom for his daily ablutions? Presumably there is a tub or shower upstairs somewhere, but I suppose he might have made do with sponge baths here, though given the tiny size of the room I'm inclined to think he used the kitchen sink instead.

The sandwiches are still heating in the oven, and Bob invites me to join him at the kitchen table, which is in such amazingly good condition that I can't help but wonder if it's a modern replica. "Can I get you something to drink?" he offers as I settle in. "I have water, sparkling water, and coffee or tea. Not much else I'm afraid."

"I'd love a cup of coffee," I say.

He has one of those modern cup-at-a-time coffee machines and in just over a minute I have a steaming mug in front of me. "Do you take anything in it?" he asks. "I have some skim milk in the fridge and sugar if you want it."

"Black is fine," I say. "Thanks."

As Bob sits down with a can of sparkling water, I say, "Danny Hildebrand doesn't strike me as a killer. He might be a cam bolt shy of being fully assembled at times, but he's basically harmless."

Bob gives me a confused look and I gather that he's never had to assemble any furniture. He sighs, his brow furrowed with doubt. "I don't know, Hildy. I've seen too many people with mental health disorders take an unexpected ride on the wild side to think they're predictable at all. Hell, plenty of so-called normal people do the same thing. If there's one thing about us humans that's predictable, it's our unpredictability."

I smile at that. "Speaking of unpredictability, what have you found out about our Mr. Fletcher? How long do you think he's been growing pot?"

"Laura got a preview of his financials at the house and it looks like the bank was about to foreclose on his farm two years ago. Then a sudden influx of cash arrived and there have been other similar deposits ever since, about once every three months. I'm not too concerned about the pot. It's going to be legalized soon enough anyway. But the other plants he was growing are certainly worrisome. The guys at Homeland Security are quite interested in Mr. Fletcher's secret garden."

I nod, feeling a worm of unease in my gut. "Any idea who he was growing it for, or where the money was coming from?"

"Laura said all the transactions she could find were cash. Nothing traceable."

"It was a daughter who called in requesting the welfare check. What does she have to say?"

"There are two daughters, actually, both married, both living in Minnesota. His wife died four years ago in a car accident. I haven't had a chance to talk to the daughters yet. The local cops in Minnesota served the death notice to the daughter who called asking for the welfare check."

"We have a positive ID then?"

Bob nods and gets up to check on our sandwiches, talking while he works. "Doc Morton was able to identify him from scars and birthmarks. Mr. Fletcher had a lot of scars from mishaps he had with his farming equipment. There was a wound on his right leg a few years ago from a machinery incident that got infected. It cleared up after some antibiotics and a few trips to Milwaukee for treatment in a hyperbaric chamber. While the wound eventually healed, it left a distinctive scar on his leg that was in the shape of a maple leaf. There was a picture of it in his medical record—or rather several pictures—taken at various stages in the healing process, including one of the wound after it was completely healed. That picture showed the distinctive shape of the scarring."

Bob dons a pair of oven mitts that are covered with burn marks and removes the sandwiches from the oven, putting them on plates. He carries them over to the table and sets them down, then shucks the gloves and retrieves a couple of forks from a drawer, and two paper napkins from a package sitting on the counter. He hands me a fork and a napkin, and then sits down and uses his fork to remove the hot foil wrapping from the remnants of his sandwich.

"Did the Minnesota cops have anything to say about the daughter's reaction when they told her?" I ask him, picking up my fork and unwrapping my sandwich. The reheating has worked well; the roll is still soft, the cheese inside the sandwich is melted nicely, and the pepper and onion toppings are steaming.

Bob grins at me. "You sure ask a lot of questions," he says. "Good ones, no less."

"So, she did say something significant?" I ask, eager for the details.

He shakes his head. "Not exactly. It wasn't anything she said, it was her reaction to the news." He pauses and takes a bite of his sandwich. After a few chews he nods and smiles at me. "This is really good," he says with a full mouth.

I set my elbows on the table, lace my fingers together, and use them as a hammock for my chin. My sandwich can sit for now and cool off a little. I suspect Bob is drawing out the telling of his story on purpose, and I'm more than happy to put the pressure on him while I wait him out. I fix him with a laser-like stare.

A hint of a smile crosses his face as he swallows, and he washes the food down with a swig of water. After dabbing at his mouth with his napkin, he finally says, "The cops up there said she barely reacted at all. She didn't seem particularly surprised or upset to hear that he was dead. Didn't even ask for any details about how he died. She just thanked the cops and closed the door."

"Wow. That's cold," I say.

"I thought so, too, so I did some inquiries. I called a neighboring farmer, spoke to Mrs. Fletcher's sister, and spoke to the minister at the Lutheran church in town because Laura noticed that despite his financial problems, Mr. Fletcher has been making regular donations to the church for the past few years. It turns out that Arthur Fletcher was driving in the accident that killed his wife."

"How awful."

"And he was drunk."

"Oh."

"Yeah. The neighboring farmer said it was well known that Artie Fletcher had a drinking problem. That's why he was always getting injured by his farm equipment. The minister said Mr. Fletcher wasn't a member of the church; his wife was. Arthur Fletcher has never set foot in the place. But he sobered up after his accident, and he's been making the donations on a regular basis ever since, in memory of his dead wife."

I decide I've waited long enough, and I finally take a bite of my sandwich. Bob takes another bite of his, too, then another, and after one more, his is gone. There is a period of relative quiet as we both chew.

Bob picks up his story after he swallows his last bite. "According to Mrs. Fletcher's sister, who lives in Chicago, the girls blamed their father for their mother's death and didn't speak to him for two years after the car accident. They were both living away from home already at the time, so it was easy to maintain an estrangement. One of them, the one who called about the welfare check, apparently forgave her father, or at least decided to start speaking to him again, and even visited a time or two over the past year. But I gather his relationship with both of his daughters is a strained one."

"What about their inheritance? Won't they get the farm?"

"Doubtful," Bob says. "The property will most likely be seized by the DEA. Fletcher wasn't actively farming other than the stuff in the barn cellar, if you can count that. He was renting out his fields to other farmers. I suppose it's possible they might sell off the property in parcels to the farmers who are renting." He shrugs. "I don't know for sure how that stuff works."

I finish off my sandwich in silent contemplation while Bob gets out some bowls and serves up the ice cream.

"Any theories about where Fletcher's cash was coming from?" I ask Bob after sampling the ice cream. For low fat, it tastes quite good.

"There are private militia groups all over Wisconsin and Michigan," he says. "Some are based on religious beliefs, some are anti-government, others have their own agendas. My best guess would be one of them. There's an anarchist group that's been compared by some to the Branch Davidians that's based in the U.P. not far from the Canadian border. Rumor has it they have recruits all over the country."

When Bob says "U.P."—local shorthand for the upper peninsula area in both Wisconsin and Michigan—it makes me snort with laughter, and that garners me a peculiar look from him.

"Sorry," I say. "I'm not laughing at what you just said. It's not only not funny, it's scary as hell. It's the mention of the U.P. that got me. One of my foster sibs used to pee in her pants whenever anyone would say U.P. and when the foster parents would question her on why she did it, she'd always say that so-and-so told me to, with so-and-so being whoever had uttered the words, or for her the command, U.P. It always made us laugh . . . us kids, that is. The grownups definitely did not find it funny."

"Why did she do that?" Bob asks, looking puzzled and perhaps a bit wary as well.

I shrug. "I think it was her way of protesting, of acting out. We all did it in one way or another."

Bob contemplates this as he scrapes the last of his ice cream from his bowl. "It must have been hard growing up under those circumstances."

"It had its ups and downs." I finish my ice cream and drop my spoon in the bowl with a clatter.

Bob snatches up both bowls and carries them to the sink. Over his shoulder he says, "Did you act out?"

"Hell, yeah. I was probably one of the worst kids."

"Really? What sort of things did you do?"

"I stole. A lot. Food, mostly." I leave out the fact that I still steal food even now and do it without realizing it most of the time. "I also mouthed off a lot, and broke my curfews, and I ran away a few times. There were some physical altercations here and there, usually with other kids."

Bob looks amused by this. "I gather you lost most of the time, just by virtue of your size."

"Actually, no," I tell him. "I was small, but I was mean, determined, and fueled by my righteous indignation. Because of my size, people were always underestimating me."

Bob has returned to the table and he's standing there looking down at me with an odd expression. "I'm betting people still do," he says.

Sensing that it's a good time to change the subject, I say, "Are you serious about wanting to redo this house?"

"I am. It's been the same for thirty years or more. I'm ready for a change."

"I'd love to help."

"I could use it."

"I'll write down some ideas and we can talk it over." I glance at my watch. "But it will have to wait. I need to go home and get ready for my shift tonight."

"Who did you say you're riding with tonight?"

"Brenda Joiner. I like her. I think it will be fun. Devo was okay, but I don't think he's bought into the whole social worker idea yet."

"Give him time. New programs tend to be a bit rocky straight out of the gate. People don't always take to change."

"Want some help with those dishes?" I say, nodding toward the sink.

"No, I can manage. It's the least I can do since you cooked. Thanks for dinner."

"And thanks for dessert."

"We should do it again some time."

"We should."

There is a long, awkward moment of fleeting glances and shuffling feet before Bob clears his throat, turns away, and makes a beeline for the front door. Neither of us says a word as we get into the car, or during the ride back to my house.

Bob finally breaks the silence as he pulls up to the curb and says, "Have a good shift." He makes no effort to move toward me, and he has a white-knuckled grip on the steering wheel as if he's afraid it will get away.

I decide to let him set the pace of things for now and simply say, "Thanks. You have a good night." Then I get out of the car and head inside. He pulls away and disappears before I reach my front door.

Chapter 13

When I get inside, I find P.J. sitting on my couch, Roscoe curled up at her feet . . . no, *on* her feet, I realize. "You two look cozy," I say.

She's having none of the small talk. "How did the date go? Did you kiss him? Did he kiss you? Did you do anything else?"

I'm not sure what P.J. knows about the "anything else" part, and I don't want to find out. "You're being rather personal," I say. "I'd like to keep things private for now. People often feel that way and it's rude to push too hard when it comes to things like that." Anyone else might take offense at my correction, but P.J., who seems to sense her own lack of social skills, takes it like a champ.

"Okay." She pulls her feet out from under Roscoe and gets up from the couch. She heads for the door and I assume she's leaving for the night, so I tell her goodnight.

She stops, looks back at me, and says, "Would it

be too personal or rude if I asked you how you learned to kiss?" I arch my brows at her, surprised, and wondering what's behind the question. P.J. elaborates when I'm not immediately forthcoming with an answer. "You know, kiss in a romantic way, not like the way you kiss a mother, or father, or brother."

"Why are you asking me that?" I say. "Are you thinking about kissing someone in a romantic way?"

"No," she says matter-of-factly. She turns to leave but I call her back.

"P.J., a couple of weeks ago you asked me a question about how to tell if a boy likes you. I get the sense that there is a boy out there that you are interested in. If there is, you can tell me."

She stares at me for the longest time, her face expressionless, revealing nothing. Then she shrugs and says, "I don't have a boyfriend if that's what you mean. I heard some older girls on the track team talking and I didn't understand some of it. They were talking about letting a boy kiss them, and how some of them don't know how. And then they were talking about playing some weird baseball game where they let the boys go to first or second base."

Oh, my. P.J. is only eleven years old, still much too young to be dealing with such things, in my opinion. Then again, I knew way more than she apparently does when I was only five. Having a mother who earns her living as a hooker tends to educate one on those matters. I don't want P.J. to lose her innocence the way I did, but I also don't want her to be ignorant of the things that could happen to her. Have her parents talked to her about the birds and the bees yet? I suspect they haven't, only because they don't seem to spend much time with the kid. When did they cover this stuff in school? Surely not in the fourth grade. Today's kids are often quite precocious when it comes to their knowledge of sexual matters, at least the nitty-gritty part of it, but I can't imagine that any official sex education starts much before middle school.

I'm tempted to brush off the matter by telling P.J. to ask her parents about it, but I know she won't. Her isolation from her parents is as much because that's the way P.J. likes it as it is her parents' laser and often singular focus on other things. No, I can't brush her off, I realize. But I'm not ready to tackle the problem yet, either. So, I stall.

"Tell you what, P.J.," I say. "You and I can talk about that stuff and I'll explain it to you. But I can't do it tonight because it's a big topic and it will take more time than I have right now. I need to get ready for my shift with the police. And I think it's your bedtime, isn't it?"

"I go to bed when I want," she says with a shrug. From any other kid I would suspect this is a bit of false bravado, but I believe P.J. She turns and heads for the door again. "I'll be by in the morning to walk Roscoe after you get home," she says over her shoulder.

"That's fine. And since I'll be sleeping for a good part of the day, would you mind walking him again around lunchtime?"

"Sure," she says, pausing in the doorway. "Goodnight." She's out the door, closing it behind her before I can say goodnight back.

I stare at the closed door for a minute or two, my mind racing. Clearly, I'm going to need to come up with a plan for dealing with this issue. And knowing P.J. like I do, I realize it will have to be sooner rather than later. She is bright, curious, and inquisitive, and when she gets a bug up her butt on a subject, she doesn't let it go until she gets the answers she's seeking. While watching a Harry Potter movie at my house one afternoon, a commercial came on about a feminine hygiene product. That triggered a host of awkward questions from P.J. that I tried my darnedest to skirt around and avoid. But over a period of several days she kept bringing the topic up, asking and prodding and digging until she felt satisfied with the answers I gave her. We waged a similar skirmish when she heard the phrase *erectile dysfunction* somewhere and started questioning me on what it meant. Every answer led to a new question, and I danced around that one the best I could using euphemisms and terms like "a circulatory problem" that were factual but also vague.

I turn and look at Roscoe, who is still lying on the floor by the couch. "Looks like we have our work cut out for us with P.J., eh?" I say, and Roscoe thumps his tail in agreement.

I go to my bedroom and pick out some slacks and a plain tan blouse to wear for my night shift with the police department. When I asked what I should wear for the job—would a uniform be required?—Chief Hanson had suggested that we start out with simple street clothes, something that

looked professional to a degree—no blue jeans—
but nothing too fancy. Basically, the same things I
would wear for my job at the hospital, accompanied by an ID badge that made it clear I was a
member of the police department. And until the
weather got too warm for it, I also had my bomber
jacket, which I considered really to be the bomb,
and which has the police department emblem
sewn onto the front of it.

I'd been relieved to learn that I wouldn't have
to be fitted for a uniform because I knew it wouldn't
be an off-the-rack affair and I'd have to arrange
for some hurried alterations. As it was, I bought a
few new clothing items as a way of celebrating my
new job: several pairs of slacks, some blouses, and
two pant suits. The blouses fit me fine since they
were short-sleeved, though they did hang lower on
me than they would on most women. The other
stuff all had to be altered and I'd taken the items
to Tamela, a fellow foster sibling I got to know
when I lived in a group home during high school.
In fact, she is due to deliver the items back to me
tomorrow evening.

After getting myself ready, I put Roscoe's vest on
him and the two of us hop in my car. The drive to
the station only takes a few minutes thanks to the
lack of traffic at this time of night, and my badge
gives me access to the fenced-in lot behind the station. I park, leash up Roscoe, and badge us into
the building via the back door, which opens into
the station's breakroom.

I'm early by half an hour, so I tell Roscoe to go
lie down and then I do some cleanup. Back when I
first saw this room, which was before I was hired

on, I was appalled at what a mess it was. And being just the tiniest bit OCD when it comes to cleanliness, I proceeded to spiff the place up. My efforts were noticed and appreciated by Brenda Joiner, the only person who commented at all. The rest of the station employees not only haven't noticed, but they've made no effort whatsoever to maintain the newly cleaned state. I'm surprised I got the job I did with this department because, apparently, being a slob is one of the criteria for working here.

Tonight's mess is the usual: crumbs on the counters, the remains of some tomato sauce that exploded from someone's nuke-a-meal inside the microwave, cup and can rings on the countertops, spilt soda on the floor and table, an overflowing trash can, and a sink half-filled with used coffee mugs and water glasses. Roscoe settles on the doggie pillow that Chief Hanson bought for him, sniffing at the food and water dishes beside it, but not sampling either. He watches me as I make quick work of the cleanup and then thumps his tail when Brenda Joiner comes in the back door just as I finish.

"Oh, Hildy, you do nice work," she says appreciatively.

"Thanks."

She walks over to Roscoe and gives him a scratch between his ears. She does this every time she sees him, which is why he started thumping his tail the minute she came through the door. "How's our boy tonight?"

Judging from the lolling tongue and look of ecstasy on Roscoe's face, I'd say he's doing just fine.

"I'm looking forward to our shift tonight," Brenda

says. "This new program is exciting. I think it's a great idea. Last night was certainly a big one, eh?"

"That it was," I agree.

"Hopefully we won't have anything quite that exciting tonight. How did you and Devo get on?"

"Well enough. It's going to take some time for people to get used to having me tag along."

"Devo's a bit old school," Brenda says, rolling her eyes. "He might take longer than some of the others. Though I can't speak for the county guys. They might take to you right away."

Her comment puzzles me. "They shouldn't have to deal with me too much," I say.

Brenda looks at me, her brow furrowed. "You know you're going to be riding with them, too, right?"

"What? No. Why do you say that?"

Brenda sighs and shakes her head. "I can't believe they didn't tell you."

"Tell me what?" I say, a sinking feeling in my gut.

"In order to get the funding approved, Chief Hanson had to expand his proposal to reach beyond the Sorenson city limits. Helping Hands is going to be a countywide program. You and Roscoe are going to be doing ride-alongs with the county sheriffs, as well. In fact, you might end up spending more time with them than with us."

I ponder this new information with a mix of irritation, excitement, and trepidation. I'm irritated that I wasn't told this before now, excited that the program would apparently extend beyond the confines of Sorenson—which, despite last night's happenings, I suspect isn't all that exciting on most nights—and trepidation because I'll be working with a group of unknown cops. I felt comfortable with the Sorenson department because I've gotten to know most of the officers through my work at the hospital. The county sheriff's department is a whole new unknown.

"Thanks for telling me," I say to Brenda. "Chief Hanson somehow neglected to share that information with me."

"Sorry," Brenda says with a grimace. "I hope it doesn't upset you."

"It's unexpected," I admit. "But I'll adapt. That's what the program is about, after all, adapting to unexpected and new situations, and helping others do the same."

"Good attitude," Brenda says. "I'm going to go check out the shift report. Meet you back here in five to ten?"

"We'll be here."

The back door opens, and Devo comes in. He nods at me but doesn't say a word.

"Ready to roll, Devo?" Brenda says.

"Sure," he answers with little enthusiasm. He follows Brenda out of the breakroom and down the hall to a front room where the shift handoffs take place. There is no fancy roll call here, or room full of coppers getting all the latest intel and info like you might see on a TV show. Sorenson only has three officers on duty on the night shift, and a maximum of five on the day and evening shifts most of the time.

Other than the murder of Arthur Fletcher, there must not be much going on in town. And judging from the fact that Brenda and Devo return from their shift report in eight minutes flat, I gather there hasn't been much progress in the Fletcher case, either.

Five minutes later, Brenda and I are cruising through town, Roscoe riding contentedly in his pen in the back of the car. There is a thin haze of fog hovering over the ground in areas, lending the night an ethereal air.

"They had a bunch of guys from the FBI and Homeland Security out at the Fletcher farm all day today," Brenda tells me. "It's obvious that Mr. Fletcher wasn't growing that much stuff just for himself, and they haven't had much luck yet tracking the cash flows he received to figure out who he was working for. They're interviewing other farmers in the area to see if any of them were approached by anyone offering cash payments for certain crops, but so far Fletcher seems to be the only one. Though that's assuming the other farmers are being upfront and honest about things. For all we know, there may be another one of those barn basements filled with death plants in the area. Farmers are really struggling these days. Can't say I'd blame them for the marijuana, but the other stuff. . . ." She shakes her head woefully.

"Do you think Mr. Fletcher knew what he was growing?" I ask her. "I mean, I'm sure he knew about the pot and I imagine he figured it was worth the risk since the stuff is getting legalized everywhere these days. It's only a matter of time before that happens here, too, I suppose. But what about the other plants? The ones used to make ricin and stuff like that. Do you think Arthur Fletcher knew that he was growing poisons for potential weaponization and bioterrorism?"

Brenda sighs. "Hard to say. I heard they found some articles on Fletcher's computer that suggest he had some strong anti-government leanings. Not hard for a farmer to think that way these days, since the government seems to have abandoned them. But we're starting to wonder if maybe he was having second thoughts. Arthur Fletcher owned a cell phone, but we can't find it anywhere, and the land line to his house was cut. The key to his pickup is also missing. Sounds like someone was afraid Fletcher might go AWOL."

"That would explain why he was killed," I say, and Brenda nods grimly.

We are driving past the cemetery, the one where Danny claimed to have seen Fletcher's ghost. Clearly, Fletcher's death spooked him, and I can't help but wonder how much Danny knew about what was going on out there at the farm. I'm about to say as much to Brenda when I see something strange near the giant oak tree in the cemetery.

And then I'm stunned into horrified silence as I watch the ghost of Arthur Fletcher emerge from the trunk of a tree.

Chapter 14

"Brenda, stop the car!" I say when I manage to find my voice.

She hits the brakes and pulls over to the curb. "What? What's wrong?" she says, looking about frantically.

I realize then what I'm about to say, that I just saw a ghost in the town cemetery. We are nearly two blocks past the graveyard already, and I glance back over my shoulder, half expecting to see Arthur Fletcher's ghost come flying down the street toward us. But of course, that doesn't happen.

"I thought I saw something . . . something odd back there at the cemetery," I say. "Can we turn around and go back?"

"Okay," Brenda says slowly, shifting the car into gear. "What is it you think you saw?"

She's going to think I'm a lunatic. And then she'll tell

Chief Hanson about it and I'll end up getting fired from this job before I've even finished the first week.

I realize how insane it's going to sound if I tell Brenda what I think I saw, so I do a quick mental scramble and come up with a version of the truth. "I saw something odd, like a weird flash of light. Maybe it's the same thing that Danny saw."

The two of us stare at the cemetery in silence as Brenda steers the car back down the street and then turns left to drive past the gated side. I see tombstones and monuments in the dim moonlight, but nothing else.

"I don't see anything. Maybe it was a trick of the light," Brenda says suggestively, and I nod. She eyes me warily and then says, "You look like you've seen a ghost, Hildy. Are you sure you're okay?"

"I'm fine," I say, though I'm not totally convinced, and I can't help but chuckle at the irony of her comment. Surely, I didn't see a ghost. I don't believe in ghosts. "It must have been an odd patch of fog that reflected the moonlight just right," I tell her. "It did look like a ghost."

We both laugh at that, though I'm aware that neither laugh is fully committed. I realize we're both feeling a little nervous, and I decide to try to shift the conversation to a more neutral topic.

"Whatever it was, it's gone now," I say. "Sorry for making you stop."

"Hey, not a problem."

"So, I hear you're dating Christopher Malone from the ME's office."

She gives me a funny look before answering, probably amused or confused by my random change of subject. "I am. For several months now. It seems to be going rather well."

"That's great."

"I hear you might be dating Bob Richmond," she counters.

I make a face. "I'm not sure you could call what we're doing dating," I say. "We've had dinner together two whole times, but it always feels more like two friends getting together, or two colleagues. I think he's interested in me in a more romantic way, but I'll be darned if I can figure out how to go about getting him to take the next step."

Brenda chuckles. "Men," she says with a woeful shake of her head. "They are complicated creatures at times, aren't they? I tried to tell Christopher once that I wanted to feel more like a woman, meaning I wanted to dress up in feminine clothes and maybe soak in a bubble bath or get a pedicure, those kinds of things. His response was to suggest that I cook more often or decorate something."

I snort a laugh. "I went out with a guy once who couldn't understand why it bothered me that he flirted with other women during our date. He kept insisting that since he was on a date with me, I should feel confident and secure in our relationship. I told him that confident and secure doesn't typically come on first dates, particularly when your date spends most of his time eyeballing other pretty women. He told me our first date would be the last because I was just too insecure. I came back with a comment about how cocky it was of him to assume I'd want a second date. At which point he said, "Why wouldn't you? I'm a catch.""

"Oh my God, he actually said *I'm a catch?*" Brenda says, giggling in disbelief.

"Yes, he did."

"Men and their egos," Brenda says. "And they're like mascara. They run at the first sign of emotion."

"Do you have a hard time at work given that you're a woman in a mainly male field?"

"Oh, the guys tease me all the time. They're crass, politically incorrect, and ribald as all get out. When we attend those employee awareness sexual harassment sessions, I realize that their behaviors are like a training video on what not to do. But I don't mind it. No one is mean to me, and I know they have my back if I need them. They may tease me a lot, but I dish it right back to them. And I know that despite it all I have their respect. The teasing is just a way to let off some steam and build camaraderie. Though I suppose my tolerance of it sets the women's movement back a decade or two every time I let them get away with something."

I shrug. "My personal feelings on the matter are that if no one is offended or gets hurt, where's the harm? I think where things go off the rails is when someone like you doesn't mind the banter and even engages in it, and then someone else comes along who doesn't like it and they complain. Sometimes it's hard for people to realize that not everyone will appreciate that sort of banter. But it's not uncommon in fields where there's a high level of stress. I see it among the medical staffers a lot, especially in the ER. And now that there are more men in nursing, and more women doctors, it's gotten worse instead of better. The sexual innuendo, crassness, and political incorrectness that flies around there is crazy. But no one seems to mind it. It keeps them laughing, and that's good therapy."

"Speaking of laughs," Brenda says, "there's this one incident that the guys tease me about all the time that still makes me crack up whenever I think about it. I arrested this guy for a B and E at a liquor store and he was already drunk as a skunk. So, I cuffed him and then proceeded to cite the Miranda warning. When I got to the part that says anything you say can be held against you, he came back with *How about your boobs?*"

I chuckle. "That was some fast thinking on his part."

"And even more impressive when you consider he blew a three-nine."

Our conversation is cut short by a call coming in over the car's radio, asking Brenda to check out a complaint about a guy who appears to be having a mental breakdown. My thoughts immediately go to Danny when I hear this, but the address isn't anywhere near his sister's house. In fact, it's on the opposite side of town. Of course, it's possible Danny might be at some other location, so I remain prepared to find the poor guy once again in the throes of a schizophrenic episode.

It only takes a few minutes to reach the address the dispatcher gave us. It's one of several duplexes on a street, some of them owned by the people who live in them, some of them rentals. There is a woman in a bathrobe, pajamas, and a cap with two points on top of it, making her look like a bat or a cat, standing in the front yard of the address we were given. Brenda pulls up to the curb and parks.

"What can we help you with, ma'am?" Brenda asks as we approach.

"It's not here. It's those people," she says, indicating a duplex across the street.

I look where she's pointing and see someone on their hands and knees in the front yard. At first, I think it's someone throwing up in the grass, but as I look closer, I realize that it's a young man crawling around and eating the grass. I give my head a shake, not sure I can believe what my eyes are seeing, and then take another look. Yep, the guy is grazing on the lawn, lowering his head to the grass, ripping out a mouthful, and then chewing.

"They're always throwing wild parties over there," the robed woman says to Brenda. "Mary Jean Homburg owns that building and she has a history of renting out to questionable people. Those of us in the neighborhood who own have asked her to be more discretionary, but she doesn't care who lives in the place because she lives across town and doesn't have to deal with them. As long as they pay the rent. . . ." The woman rolls her eyes. "I want you to arrest Mary Jean for this," she continues, glaring at Brenda. "Maybe then she'll see the light. I'll file charges or whatever it is I need to do."

"I can't arrest the landlord because of what the tenants do," Brenda tells the woman.

"Why not?" the woman asks, her voice rife with indignation. "What the hell do I pay taxes for? You're a civil servant, aren't you? Don't you have to do what I tell you to do?"

"No ma'am, I don't," Brenda says with admirable patience.

"What a load of horse pucky!" the woman snaps. "You police are useless. I don't know why you bother carrying those guns if you aren't willing to use them." She shakes her head in disgust. "Someone needs to grow a pair," she mutters. She stares at Brenda and then looks at me. We both smile back at her with questioning looks.

"Oh, for Pete's sake," she grumbles. "It's a saying. You know what I mean." With that, she turns and storms back toward her house.

Brenda gets on her radio and calls for backup. Then she says to me, "Keep an eye out, Hildy. Lord knows what we're going to find over there, but I'm also worried about this one." She gestures toward the robed woman, who is disappearing through her door. "I wouldn't put it past her to come back out here with a gun to try to deliver a little justice of her own. In fact, maybe you should wait in the car."

"I'll be okay," I tell her. "I'll stay alert and if anything starts to look hinky, I'll get out of the way."

Brenda looks at me and smiles. "Hinky?"

"Yeah, you know, worrisome, weird, potentially dangerous."

"Got it. Stay behind me, okay?"

She doesn't have to tell me twice. For once I'm glad I'm a short person. Brenda isn't tall; she's around five six, but that's tall enough to cover me, at least vertically. Horizontal is another matter, but at least if I get hit with some wild gunfire that makes it past Brenda, I figure my love handles will take the hit and there aren't any vital organs there.

We cross the street, Brenda eyeing the surrounding houses warily. Just as we reach the lawn where the fellow is grazing, another cop car pulls up and Devo gets out. He hurries over to us on the lawn where the young man, who is wearing nothing but boxer shorts and a T-shirt, is still grazing away, seemingly oblivious to our presence.

"Sir?" Brenda says, touching him on his shoulder.

He looks up at her briefly, strands of grass hanging out of his mouth, his jaws grinding away. Inside the house we hear a loud crash and some raucous laughter, and Brenda looks at Devo. "You want to keep an eye on Elsie here while we check out the rest of this group?"

"I suppose," Devo says. "Is that why you called for backup? For a babysitter?"

Brenda narrows her eyes at him, her lips pursed. I expect her to chastise him, but instead she says, "And watch out for the crazy bat lady over there." Brenda nods toward the robed woman, who is back outside, standing on her porch glaring at us, toe-tapping with irritation, arms folded over her chest.

Brenda and I continue toward the house. The front door is wide open, and light spills out from a foyer onto the small porch. Inside to the left is a large open space, a combined living and dining area. It is occupied by several people who all look to be in their twenties or thirties and out of their minds. A girl is kneeling in front of a couch, repeatedly licking the cushions, slowly dragging her tongue over the nubby material. In the middle of the living room area is a guy on his knees on the floor trying to pick up a leaf that is woven into the pattern of the area rug. His fingers scrape along the surface as he tries to pry up edges that aren't there, his focus on the leaf singular and laser-like. Seated in an armchair is a woman who is holding a table lamp, waving it around in front of her, *ooh*ing and *aah*ing over the light patterns it's making on the ceiling. Rounding out this circus is a guy standing in the far corner of the dining area with his face to the wall as if he's being punished. Behind him, on her hands and knees, is a young woman barking like a dog.

Near the center of the room is a large, square table with a variety of Chinese takeout containers scattered over it. Paper plates covered with partially eaten helpings of lo mein, fried rice, steamed dumplings, a beef and broccoli dish, and spring rolls are interspersed in between the containers. Fortune cookies, still wrapped in cellophane, are strewn about the floor.

"Oh my," I say, "These people must be on some heavy-duty stuff."

"You think?" Brenda says with no small amount of sarcasm. "LSD is my guess." She looks around the room and then points to a sheet of paper on the coffee table that looks like a page of old-fashioned green stamps. Several of the stamps are missing. "Whatever you do, don't touch that." She talks into her radio and tells Devo to come inside the house. A moment later he's standing beside the two of us gaping at the craziness before him.

"So, what do you do with them?" I ask.

Brenda sighs. "They aren't breaking any laws, other than possession, and you can bet your booties that no one in this room will be able to provide a straight answer as to whose drugs those are. And they don't appear to be engaged in any activities that put them or anyone else at risk."

"Unless the front lawn has recently been sprayed with pesticide or some such," Devo observes.

"Good point," Brenda says. "Maybe we should take that guy to the ER to be checked out. But these others . . ." She shrugs. "Unless we get another call that says they're doing something reckless or dangerous, I say we confiscate the drugs, shut the front door, and leave them be."

Devo dons gloves and gets a plastic bag from his car that he then uses to snag and bag the sheet of presumed LSD stamps. I meander back outside and keep an eye on the grazing cow guy, who is now lying on his back in the grass, staring up at the night sky, his lower face stained green from the freshly mown lawn.

An ambulance arrives to escort Mr. Cow to the ER for observation and evaluation, but the others in the house all seem to be fine physically, albeit high as kites. I look for anything I can do within my job description, but there is nothing. I don't want to let Roscoe out anywhere near these people for fear that there may be lingering bits of drug that he could lick or sniff. There is little I can do for these people in their current state. They are adults, the house is well kept and neat, and no one appears to be in any danger or in any state of emotional upset. In fact, they all look downright peaceful and happy.

Once the ambulance has gone and the front door to the house has been closed, Brenda says, "Come on, Hildy. We'll roll back by here a few times to check on them and make sure they're okay, but there's no point in hanging out."

Back in the car, I say, "I've never understood the urge to take mind-bending drugs like that."

Brenda looks over at me. "You never tried any of them?"

"Nope."

"Not even pot?"

"Nope, never did, though not from a lack of opportunity. I had plenty of chances. Some of the foster homes I spent time in had kids who kept stashes of the stuff, and most of the kids in the group home I lived in during my high school years did pot, cocaine, narcotics, even some meth. But I wasn't tempted. Maybe it's my OCD but I've never liked the idea of not being in full control of my body and my immediate surroundings. Heck, I don't even drink all that much for the same reason."

"I imagine the fact that your mother was murdered plays a role in that thinking," Brenda says.

"You know about that?" I say. I knew Bob Richmond was aware of my history, but I hadn't mentioned it to anyone else at the station and didn't think the others knew, particularly since it was such old news. My mother's murder happened over twenty-five years ago.

"Chief Hanson filled us in," Brenda explains. "He wanted us to know because he thought you might have some lingering emotional issues that could arise if you ended up at a murder scene. He wanted us to be aware, be on the lookout, so to speak."

I think back to the night before and the scene at

the farmer's house. Had Devo been evaluating me and my reaction to the scene all that time? If so, he was quite subtle about it. Though I suspect the more probable answer is that he was so caught up in the situation and trying not to toss his cookies that he forgot about me and my history entirely.

"How did it go last night?" Brenda asks. "Out at the farm. Was that upsetting for you?"

"You're not going to try to shrink me, are you?" I ask in a teasing tone. "Because I already have a shrink."

Brenda smiles. "Nah, just curious. You seem to be impervious to a lot of this stuff, but I don't want to make assumptions that might cause me to miss something critical happening with you."

"I'm fine, I promise. But thanks for looking out for me."

"Of course." Brenda falls silent, but I sense there is something more coming. A moment later, she proves me right. "I'd like to hear about what happened to your mom. Is it something you feel comfortable talking about?"

"Depends," I say, studying her face. "Why are you asking?"

She thinks about her answer for a moment, and I'm not sure what to make of that. "A couple of reasons," she says finally. "General cop curiosity, to start with. Cold cases are a hobby of mine. I'm not a detective, but I'd like to be one eventually, so any cold cases I can help solve will look good on my resume. Plus, it doesn't hurt to show the guys up from time to time," she adds with a wink and a grin.

"And why else?" I ask, sensing that there is another, deeper cause that's driving her.

"Empathy," she says. "My brother was murdered when I was seven. He was two years older than me. Someone snatched him when he was out riding his bike and his body was found over a year later, dumped in some woods thirty miles from where we lived."

"How awful," I say, trying to imagine the emotional wreckage that had to have caused. "Did they ever catch who did it?"

Brenda shakes her head. "It's a cold case, nearly as old as yours. I've looked into it, of course, but I've never been able to make much progress. The cops really bungled the investigation and some of the evidence has gone missing." She pauses and sighs heavily. "I'm more or less resigned to the fact that Ben's case will never be solved, but it helps me to work on other cold cases."

"Fair enough," I say. And since I'm eager to find someone, anyone who can help me investigate my mother's murder, I fill her in on my story.

Chapter 15

"I was seven when my mother was killed," I tell Brenda. "So, we have that in common."

"It's much too young to have to face something that awful," Brenda says, and I see hints of the pain she's been carrying all these years hidden in the lines of her face. It's a pain I know well, and I nod my agreement.

"My mother was a single mom with no family support who struggled to make ends meet. I have grandparents, or at least I think I do—I'm not sure if they're alive or dead—who live in Iowa and who belong to some type of strict religious sect. When they found out my mother was pregnant after a few rolls in the hay—literally—with a city boy, they ostracized her. Tossed her out of the family home and told her to never come back. They sent her on her way with no money, no car, not even a sack lunch. She barely had time to gather up a few changes of clothes, and then she had to leave under threat of a beating. She was sixteen."

"Oh my God," Brenda says, looking horrified. "How awful."

"Yeah. So, you'll understand why I've never tried to find or contact them." Brenda nods. "Anyway, Mom told me she walked into town and went to a few of the fast food joints looking for work. Most of them turned her away; the managers and owners wouldn't even talk to her. That's because they belonged to the same religious group as my grandparents, and they knew why my mother had been ostracized. It meant she was no longer welcome at their places of business, either."

"She went to the home of her boyfriend, thinking he might be able to put her up, but his parents had gotten wind of the situation and had sent him away to a military school. They refused to help my mom and she spent that first night sleeping on a park bench. The next day she went to a fast food place that was new in town and they offered her work. They also let her bunk in a room at the back of the store. But after a week of my mom working there, the owners realized that the rest of the town was blacklisting their establishment because they were helping her. Their business died away to nothing, so they had to let my mom go. They were kinder than the other town folk in that they gave her a bit of money on top of the wages she'd earned, along with some food and clothing, and then they bought her a bus ticket to Madison, Wisconsin."

"Wow," Brenda says. "Your mother must have been a brave woman."

"Or desperate. What else could she have done? I don't know what would have happened to her if not for the kindness of those people at the last."

"So, your father was some kid in this Iowa town?" Brenda asks.

I shake my head. "No, my mother lost that baby. She didn't get pregnant with me until a few years later. And by that time, she was earning most of her income from prostitution, so she didn't know for sure who my father was. Or so she claimed."

"You didn't believe her?"

I shrug. "I suppose it might have been the truth," I say doubtfully. "But there was one man in her life who came around more regularly than the others. I think he was paying the rent on the house where we lived, and there were other things I know he paid for. Mom still saw other men, but whenever this particular guy came around, she wouldn't entertain anyone else."

"And you think he might be your father?" Brenda asks.

"I think it's possible, even likely. I found some letters among my mother's things after she died that hinted at him being someone special. And even though Mom always made me stay with the neighbor lady whenever this guy came to town so the two of them could go off together—sometimes for days at a time—I overheard snippets of conversations. The place we lived in had once been a carriage house and whoever owned the main house put up some walls and turned it into an apartment. The main house was converted into a two-flat, and it was one of the renters in the main house who took care of me when my mother needed her private time.

"I think that lady—her name was Martha—was the closest thing to a friend my mother had. Whenever Mom dropped me off, I'd be told to go into one of the bedrooms and shut the door. There was a TV in there I could watch. Then my mother and Martha would have a cup of coffee and talk. I know they thought I couldn't hear them, but if I put my ear to the heat register in the floor, I could hear every word they said.

"I learned that my mother had a long-term relationship with this man going back years, and that at one time she considered her relationship with him to be an exclusive one. That was before I was born, around the time I would have been conceived, and at the time she was trying to make a living through waitressing and other legitimate jobs, though I think this man was supplementing her. My guess is that he was married, and he couldn't have a regular relationship with my mother, so he set her up as his mistress."

"What did he look like?"

I shrug. "I never saw him full face. My mother was always careful to make sure I wasn't around when he came. I caught a glimpse of his profile once when I sneaked a peek out the neighbor lady's window as he and my mom were leaving. But aside from knowing he had blond hair, was a few inches taller than my mother, and was a little on the chunky side, I have no clue."

"And what about the man who killed her?" Brenda says. "Assuming it was a man. Any idea who he was?"

"Not really, though I was there when it happened."

"You were there?" Brenda says with obvious horror, swerving the car slightly as she whips her head around to look at me. "Geez, Hildy, that's awful!"

"I didn't see anything, at least not anything related to her killing," I tell her. "My mother used to shut me in my bedroom whenever she entertained men and I wasn't allowed to come out until she opened my door, or the sun was up. I was in my room but awake when the man who killed her came over. I peeked through the keyhole and saw his legs and shoes, but nothing else. Based on the time of death, he was the one who killed her, but I didn't hear or see anything. I went to bed and fell asleep shortly after he arrived."

"Good heavens," Brenda says. "You're lucky he didn't kill you, too."

"I think he considered it," I tell her. "When I woke the next morning, my bedroom door was open, and my mother wouldn't have opened it unless the man had left and no one else was coming. She never got the chance. It had to have been him who opened it. The thought of him standing there watching me sleep, contemplating whether to kill me, after he'd just stabbed and strangled my mother to death, haunts me to this day. That, and the fact that I didn't do anything to save her."

"Sheesh, you were just a kid," Brenda says. "Even if you'd known what was happening, you couldn't have done anything to save her. If you'd tried, you'd likely be dead now, too."

"I know," I say with a sigh. "But it doesn't make it any easier. I couldn't help her then, but maybe I can find the man who killed her and bring her some justice."

"Any ideas at all?"

"I do have some leads, and I have a copy of the police file from the investigation, though it's not much help. I gave a copy of it to Mattie Winston over at the ME's office and Bob Richmond has one, too. He said he might try to look into it if he has some extra time."

"Where was she killed? I mean where were you living at the time?"

"Milwaukee."

"Not exactly in our jurisdiction."

"I know, but I think the killer might have been from Sorenson."

"Really?" Brenda gives me an intrigued look. "Why do you think that?"

"I saw bits of him though the keyhole that night. His right hand was missing the pinky finger and there was a ring on the next finger . . . a class ring, I believe. It had a large red stone in it. And the Sorenson High School rings have large red stones in them."

"Okay, but there must be plenty of other schools that have red stones in their class rings," Brenda says. "High schools and colleges."

"I know. But I also overheard my mother on the phone making the arrangements for her visitor. She said the name Sorenson at one point, in a surprised tone, and then said that seemed like a long way to come. And it took the guy nearly two hours to get there after the call."

Brenda rakes her teeth over her lower lip and shoots me a look.

"What?" I say.

"Don't get mad at me."

"Mad at you for what?"

"Hear me out. You think your father is from Sorenson, and you also think the man who killed your mother is from Sorenson. This town isn't that big, and you didn't even live here at the time. You were two hours away. What are the odds?"

"You're suggesting that it might have been my father who killed my mother?"

Brenda shrugs. "It seems plausible, don't you think? And it might explain why the guy looked at you while you slept but didn't kill you."

"No need to worry. I'd already come to that possible conclusion a long time ago. But I don't think it was my father who killed her. According to the police file, a dark hair was collected at the scene and my father, or the man who I think might be my father, is fair-haired. Of course, that hair could have come from any number of men. My mother had several men in her bed on a busy day, and while I'd love to say she washed the sheets several times a day, if they were done once a week, she was doing good."

The very idea of those sheets makes me shudder, and I have a sudden urge to wash my hands.

"Anyway," I go on, shoving my hands beneath my thighs to keep from subconsciously rubbing them together, "I also heard the voice of the man who killed her as well as that of my father. When I heard my father's voice it was distant and I couldn't make out any words, but I heard it well enough to know it was different from the killer's voice. The man who killed her had a Southern accent, and his voice was deep and gravelly. My father had more of a tenor voice."

"So, the fact that they were both from Sorenson—at least you think they were—is just a coincidence?" Brenda says.

"I suppose so, yes."

"I don't believe in coincidences," Brenda says firmly.

I sense her growing interest on the topic and realize I might have finally found an ally to help me investigate my mother's murder. But even as I'm thinking this, a call comes in over the radio and we are forced to refocus. This time it's a domestic situation, one of the cops' most hated calls, and it's at the home of someone the cops know well. As it turns out, so do I.

Chapter 16

I know that the scene at the house we're headed for will turn the domestic violence stereotype on its head. The victim is most likely the husband, Stewart Riley, a kind, intelligent man who is hopelessly in love with his wife. Stewart is a small man, standing about five-five and weighing maybe one-thirty. His wife, Marla, is several inches taller, at least forty pounds heavier, and strong as an ox. Marla spent time in the military and saw some action in Iraq, where a vehicle she was riding in hit an IED. The resultant explosion killed everyone except Marla, though she was badly wounded.

Marla recovered physically, but her mental wounds have proven more stubborn. She retired from the military with PTSD and developed a significant drinking problem. Unfortunately, Marla is not a very nice drunk; alcohol brings out the worst in her temperament. Also, unfortunately, her husband, Stewart, who has consistently stayed by her side, encouraging her to get help, is often the primary target of her rages. It started with verbal and emotional abuse, but it didn't take long for things to escalate to the physical. I've seen and spoken with Stewart half a dozen times in my years at the hospital, and I knew of other visits he had when I wasn't on duty.

I was the one who finally got the truth out of Stewart. In the beginning, either out of embarrassment or a desire to protect Marla, he tried to explain away his injuries with lies. For the most part, his stories were plausible. I finally got him to admit to the abuse one night when he came to the ER with a broken arm. It was what the doctor called a spiral fracture, an indication that the arm was twisted violently, making the break literally spiral around the bone. It's a type of fracture that cues medical professionals to suspect abuse in children when they see it—the same type of fracture that put Child Protective Services onto Al Whitman's family. Such a break in the arm of a grown man is less suspect, and the explanation Stewart gave made some sense. But one savvy, alert nurse saw something in the way Stewart answered certain questions and refused to look at her, and she called me in for a referral.

It took me about thirty seconds to decide the nurse had been right to be concerned, but it took much longer to get the truth out of Stewart. I'd seen Marla in the ER a few times, too, on those rare occasions when she'd let Stewart bring her in for detox, and I knew what she was like when she drank. Looking back at the number of times Stewart had been in with injuries, I commented that he seemed to be awfully accident prone. A few more comments and some hems and haws from Stewart eventually led to his breakdown confession. His wife regularly beat up on him when she drank, and he, believing that women were the weaker sex and that physical violence isn't the answer to anything, never retaliated or reported her. This, combined with the difference in their sizes and strengths, often made him a helpless victim.

I spent some time with Marla after that, talking to her when she'd show up in the ER, occasionally letting Roscoe work his therapeutic magic on her if I happened to be rounding with him when Marla was in the hospital, and trying to help her find better ways to deal with her PTSD. She would improve for a while, but inevitably the lure of the bottle would call her back and, when she started drinking, the cycle would repeat itself.

"Brenda, I know this couple well," I say as she steers the car toward the Riley house.

"As do we," she says with a sigh of impatience. "That woman is a beast."

"She can't always help herself," I explain. "She has PTSD and when her bad spells come on, she gets so frantic and desperate that she drinks too much to try to dull the pain. If you get in her face when she's like that, it only makes things escalate."

"Oh, I know," Brenda says wryly. "I've tussled with her before."

"Let me approach her, with Roscoe. I've dealt with her before using Roscoe and he has a definite calming effect on her, even when she's drunk. Her unit adopted a stray dog over in Iraq, and Marla spent more time with it than anyone else."

Brenda eyes me, thinking about my suggestion. "I don't know, Hildy. She'll take a punch at anybody, and if she has anything she can use as a weapon, heaven help you. She came at me once with a toilet plunger and rang my bell something fierce."

I smile at the image of Brenda getting clocked with a plunger. "Tell you what," I say. "Why don't we approach her together? You be on the ready in case she goes bonkers, though I don't think she will if I have Roscoe with me. She knows him and he always calms her down."

"Even when she's half out of her mind with alcohol?"

"Even then," I say. "Dog love is universal and pervasive. Trust me."

"Famous last words," Brenda says with a frown. "An old boyfriend told me to trust him right before he eloped with my best friend."

"Ouch!"

"Yeah, but I got my payback. I confronted him and then I Tased him, right in his junk. Got canned from my last job because of it and that's how I ended up here, but it was totally worth it."

"Too bad you didn't get back at your supposed best friend."

"Oh, but I did," she says with a wicked grin.

"Do tell."

"Another time. Let's deal with Marla first."

"Okay." And then, with my own wicked grin, I add, "Let's go flush her out."

Brenda doesn't miss the innuendo. "You are evil, Hildy," she says with a grin of her own. "I like that in a woman."

The front porch of the Riley house is dark, the

light fixture lacking any bulb. There is a picture window off to the left and faint, filtered light sifts through it, eking its way through closed, vertical blinds. No sooner do we get out of the car than I hear Marla's slurred but booming voice coming through the walls.

"Ish not funny, Stewie," she says in a sneering tone. "They're gonna get me. I know it. They're coming and you probly called 'em."

We hear Stewart's voice, next, but his is calm and low and it's impossible to make out what he's saying. Brenda makes Roscoe and me stay behind her and she steps up onto the porch and bangs hard on the front door.

"Sorenson Police," she says loudly.

Everything falls quiet. I look around at the nearby houses and see several curtains flick into place. The neighbors are watching.

A few seconds later the front door opens, and we see Stewart standing there, looking relieved. There is a nasty gash on his forehead that is bleeding, though not heavily. Most of it has crusted over, but the dried blood on his shirt tells us that it bled profusely at some point.

"Come in," he says. "She's in the kitchen. I've never seen her like this before, this bad. She's super paranoid and it's like she's completely lost touch with reality. I'm starting to wonder if she's on something more than just alcohol."

"Are you okay, Stewart?" I ask, nodding toward his head wound.

"Oh, this," he says after a moment of confusion, touching the spot with two fingers. "She threw a glass across the living room, not at me, at some imaginary person. It hit the fireplace surround and the glass broke and splintered in several directions. A piece of it nicked me. It's not deep."

"Why don't you wait out here for a few minutes," Brenda says to Stewart. "Let us approach Marla on our own and see what we can do to calm her down. Hildy says her dog, Roscoe, has a calming effect on her."

"That he does," Stewart says with a meager smile. He walks over and sits on the steps, looking tired and defeated.

Brenda nods to me, and then she starts down the hallway that leads from the front door to the back of the house, which is where the kitchen is located. We can see a small bit of the room from here: the sink with a window above it, faux-brick patterned linoleum, and some type of cloth lying on the floor, probably a towel.

I lead Roscoe on his leash, sticking close behind Brenda. Roscoe's steps are tentative; he senses the mood here is tense, and he's wary.

Brenda reaches the doorway to the kitchen and looks to the left and then to the right. It's quiet, so I gather Marla isn't in the throes of a major meltdown, and I risk coming up alongside Brenda.

The kitchen is a mess, dishes piled up in the sink, a half-eaten sandwich on the table, spilt milk on the countertop, and an open package of Oreo cookies sits on the floor, several of the cookies strewn about. I see Roscoe's nose twitching as he eyes the cookies and I tell him, "Leave it," in a low but firm tone. He obediently disregards the cookies and focuses his attention on Marla Riley instead.

Marla is standing in the doorway of a small bathroom—nothing more than a toilet and a sink like the one I saw at Bob Richmond's house—that's located off the kitchen. Her eyes are wide open and crazed, making her look both scared and a bit demonic. Her hair, which is long, dark, and curly, is a tangled, wild mess encircling her head. She's wearing leggings and a threadbare blue robe that is open in front and nearly off her right shoulder, revealing a tank top underneath. Her hands are tightly clenched at her sides.

When she sees us, her eyes widen even more. "We have to get them," she says in a low, paranoiac voice. "We have to get them before they get us. Guns and bombs everywhere." Her voice escalates in both volume and tenor.

"Marla, you're not in Iraq, you're at your home here in Sorenson," I say. "Look at your kitchen sink, and the table over there." I point to a small wooden table and two chairs located on the other side of the room. "There are no weapons here, just your husband, and some friends. Do you remember me? Hildy Schneider? We met several times at the hospital here in town."

There is a slight relaxation in Marla's taut shoulders as she looks around the room, though her eyes are still wide with fright.

I tell Roscoe to sit and stay, and I unhook his leash. Then I slowly move out into the kitchen and start gathering up the cookies. "Look at these, Marla," I say. "When did you ever see Oreo cookies in Iraq?" I shove the loose cookies back into the open package and set it on the table.

"Do you remember Roscoe?" I continue, hoping

to maintain my momentum. I walk over and pet Roscoe on the head, and he wags his tail tentatively, thumping it on the floor.

Marla's eyes shift to Roscoe and her expression softens. Tears well in her eyes. Then Marla's hands come up from her sides and I see the glint of something in one of them.

"Marla, what's in your hand?" I ask.

Marla shifts her gaze from Roscoe to me, looking mildly bemused. "My hand?" she echoes. She then looks at her left hand, which is empty, followed by her right hand, which is holding a knife.

"Marla, put down the knife," Brenda says. She removes her Taser from her belt as she speaks, moving slowly and with her body turned in such a way as to prevent Marla from seeing what she's doing.

Marla looks at the knife in bewilderment for a moment, as if unsure how she came to be holding it. Then she snaps her attention back to us. "I need my weapons," she says hurriedly. "I need to defend myself."

"Roscoe will protect you," I say in a calm voice. "But I can't let him be with you if you're holding the knife. He might get hurt. Sharp things scare him."

Roscoe, as if he understands what I've just said, whimpers. At the sound, Marla's hand opens and the knife clatters to the floor. Brenda, still with her Taser at the ready but held close where Marla can't see it, moves toward the knife and kicks it away. It scuttles across the floor and for a second Marla's attention is distracted from me and Roscoe as she pins her stare on the knife. Just as I'm thinking things might turn very bad very fast, Marla looks back at Roscoe and squats on the floor, her arms extended.

"I don't see any other weapons on her," Brenda informs me, and then I tell Roscoe to go to Marla. The dog dutifully walks up to the woman, slowing as he nears her, and gently rests his head on one of her knees, his big brown eyes looking up at her with the soul of unadulterated, unconditional doggie love.

Marla lets her hand rest atop his head, and she strokes him once. Then she collapses the rest of the way to the floor, a heap of sobbing human. Roscoe nuzzles her hand with his nose and lies down next to her.

"Wow, he's good," Brenda says appreciatively. "Why can't men be more like that?"

I clear my throat, and she looks at me quizzically. I roll my eyes back over my shoulder, a reminder that poor Stewart isn't that far away and might be listening.

"Oh, right," Brenda says quickly and half under breath. She clicks a button on her shoulder radio, informs the dispatcher that things are under control and then asks for an ambulance to be sent to the address.

I walk over to the huddled mess that is Marla and stroke her hair with one hand while I pet my dog with the other. We stay like that until the EMTs show up, and then there is a half-whispered side discussion about how safe it will be to transport Marla to the hospital without restraints or a police escort.

"Let me and Roscoe ride in the rig with her," I suggest. "I think she'll behave if Roscoe is there."

Judging from her expression, Brenda is clearly on the fence with this idea. "Okay," she says finally, "but I'm going to follow right behind you. If she starts to act out in any way at all, you pull over immediately and I'll be on it, okay?"

The EMTs are fine with this idea, and after they look over Stewart and clear him to drive himself to the hospital, we pile into our various vehicles to head out. Marla gives us a moment of grief when she tries to get off the ambulance cot when the EMTs go to strap her in, but I tell her that it's for everyone's safety and that even Roscoe will need to be restrained inside the ambulance.

Marla does fine in the ambulance with Roscoe at her side. It's a relatively short ride of just under ten minutes, and by the time we hand Marla over to the ER staff, she is glassy-eyed and meek, worn out from her alcohol- and adrenalin-fueled breakdown.

The staffers are all familiar with both Marla and Stewart, and I can see the weary determination on their faces as they gird themselves for yet another round in this family's drama. Marla never adheres to any of the plans put in place for her for long-term care, in part because she refuses to get any of her care through the VA, and her short-term commitments never last long, either.

While Brenda is chatting with the ER staff and Stewart so she can write up her report, I give Roscoe a quick walk and then put him in the carrier in the back of Brenda's cruiser. It's cool enough outside that he should be fine in the car while we tend to our ER needs.

Once inside, I go into Marla's room to talk to her, hoping that maybe this time she can be convinced to stick with whatever plan we put together for her. Despite her history, I know from caring for other patients that it only takes one time, one bit of dogged determination, one moment of desperation and commitment, to turn a life like Marla's around. You never know when that moment will come. For some, it's never. For others, it may be the fourth or fifth or twentieth time they try to get clean. I try never to give up on anyone.

A nurse has already started an IV and she is in the process of giving Marla some medication through it that will sedate her and keep her from going berserk again. Under the bright and somewhat harsh lights of the ER, I see a glimmer in Marla's eyes that I've never seen before, and I realize with a sinking heart that she is much worse this time. That glimmer I see isn't one of hope, it's the too-bright spark of someone who has gone over an edge, taken one step too many and fallen into the abyss. She looks at me with a maniacal smile.

"Hildy, we're going to get them good this time," she says excitedly. "We've got new weapons!"

"Marla, you aren't fighting the war anymore. You're home now, remember?"

"Of course, I do, silly," she says with a tolerant smile. "That's what's so great about it! We're fighting the war right here at home." That glimmer in her eye is starting to fade, and her lids are growing heavy. "Right here in Sorenson," she continues, but slower now. "We're making poisons that will kill them, growing . . . them . . . right . . . here."

Her words raise the hairs on my neck and arms, and it's as if my feet are frozen to the floor. For a moment I feel incapable of movement, but I manage to ask, "Marla, what poisons?" But the drugs Marla's been given are doing their magic and she's off in la-la land.

The thoughts now running through my head kind of make me wish I could join her.

Chapter 17

Stewart is being treated in a different cubicle in the ER and I make my way there. I see Brenda standing by the ER desk area chatting with a nurse, and I wave her over. One look at my face must convince her that it's serious because she comes right away.

I enter Stewart's room and call out. "Stewart, it's Hildy. Can Officer Joiner and I come in?"

"Sure."

I push aside the curtain surrounding his stretcher with Brenda on my heels. Stewart's head wound has been numbed up but not sutured yet, and tiny trails of blood have tracked down one side of his head into his hair.

"Stewart, what did Marla do in the military?" I ask him.

"She was some kind of weapons specialist," he says. "I don't know the details. Whenever I try to get her to talk about her time in the military, she shuts down."

"Has Marla changed her behavior recently?"

"How do you mean?" Stewart furrows his brow, triggering a fresh trickle of blood down the side of his forehead.

"I mean, has she been leaving the house more than usual, or hanging out with people who are new in her life?"

"Marla never used to leave the house at all," Stewart says, eyeing me with worry. "But yes, she's been venturing out lately, taking drives in the car. And then there's her support group."

"Support group?"

"She says there's a support group for veterans that she attends a couple of times a week."

"Where?" I know about all the support groups in the immediate area and I have a suspicion that Marla hasn't been attending any of them.

"I don't know," Stewart says. He sighs and motions toward the wound on his head. "I've learned not to question her too hard."

"What are you thinking, Hildy?" Brenda asks.

"I don't know," I say, a lie, but I don't want to air my suspicions in front of Stewart, at least not yet. "Stewart, would it be okay if we looked around your house? I think I might be able to help Marla get the help she needs if I can find some information on these support groups." This is hogwash, and most people would pick up on that immediately. But I know how utterly committed Stewart is to Marla, and the mere suggestion that I'm trying to find a way to help her is enough for him. I *am* trying to help her, just not in the way he thinks.

"Sure," Stewart says. "I don't know how much longer I'll be here, though. And I kind of want to stay by Marla until we figure out a plan for her."

"She's going to be out of it for a while," I tell him. "The doctor gave her something that knocked her out."

"And I'm thinking of putting a legal hold on her so that she can't leave the hospital unless she's in police custody," Brenda says. "That's assuming you press charges against her for assault."

I see the reticence on Stewart's face and sigh. He always threatens to file charges against Marla but to date he has never gone through with it. It's a common occurrence in domestic abuse cases. But if what I'm starting to suspect about Marla is right, we won't need Stewart to file charges. If I'm right, will he still be championing her cause, I wonder?

"Stewart, something has to change," I say. "You two can't keep going on the way you have been. Marla needs help and she doesn't seem to be able to commit to getting it voluntarily. Every time she enters a program she quits before it can do her any good. If you really want to help her, and help yourself, it's time for the tough love. She's shown she can't do this on her own."

Stewart doesn't look convinced, and I decide I need to show a couple of my cards.

"I don't think she's been attending any support groups," I tell him. "At least not now. She might have gone to one or two meetings in the past, but I don't think that's what she's doing now. I suspect she's fallen in with a group of people who aren't doing her any good, people who don't have her best interests in mind."

Stewart is frowning at me, and he still looks skeptical, so I up the ante.

"I think she's in danger, Stewart."

Stewart sits up straighter. "Danger? What kind of danger?" Judging from the look Brenda's giving me, I gather she's wondering the same thing.

Time to show my hand. "The kind that might get her killed. Her and a lot of other people." Brenda and Stewart are both staring at me with confused expressions, momentarily speechless. The silence is darned near perfect. All I can hear is the three of us breathing. Then a nurse bursts into the room carrying a suture kit.

"Are you numbed?" she asks Stewart in a cheery voice. "The doctor is coming in to sew you up."

As the nurse goes about setting up the suture materials on a stand in the room, Brenda grabs me by the elbow and tugs me toward the door. Stewart looks at us anxiously and I tell him, "Get fixed up and we'll be back to talk some more." Then I let Brenda steer me from the room and down a hallway to an area where there are no potential eavesdroppers.

"Hildy, what the heck were you talking about in there?"

"I think Marla might be involved in that business out at the Fletcher farm," I tell her. "Think about it. She was a trained weapons specialist in the military and she's vulnerable from her PTSD and her drinking problem. How hard would it be for someone to turn her, to get her to help them in developing the kind of deadly weapons that can be made from those plants we found out there at the farm?"

Brenda contemplates this, her brow furrowing. "Kind of a wild leap, isn't it?"

"You didn't hear what Marla said to me right before she passed out from whatever medication they gave her. She said, *We've got new weapons we can use.* I tried to reorient her to the fact that she isn't fighting the war anymore, that she's safe at home now, but then she said, *We're fighting the war at home, right here in Sorenson.*"

"So, she's having flashbacks or something like that and thinks the enemy is here," Brenda says.

I shake my head. "She was happy, gleeful even, not fearful or angry. And then she said that they're making poisons that will kill them, making them right here in Sorenson. Except she used the pronoun we. *We're* making poisons."

Brenda's scowl deepens. "I don't know, Hildy," she says.

"Stewart said she was going to some support groups, but I know the people that run the veteran support groups in the area, and I contacted them a year or so ago and told them about Marla because I was encouraging her to go to one of them. I asked the group leaders to let me know if she showed up so I could reinforce the behavior on my end given how often I was seeing her and/or Stewart here in the ER. The guy who runs the veteran's support group here in town told me she came to his group twice last year, but then she stopped showing up and never came back. He said there were some troublemakers in the group, some guys who showed up on occasion and tried to peel off some of the other attendees to come to a group of their own making. This other group is reported to be an offshoot of a radical anarchist type militia that promotes violence, racism, and the like."

Brenda nods. "I've heard about them from the county guys. There are some rumors that they were behind that bombing in Milwaukee last year, but no one could prove it."

"If Marla got hooked up with them, she could also be involved with whatever was going on out at the farm. If we look around her house, we might be able to find something that connects her to them."

Brenda nods. "She *would* be an asset to that militia group with her weapons background."

"And with her drinking issues and her PTSD, she's also prone to manipulation. It wouldn't take much."

Brenda sighs. "I need to call Bob Richmond and run this by him. I want to make sure we do everything by the book." She takes out her cell phone and punches a number. "I hate calling him in the middle of the night," she says as she puts the phone to her ear. "It always takes him a little while to wake up fully and remember where he is."

Before I can comment on this intriguing glimpse into Bob Richmond's life, Brenda says, "Hey, Bob," into the phone. "I need to run something by you, and it's important. So, I need you to get out of bed and walk around."

In my mind's eye I envision Bob doing as instructed, hair mussed, eyes puffy with sleep, feet shuffling around a bed, though I didn't get to see the bedrooms when I was there, so my imagination fills in the picture. Then Brenda shatters my imagined image.

"Oh, you are? I figured you'd be asleep this time of night." She listens a moment and then says, "Oh, right. She lives in California now, doesn't she? Two hours behind us."

I know from rumors I've heard and things that Bob himself has told me that he was dating a divorcee here in Stoughton last year until the woman moved to California. I feel a jealous twinge as I realize he was probably talking to this woman and that's why he is awake at nearly two in the morning.

"Yeah, it's about the case at the Fletcher farm. We may have discovered another connection here in town. Hildy figured it out."

I listen as Brenda explains the situation with Marla and Stewart, and the things we've discovered, surmised, and hypothesized. When she's done, she listens for a few seconds and then says, "Stewart seems agreeable to letting us look around the house but he's also very protective of Marla." Another brief period of silence as Brenda listens, and then, "I know, I know. I don't get it either, but we see it all the time."

I gather from this that Bob has expressed confusion over Stewart's undying devotion to the spouse who keeps abusing him physically, mentally, and emotionally. It's an area of frustration to those of us who see it on a regular basis because we don't understand and are often helpless to do much about it. Even if the perpetrators get arrested, the charges often get dropped and the abused parties frequently return to the relationship, convinced by the perpetrator's vows to do better, the profuse apologies, and a perverse, underlying sense that even though they are the victims of the abuse, they are also somehow guilty of provoking it.

Brenda says, "Okay," into the phone and then disconnects her call. "Bob is going to meet us at Stewart's house. I'll send him a text when we're ready to leave here. In the meantime, he's going to try to get a search warrant to make our look around the house a legal one, but he's not hopeful that he'll get one at this hour since it's Judge McAllister on duty this weekend and he's a tough nut to crack. Plus, we're basically acting on little more than speculation and supposition."

"And my gut," I say. "It's proven to be quite reliable over the years."

Brenda gives me a conciliatory smile. "I think your gut is as reliable as anyone else's but I don't think it will sway the judge."

She's right, of course, so I gear myself up to be the Great Convincer for Stewart, cajoling him, reassuring him, and maybe even stretching the truth a tad to make sure he has no misgivings about letting us search his house. Because I feel certain that if he fully understands what it will mean for Marla if we find anything that convincingly ties her to the stuff at the Fletcher farm, he wouldn't let us touch his house with a ten-foot pole.

Before I have a chance to gird my loins for the battle ahead, the chipper nurse approaches and informs us that Stewart is about to be discharged. Brenda and I exchange a look, and then she gives me a nod of approval. I hurry back into Stewart's room and start preparing him for what's to come. He's going to know this isn't just a quick look around his house when he sees Detective Richmond there, and my job is going to be to convince him that what we're doing is in the best of interests of him and Marla. But is it? Just how devastated is Stewart going to be if Marla is arrested and imprisoned? It will put an end to the abuse she pours down on him, but I'm not sure it will do much to improve his state of mental health. This is going to be a delicate tightrope for me to navigate and I don't want to mess it up. I don't want to see anyone get hurt, but there isn't going to be much I can do for Marla at this point, at least from a legal standpoint.

Stewart confirms my worries when he insists on saying goodbye to Marla even though she's essentially unresponsive at this point. Tears form in his eyes as he kisses her on the cheek and whispers something I can't hear in her ear. I sense his reluctance to leave her and give him some gentle encouragement with a slight tug on his arm and some words I hope he finds reassuring.

"We need to let her rest and allow the drugs to do their magic," I tell him. "And then we need to make sure she gets the help she needs. The best thing you can do for her right now is leave her to the professionals."

Reluctantly, Stewart exits his wife's room and follows us out to the parking lot. There is a chill in the night air, and I shove my hands in my jacket pockets to keep them warm. That's when I discover two Oreo cookies in one pocket, and something hard and crinkly in the other—a fortune cookie. I frown because per usual, I have no recollection of putting anything in my pockets. I'm tempted to try and toss them, but fear that if I do it now, someone will see and that will lead to questions—questions I don't want to answer.

As Brenda and I watch Stewart walk to his car, I give Roscoe a scratch behind his ears, a brief, "Good boy!" and a treat from a box that is kept in the rear area of the car. As soon as Stewart gets his car started, Brenda and I climb into our seats and take off behind him.

"Devo went by the LSD house and checked on the occupants. They all seem to be sleeping it off at this point."

"Good." *I hope they won't miss one of their fortune cookies.* "And the irate neighbor lady?"

"No sign of her," Brenda says. "Though something tells me we haven't heard the last from that lot."

Both Devo and Bob are already there when we arrive at the house, and I hurry out of the car and over to Stewart, wanting to be near him when he sees that there is another cop and a detective present. A quick glance at Bob's car tells me that he's on his phone, probably still trying to get a search warrant. A quick glance toward Stewart tells me that he hasn't seen Bob yet, so there's time.

Stewart gets out of the car and walks toward his house, his posture stooped. His expression is morose, and I wonder if it's only because he had to leave Marla behind, or if he's realized the implications of what we're about to do.

Bob opens his car door and gets out. The movement catches Stewart's eye and he glances over at the detective with a momentary look of confusion. I see his wheels turning, sense the dawning realization that's settling on him, and brace myself.

"Stewart," I say, placing what I hope is a reassuring hand on his arm.

Before I can say another word, he looks down at me, his expression even sadder now. "This is getting very serious, isn't it?" he says.

I look up at him and nod.

"Oh, dear," he says. And then he collapses onto the ground.

Chapter 18

I squat down next to Stewart as his eyes flutter open. He looks up at me in bewilderment and says, "What happened?"

"I think you fainted."

He struggles to sit up, blinking his eyes hard. "How embarrassing," he mutters. He looks around, sees Bob Richmond standing there, and I see the dawning wash over his face. "Oh, right," he says. He runs a hand through his hair, wincing as his palm hits his sutured wound. No doubt the local anesthetic is starting to wear off.

"Maybe we should take you back to the hospital," I say, and I see Brenda and Bob exchange a look.

"Hildy, can I talk to you for a minute?" Bob says, gesturing with a sideways nod of his head to a spot several feet away. I get up and go over to him, and he leads me a few steps farther away from Stewart.

"I want Stewart here if we're going to look around

his place," he says, bending over and speaking into my ear just above a whisper. "I wasn't able to get a search warrant and without Stewart's permission and presence we run the risk of any inculpatory evidence we find being excluded later at trial because the search will be declared illegal."

"Inculpatory, schmulpatory," I say. "I won't risk the life of one of my patients just so you guys can get some evidence that may or may not exist."

"Hey, this was your idea," Bob says with a shrug.

"And it was a good one. Which shows you I'm smart. Which suggests that maybe you ought to listen to me." I glare up at Bob, hands on my hips, my expression determined. He stares right back at me for several seconds and then shakes his head. I see a hint of a smile creep in at the corners of his mouth and know he's not truly angry. I return to Stewart, who is struggling to stand, brushing at clips of freshly mown grass stuck to his backside.

"I'm okay," he says before I can ask. "I think seeing all these cops here made me realize how . . . serious the situation might be. And that took the wind from my sails, you know?"

I nod. "I know how much you love Marla," I tell him. "And I know that this isn't easy for you. But I do think it's time for some tough love from you. Marla may have gone too far, and you aren't the only person who's at risk." I see a cautionary look come my way from Bob. Then Stewart shows he's not as dumb as we may think.

"Marla's been talking in her sleep a lot lately and it's been . . . disturbing, scary stuff. Things about bombs and poisons and killing lots of people all at once." He winces and looks at the cops then back to me. "I thought she was having flash-backs, or dreams based on what she did when she was in Iraq, but you think she might be involved in something here, don't you? A local terrorist plot or something?"

Before Bob or the others can interrupt or stop me, I say, "Do you have reason to think she's involved in a local terrorist plot?"

Stewart looks sadder than I've ever seen him. "She's been different lately. More secretive, more . . . I don't know . . . judgmental." He sighs and then heads for his front door. "Let's get this over with."

Bob has a video camera and he turns it on once we're inside the house and prefaces the footage with where we are and who is present, and then he asks Stewart if it is okay to look around the house for things related to comments made by his wife about killing lots of people. Stewart agrees, looking like he just issued a death sentence to his best friend.

Bob asks Stewart if Marla has a cell phone.

He shakes his head. "She doesn't like technology and she's always said cell phones are a way for the government to track and listen in on you."

Brenda and Devo take Stewart into the kitchen and have him boot up a laptop computer that's sitting atop a small desk tucked in one corner of the room. According to Stewart, this computer is primarily his though he admits that Marla has used it from time to time. While Brenda and Devo are examining the computer content, Stewart sets up a coffee pot and starts it. Bob heads for the extra bedroom that Stewart has said Marla uses as her quiet room, a place to go when her PTSD is particularly bad, or when she simply feels the need to escape from life for a while. There is a laptop computer in this room, too, and Bob doesn't bother looking at any content. He simply tags it and bags it.

I look around the room, which has more of a feminine touch to it than I would have expected from Marla since every time I've seen her she's been outfitted in stuff that is either androgynous or leaning toward male attire: camouflage pants and tees, heavy work boots, jeans and denim shirts—that sort of thing. I don't think I've ever seen her wear any makeup. Yet this room has pale yellow walls, lace curtains on the window, a white desk with gold-colored hardware, a pink fleecy throw draped over a floral-patterned daybed, candles that lend the room a strong eucalyptus scent, and a large, framed black-and-white poster of a dozen ink-drawn Gibson girl-era women's portraits, their bright red lips a stark contrast to the otherwise colorless lines. A five-by-seven throw rug at the center of the room boasts a mosaic pattern in shades of lavender, pink, yellow, and seafoam green.

I walk over to the desk and look at the stuff remaining on top of it after Bob has taken the computer. There's a small set of speakers and I wonder what kind of music Marla listens to. A day calendar book sits off to one side and I flip it open.

"Please wait," Bob says.

I withdraw my hand and let him focus the camera on the day calendar book and start flipping through the pages. Every Tuesday and Thursday evening since January she has written in *Support Group* at six o'clock. I point to it and say, "The support groups for veterans that are in the area all start at seven."

Bob nods and flips more pages, still filming. When he gets to the current date he stops and steps back. "Which drawer should I do first?" he asks, eyeing the matching drawers on either side of the desk. Both are about six inches high, not big enough to store hanging files.

"Go with the one on the left," I say. He opens it and films the contents, none of which prove too exciting. There are the usual office supply kinds of items: pens, pencils, a ruler, some index cards, a box of staples, a box of paper clips, some rubber bands, several pads of sticky notes, and boxes of replacement ink cartridges for the printer that is sitting atop a small bookcase off to the right.

As Bob shuts the drawer and moves over to open the other one, I walk over to the bookcase and examine the titles. It's a collection of suspense novels with a few mysteries mixed in, and one other book that doesn't seem to fit in with the rest.

"Bob, look at this," I say, pointing to the book. On the spine is the title of the book: *A Guide to Botanical Poisons*. Bob abandons the drawer he just opened, which is filled with a stack of printed papers, and zooms in on the bookshelf and the book's title. Then he takes the book out and opens it, flipping through the pages.

"Wow, this is basically a cookbook for poisons," Bob says. He turns off the camera and sets it down, then he tags and bags the book and places it on top of the computer, which is sitting on the floor by the door to the room.

Before he can pick up the camera again, I say,

"So, Brenda made it sound like you were talking to someone out in California when she called you. Isn't that where the woman you were dating is living now?"

Bob narrows his eyes at me and screws his mouth up like he just tasted something awful. "It is," he says after a moment. "She called me," he adds quickly, as if to defend himself.

"Is there still something going on with you two?" I ask. "I got the impression that your relationship with her was over, but if that's not the case, I'd like to know."

"She wants me to move out there," Bob says. "That's never going to happen."

"Do you think she might move back here?"

He shakes his head. "She bought a house out there. And she has kids living out there. She wants to be close to her grandkids."

"I see."

Bob cocks his head to one side and smiles at me. "Do I detect a hint of jealousy, Hildy?"

"More like practicality," I tell him. "I don't want to put a lot of time and effort into a relationship with someone who is stuck on someone else."

"I'm not stuck on anyone," he grumbles. "And you had dinner with Jonas Kriedeman, so it's not like you're giving me all of your attention."

"Do I detect a hint of jealousy, Bob?"

He huffs in irritation, but then cracks a smile. "Look, I'm not interested in moving to California, and that relationship is done. But understand that I don't have a lot of experience with this kind of stuff. I need to take things slow."

"I'm not getting any younger, Bob," I tell him. "And neither are you."

He sighs. "I know. But that just goes to show you how set in my ways I am."

"Change can be a good thing. You've started with the décor in your house and that seems to have you revved up. Making a change in a more personal aspect of your life can be just as fulfilling."

"This from the woman who once said she was going to join me at the gym as often as possible."

Now it's my turn to sigh. "Yeah, truth is I don't think I'm cut out for a regular gym visit kind of life, particularly now that I have two jobs to balance. My free time is severely limited."

Bob gives me an acquiescent nod. "Fair enough. I can't argue that point. Even I have a hard time getting there as often as I'd like, and I only have one job to deal with."

"Speaking of which . . ." I nod toward the papers in the drawer.

"Right." Bob picks up the camera and turns it on. Then he looks at me. "Would you mind holding and filming while I look through these papers?"

"Sure." I take the camera from him and focus in on the top sheet in the drawer, watching on the tiny screen. The lens adjusts itself a smidge to bring the print in clearer and my stomach sinks when I see what it says. I keep filming as Bob goes through the stack one page at a time, stopping about halfway through.

"I think we have enough to hold Marla," he says.

"These pages are a manifesto and construction guide for destruction of all kinds—bombs, poisons, gun alterations . . . you name it."

"Marla is a damaged woman," I say. "Between her drinking and her PTSD, I don't see how she could be any sort of mastermind for something like this. We need to figure out who it is she's working for, or with. And if you just toss her in jail, I don't think you'll ever get anything useful out of her. She needs therapy, and lots of it."

"Are you suggesting that you're the person to do that?" Bob asks me.

I shake my head. "She needs more than what I can offer. But I think Dr. Maggie Baldwin might be willing to help her, and in doing so she might just help us."

"Us?" Bob says, unable to suppress a smile.

"You and I are a team, right?" I say with a wink.

He doesn't say no.

Chapter 19

The search of the house doesn't turn up anything more of interest, but we already found enough to implicate Marla in some bad stuff. I tell Bob that I'll put in a call to Dr. Maggie Baldwin, who just happens to be my personal counselor as well, though I leave that tidbit of information out. He puts in a call to the County Sheriff's Department and updates someone there on what has happened, suggesting that they make arrangements to put a police hold on Marla Riley while she's in the hospital so she can't just leave, and maybe even put a guard at her door. By the time all is said and done, and after hauling the collected evidence back to the station, the night shift is at an end and the day staffers are coming on duty.

I give Roscoe—who had a rather boring rest of the night stuck in the car for the most part—a quick walk so he can relieve himself. P.J. will give him a longer walk once I get back to my house. Before going home, I pop my head into the front area of the station and say hi to Miranda, the dispatcher who was working all night.

Just as I'm about to depart for home and my bed—which I can hear calling to me—Bob grabs me and says, "Hildy, can you hang out for a bit longer? Arthur Fletcher's daughters have arrived in town and they are coming down to the station. I want to chat with them, and I'd like you to sit in. See if there's anything that pops into your head that you want to ask them about the situation. Sorry for the short notice, but I only just now found out that they were here. They didn't tell anyone they were coming."

"Okay," I say tiredly. I glance at my watch, see it's almost seven-thirty, and ask, "What time are they due to arrive?"

"Eight. I can put on a fresh pot of coffee if that helps."

"It would," I admit. "Is it okay if I run Roscoe home and then come right back? He could use a long walk and I'm sure P.J. is eager to give him one."

"Absolutely. I'll keep the daughters waiting until you get back."

"I should be back before eight." With that, I head out the door to my car and take Roscoe home. P.J. is sitting on my front porch waiting for us.

"Thought you'd be home closer to seven," she says.

"So did I."

"You going to bed right away?"

"Actually, I'm going back to the station for a while. I've got some things to do and since I don't have to work at the hospital today, I figure I can hold off on sleeping."

P.J. cocks her head to one side and studies my face. "You look okay, so I suppose you can go back."

"You suppose I can go back?" I echo sardonically. "What are you, my mother now?"

"No. Your mother is dead." P.J. says this matter-of-factly, without emotion. It's a typical response from her, a simple stating of the facts. After uttering her comment, and with me still a bit taken aback by the bluntness of it, she grabs her backpack from the porch step and slings it on; then she takes Roscoe's leash from my hand and walks him off the porch. "I'll come by and walk him a couple of times later on today," she says over her shoulder. "You'll probably be sleeping by then." Without another word, she skips off with Roscoe happily trotting along beside her.

I take a moment to run inside the house and hit up the bathroom, checking my face to see if I need a fix-up. While I'm there, I take out the Oreos and the fortune cookie to toss them. On a whim, I decide to tear open the fortune cookie and break it in half to check the fortune. It reads: *I see lots of money in your immediate future.* I toss it in the trash, and then head back to the police station.

It's right at eight o'clock by the time I let myself in and make my way to Bob's office.

"Oh, good," Bob says. "The daughters got here early. They've been waiting out front for about ten minutes now and according to the dispatcher, they are none too happy about it."

"Sorry."

"Don't be. I like making people wait. If you get

them revved up over something, they tend to drop the masks and filters more easily. You get more honest responses that way. You want a cup of coffee before we go in there?"

"Maybe the whole pot," I say.

"Go get yourself what you want, and I'll fetch our visitors. Meet me in the conference room."

I fix myself a cup of coffee with sugar in it—I don't usually do the sugar unless I need a little extra pick-me-up—and make it into the conference room before Bob or our visitors do. Their imminent arrival becomes apparent a moment later when I hear them arguing as they walk down the hallway.

"Of course, it's all about you, Ruth," says an irritated female voice. "It's always about you, isn't it? You're the most selfish, egotistical person I've ever met."

"Seriously, Rebecca?" sneers another feminine and nearly identical voice. "Talk about the pot calling the kettle black. At least I tried to help Dad out after Mom died. All you did was run off and do what you wanted to do. The hell with everyone else right?"

"I offered to come and help him," the first voice says, much closer, and consequently, much louder now. "He told me he didn't need me."

"That's because I was doing it all, you moron!"

With that, the door to the conference room opens and a harried-looking Bob Richmond holds it for the two women, who enter the room like cold gusts of wind. They not only sound alike, they look a lot alike. I don't think they're twins, but there's little doubt that they sprang from the same genetic pool. Both are medium height with slender hips and large chests, strawberry blond hair that, judging from the eyebrows and lashes, is their natural color, and huge green eyes. I'd peg them to be around my age, maybe a smidge younger: early to mid-thirties.

After entering the room, they both stop, look at the table, chairs, and then the rest of the room. This garners a grimace from both women before they make for the seat at the head of the table. One woman grabs the chair from the left, the other from the right. There is a brief tug of war as the two of them glare at one another, their eyes narrowing, their nostrils flaring, like two bulls about to charge.

"That seat is mine," I say loudly, hoping to defuse the explosion that seems to be building. This isn't true—most of the other times I've been in this room with Bob I sat beside him on the side of the table by the door. The chat with Danny and Allie yesterday is an exception and that was because I wanted to serve as a buffer and keep Roscoe close to me as well as Danny.

The two women turn in unison after my declaration and look at me with identical expressions of dismissive skepticism.

"You ladies can sit on that side of the table," Bob says, pointing to the far side.

The sisters look back at one another one last time, release their respective grips on the chair, and move to the other side of the table, where each one picks a seat and settles into it, their movements perfectly in sync as if they are operating from some sort of hive mind. This makes me reconsider their relationship. Maybe they're twins after all, not identical, obviously, but fraternal. They appear to have the type of mind link that twins often share.

I start to move toward the seat at the head of the table, but at the last second, I decide to take one beside Bob instead. I watch the two women for a reaction. The one on the left shrugs and smiles, the one on the right cocks an eyebrow at me and shakes her head.

Bob hits a switch under the table to start up the AV equipment built into the room so we can record the session. He then does the introductions and I learn that the woman on the left is Ruth and the one on the right is Rebecca. I'd wager that Rebecca is the older of the two even if it's only by a matter of minutes because she has a take-charge attitude, as evidenced by the way she launches the conversation after Bob finishes the introductions.

"I don't understand why you've asked Ruth and me to come into this . . . this . . ." She looks around the room and her upper lip curls in disgust. "Ugh." She shudders. "Why aren't we allowed to go to the farm? It's our childhood home and there were cops there who wouldn't even let us drive onto the property. Aren't we suffering enough already with the fact of our father's death?" She glares at Bob, eyebrows raised in question.

Ruth, who is also looking at Bob but with a more troubled expression, says in a quiet voice, "Do you think he killed himself?" I gather from their questions that they haven't been filled in on a lot of the details surrounding their father's death. This should be interesting.

Bob immediately shifts his attention to Ruth, which seems to irritate Rebecca. "Why do you ask?" Bob says.

"The officers who notified me of Dad's death said it might have been a suicide, but he wasn't the type to do that," Ruth says, her brow furrowing. "He just wasn't. Though I get why you might think it, given all the hardships and bad luck he's had over the past few years. First Mom's death, then the constant financial losses for the farm, and having the bank try to foreclose on the place. Plus, Dad was diagnosed with cancer last year."

"What?" Rebecca snaps, her head whipping around to stare at her sister. "Dad had cancer?"

Ruth looks at her sister and nods. "Lung cancer. The doc said it was likely a combination of pesticide exposure from spraying crops and, of course, his smoking habit."

"Dad quit smoking years ago," Rebecca says.

"He started again after Mom died. He just managed to quit again a little over a year ago, but by then it was too late."

Rebecca looks confused. She straightens in her seat and spits out, "Why the hell didn't you tell me about any of this?"

"You were always too busy with your own life," Ruth says with a shrug. "I tried several times over the past year to get you to come home for a visit, but you were always too busy with your work, or your love life, or some other excuse."

"Oh, for God's sake, Ruth," Rebecca mutters irritably. "If you had told me how serious things were, I would have made more of an effort."

"Dad wouldn't let me tell you," Ruth says. "He

said he wanted you to come visit because you wanted to see him, not out of some sense of duty or obligation."

This seems to hit home with Rebecca. She sags back into her seat and a look of shame flits over her face.

"Anyway," Ruth goes on, "he seemed like he was doing better lately. For the past several months he's been very upbeat about things. He said his cancer was in remission, and that leasing out his fields and selling off some farm equipment staved off the bank and helped him catch up on the bills."

Bob and I exchange a look. It's clear that Arthur wasn't totally honest with his daughter about the source of his income. I wonder if his cancer diagnosis had any impact on his decision-making with the plants he was growing under the barn.

Neither of the girls misses our look and Rebecca calls us on it immediately. "What?" she says, folding her arms over her ample chest. She sighs with impatience. "What aren't you telling us?"

Bob looks at Ruth and says, "Did you know about the stuff your father was growing beneath the barn?"

"Beneath the barn?" Ruth says, giving him an indulgent smile that suggests she finds the idea ridiculous at best. "The only thing my father ever kept in that nasty cellar area was rusted old farm equipment and the setup for his homemade wine."

"Apparently he upgraded the space," Bob tells her. "He had a nice greenhouse down there."

"A greenhouse?" Ruth's voice is rife with skepticism. "He told me he was done with crops. His fields are all rented out, so he couldn't plant in them even if he wanted to."

"I don't think the plants he had beneath the barn were ever meant for the fields," Bob says. "The bulk of it was marijuana."

"Oh, for God's sake," Rebecca says, rolling her eyes. She unfolds her arms and rakes both hands through her hair. "Is that what he was doing? Growing pot?" She laughs loudly, a bitter, ironic sound.

Ruth says nothing at first, staring at her clasped hands on the table. Then she looks at Bob and says, "That makes a weird kind of sense."

"How so?"

"I went with Dad to one of his oncology appointments months ago, and he was complaining to his doctor that the nausea medication he was prescribed wasn't working very well. The doctor prescribed him something stronger, but it didn't work either. I told Dad about a friend of mine who was getting chemo and who swore marijuana helped immensely with the nausea as well as with general anxiety. Dad pooh poohed it at the time, but he must have rethought things and decided to try growing his own."

Bob sighs and licks his lips. I can tell he isn't crazy about what he has to say next, so I decide to jump in.

"Your father wasn't growing a few personal plants. He had hundreds of them down there." I pause and look at Bob, unsure how far he wants to go. He waves a hand over the table, an indication to cut it off there.

"We're not sure of how involved he was beyond

the growing and processing of the plants," Bob says, taking over. "Did he give either of you any indication of what he was doing? Did he mention anything about a financial windfall or the potential for losing the farm?"

"He's been losing that damn farm for the past four years," Rebecca says with a roll of her eyes.

"How the hell would you know?" Ruth snaps at her sister. "Have you bothered to come around at all? Have you taken the time to sit down with Dad and talk to him about the state of things? No, of course you haven't, because you're too caught up in your own life and your own selfish needs to have time for anyone else."

"Dad might not have shared anything with me recently," Rebecca says, "but he told me several years ago that he was likely going to lose the farm. He was trying to talk me into taking it over." She scoffs. "Like I'm that stupid." She looks from her sister to Bob. "My father is . . . was a stubborn old fool who loved that farm beyond reason. He would have let the whole thing fall down and rot all around him before he would have given it up and moved away."

"It was his love of the place that turned it around," Ruth argues. "He came up with the idea of leasing out the fields and it must have been working for him because he told me a few weeks ago that he'd paid off all of his debt and was thinking of doing some fix-ups on the house."

"That's because he was growing pot in the basement," Rebecca reminds her. "And I assume he was selling it."

Ruth appears taken aback by this. She starts to say something, but the words never come out.

"Who was my father selling this stuff to?" Rebecca asks, turning back to Bob.

"We're not sure. We've been going over his financial records, but we haven't been able to track down anything other than some large cash deposits that he made. In addition to the plants, there's also a small laboratory area beneath the barn," Bob says. "Do either of you know why it's there? Does it have something to do with the day-to-day running of the farm?"

Ruth looks surprised. "A laboratory? Are you sure?"

"It's a small, enclosed area with Bunsen burners, flasks, a stove, a sink, and some containers of fluid that we couldn't identify."

"Maybe he improved on his wine-making efforts?" Ruth poses, but Bob shoots that idea down with a shake of his head

"Maybe he was cutting the weed with something?" Rebecca suggests, looking appalled at the idea. She puts her elbows on the table and buries her face in her hands. "Man, this isn't going to play well in the news," she says. "It can't be good for my career."

Ruth turns and gapes at her sister with a look of disbelief. "You're a real piece of work, you know that?" she says. "Is that all you can think about right now?"

"Well, I need to make a living somehow," Rebecca counters, her voice a bit whiny. "What do you want me to do, go back to waiting tables? I'm a celebrity in Minneapolis, and I have a reputation to protect. If it gets out that my father was a drug dealer, I'll never get work again."

"Boo-hoo," Ruth says, the words dripping sarcasm. "Maybe it's time for you to consider a real career. It's not like you're making big money doing what you're doing. And if you're a celebrity, I'm Martha Washington."

"You are such a bitch," Rebecca sneers. Her hands are opening and closing into fists.

"Now ladies, I think we need to take a few deep breaths and a step back," I say. "We're here to help you get through this and we need your help, as well. Can we please try to put aside past grievances, shelve the vitriol, and deal with the issues without all this rancor?"

"What are you putting on a shelf?" Ruth asks, looking confused.

"It was a metaphor," Rebecca says with an irritated huff. "Vitriol means meanness and hateful criticism. If you hadn't dropped out of high school so you could drop your panties for Horny Hopper, you might know that."

"His name is Henry Hockner," Ruth says irritably.

"Not amongst those of us in the know," Rebecca says with a mean smile. "Given the way he hopped from one girl's bed to another, I think our name was the more appropriate one."

Bob gives me a pleading look and I shrug. These two are a definite challenge and I'm not sure how to get them to stop their bickering.

"Have the two of you made any plans for your father's funeral?" I ask. "Because I can help you with that if necessary."

This stops the bickering and the two of them look at one another with dawning expressions. Just when I think I've got them thinking along more amicable and practical lines, they prove how wrong I am.

"I want mother's pearls and her diamond ring," Rebecca says. "She told me I could have them back when I was in high school."

"Dad sold her ring two years ago," Ruth says. "He needed the cash to try to stave off the bankers."

Rebecca looks furious, her teeth clenched, her eyes narrowed in anger. She shifts her gaze to Bob, who looks a little shell-shocked, and says, "Can we go out to the farm and have a look around the house? Maybe collect some personal things? We tried to go there when we first got to town last night but there was a guard at the base of the driveway who wouldn't let us go up. Said we'd have to wait until this morning and talk to you."

"Let me check on something," Bob says. "I'll be right back." With that he gets up and exits the room, leaving me there with the two daughters.

"When is the last time either of you saw your father?" I ask.

Ruth says, "About six months ago. I came here for a visit for a few days to see how he was faring with his cancer treatments. He seemed fine, great, in fact. I would have stayed longer but I have two kids, ages seven and eight, and keeping up with all their activities and such is a full-time job."

"Yeah, and I'm betting Horny Hopper isn't a lot of help," Rebecca sneers.

"Henry helps," Ruth counters. "He works full-time, so he can only do so much. When's the last time you came to visit Dad?" she challenges, deftly changing the topic and putting her sister in the hot seat.

"I called him," Rebecca says defensively.

"Really? When? A year ago? I called him every week and visited whenever I could."

"Well, aren't you just the little saint," Rebecca sneers. "My last play went on for six months, so it wasn't like I could just drop everything and come for a visit."

"Your role in the play was a two-minute walk-on character that anyone could have played," Ruth says with a roll of her eyes.

"It may not have been a big part, but it was a very nuanced one," Rebecca says. "And I didn't have an understudy."

"That's because the part was too small to need one. Hell, anyone in the audience could have played the part with a minute or two of prep time."

"You're just jealous because you don't have a life outside of running your kids around and trying to keep Horny Hopper from straying into other women's beds."

Oddly enough and, if I'm honest, to my shame, I find I'm rather enjoying these two going at it, but Bob returns and cuts things short.

"I have clearance to take the two of you out to the farm to look around the house. I can't promise you that I'll let you take whatever you want from there. We'll make those decisions on a case-by-case basis. And parts of the house will be off limits. It's still considered a crime scene and certain key areas are cordoned off."

"A crime scene?" Rebecca says. "Why? Because of the stuff he was growing in the barn?"

"That's part of it," Bob says. "But I'm sorry to tell you that it appears your father didn't commit suicide after all. He was murdered."

For once the two women are both dumbstruck. They gape at Bob with matching expressions of shock and horror.

Then Rebecca looks at Ruth and says, "This is all your fault for suggesting that he try using marijuana for his nausea problems. You started him down this path. He was probably killed doing a drug deal."

Bob and I exchange looks of exasperation.

"Oh, for heaven's sake, Becca, this isn't one of your dramatic plays. Dad wasn't a drug dealer. Why do you have to turn everything into—"

"I'm going out to the farmhouse now," Bob says, interrupting their latest battle. "I would suggest you two head there as well, if you don't want to miss your chance."

With that, Bob leaves the room. Not wanting to be left alone any longer with the two women, despite how entertaining they are, I follow him. Bob walks out to the main hall and pokes his head into his office, which he shares with Detective Steve Hurley and Detective Junior Feller. Detective Hurley's desk is vacant, but Junior is in the office and Bob speaks quickly to him.

"I'm headed out to the farmhouse site. When those two yahoos in the conference room come out, would you please see to it that they exit out the front? And then turn the recording equipment off for me?"

"Will do," Junior says.

"Come on," Bob says, steering me to the back of the station. When we reach the break room, he says, "Those two harridans have given me a doozy of a headache." He massages his temples to punctuate the statement.

"Shouldn't we be leading them out to the farm. Or driving them?"

"I think I'd rather have someone pull my toenails out with pliers before I'd agree to ride in a car with those two. Let them drive themselves out there. They won't get any farther than the base of the driveway." He stops his massage and looks at me. "You've been up all night. You don't have to go out to the farm if you don't want to."

"You've been up all night, too," I point out. "And I wouldn't miss this circus for the world."

Chapter 20

"Do you want to ride with me or take your own car?" Bob asks.

"I'll drive myself. I don't want to get hung up at the farm. If things get crazy, I want to be able to escape and go home to my bed."

"Are you okay to drive? I don't want you falling asleep behind the wheel."

"I'm okay. It's more of a body weariness. And I'm going to stop and grab a coffee on the way as insurance. Want me to get you one?"

Bob shakes his head. "Won't the coffee make it hard for you to get to sleep when you do go to bed?"

I shake my head. "Never has. I can drink a cup of coffee, go to bed an hour later, and fall asleep without any problem. Insomnia has never been an issue for me."

"Wish I could say the same," Bob says. "I'll see you out there."

I head for my car, pull out of the secure lot, and go straight to the drive-through coffee shop in town. I order a large coffee and sip on it as I drive out to the Fletcher farm. The officer parked at the bottom of the driveway waves me on through without question, so I'm guessing Bob must have told him I was coming. When I get to the house, I see that Bob and both Fletcher women are already there standing by the front door, and the women don't look happy. There is also a uniformed county sheriff at the entrance to the house, one hand on his Taser as both women yell at him.

I park as close as I can and hurry over to the group.

"This is our house, our property," Rebecca yells at the sheriff. "You have no right to block us from entering."

The sheriff opens his mouth to counter this statement but both Bob and Ruth speak before he can utter a single word.

"We do have the right to keep you out," Bob says. "And if you don't behave, that's what I'll do."

"Rebecca, you're not helping matters," Ruth whines.

"Oh, shut up," Rebecca snaps to her sister. "You're always such a brown-noser. Stand up for yourself for once, why don't you."

Ruth does just the opposite; she withers away, backing up several feet.

"Ms. Fletcher, if you don't knock it off right now, I'll have you arrested," Bob says in a surprisingly calm voice. "I'll let you both enter the house, but it will be under my direction and you will only go where I say you can go. You will not touch anything while you are inside without checking with me first. Do I make myself clear?"

Ruth nods immediately. Rebecca glares at Bob, looking like she wants to challenge him. Fortunately, she apparently decides otherwise and with a huff of irritation says, "Fine. Can we please get on with it?"

Bob nods at the uniformed officer, who proceeds to step aside. Bob takes out a pocketknife, slices through the evidence tape on the front door, and then opens it a foot or so. Then he stops and turns to the women. "I have to warn you that the kitchen area is off limits. While we won't be entering it, we will be walking past it. I wouldn't advise looking in there, but I can't stop you. I should also warn you that there might be a smell associated with some of the . . . um . . . remaining residue."

Ruth winces and looks like she might be ill. Rebecca just rolls her eyes, tapping one foot impatiently.

Bob enters the house and we follow him in, me bringing up the rear. We gather in the living room so Bob can reassess everyone's willingness to continue. The air has an odor like that of spoiled meat, but it's more subtle than I expected. It was so carnal and fresh when I was here the other night, though I suppose removing the body also removed a large part of the source.

"I'm guessing you'll want to check out the bedrooms mainly?" Bob says.

"I'd like to see Dad's office first," Rebecca says, nodding down a hallway off the living room.

Bob gives Ruth a questioning look, silently asking if she agrees with this plan and is still okay to be here. Ruth swallows hard but nods.

Bob heads down the hallway with Rebecca hot on his heels. At the end of the hall is the entrance to the kitchen, taped off from the rest of the house, and I watch as Rebecca peeks at it, curiosity getting the better of her. If the sight bothers her, it doesn't show. She doesn't miss a step as she follows Bob into the small room on the left, a room I assume is Fletcher's home office, though I never got to see any part of the house beyond the kitchen.

Ruth is still standing in the middle of the living room and she cups a hand over her nose and mouth. Her eyes close, but she opens them seconds later and with a straightening of her shoulders, heads down the hallway. I can't tell if she looks into the kitchen at all, but I gather from the somewhat serpentine path she takes down the hall, and the way one hand is extended out at her side like a feeler, that her eyes are closed.

The room Arthur Fletcher used as a home office is small. It wouldn't comfortably work as a bedroom with anything bigger than a twin-size bed, and I'm not sure what it was meant to be originally. There is already a separate dining room on this floor, and given the office's proximity to the kitchen, I wonder if it was once a butler's pantry that was converted into a separate room. It has a single window that looks out onto the side yard, a pair of dingy, lacy sheers hanging from an overhead rod. I suspect the curtains are a remnant from Mrs. Fletcher; they give off a distinctively feminine vibe. There is no closet in the room and a worn denim jacket is hanging from a hook screwed into the back wall.

The desk is a battered and dented metal piece that looks like old military issue, and the chair behind it is a basic wooden one with a ladder back. On top of the desk is a blotter, its surface stained with coffee rings, and while there is no computer, there is an obvious void in the dust where it appears a laptop had been. I assume the feds have it now. An old mug is doing double duty as a pen and pencil holder, and there is a small dish filled with a dozen Werther hard candies beside it.

There is a three-drawer, gunmetal gray filing cabinet in one corner, its drawers open and empty, most likely courtesy of the feds, and in another corner by the window there is an old, wooden rocker. The rocking chair seems out of place somehow, and I wonder why it's there. Had Fletcher's wife spent time in here with him, sitting in the rocker, perhaps crocheting the afghan I saw draped over the back of the living room couch?

I watch the two women, curious about their reactions. Rebecca, not surprisingly given her behavior so far, looks miffed about something. Ruth just looks sad.

"Where is his computer?" Rebecca asks. "And his papers? How are we supposed to figure out his estate? And our inheritance?"

"Oh, for cripes sake, Becca!" Ruth says, nearly in tears. "He isn't even buried yet!"

"My bills aren't going to wait for him to be buried," Rebecca snaps.

"Well, maybe if you got a real job you . . ."

And they're at it again. I tune them out, thinking it's probably time for me to go home and go to bed. There is a framed picture of the family hanging on the wall beside me: Arthur and his wife, young and healthy, the two girls, around the age of five or six I'd guess, smiling as they stand in front of them. In the background is the barn, but many of the other outbuildings aren't there. They must have come later, back when the farm was in its heyday. It's the only picture in the room, save a framed ten-dollar bill hanging on the wall next to the window.

The two girls are shouting back and forth at one another, and I feel my stress level rising. This sort of thing may be part of what my new job is about, but I don't want to deal with these two any longer. I look again at the family picture, which is hanging slightly crooked. It's an offense to my OCD sense of order and with my rising stress level, I feel compelled to straighten it. Maybe if I can draw the women's attention to this picture of a happier time, they'll stop their endless bickering.

I reach up and nudge the lower corner slightly to straighten it up. It falls to the floor with a crash, tiny shards of glass flinging out in all directions. A gasp escapes me when I realize I may have just ruined the only family picture the Fletcher women have when I hear Rebecca say, "Well, look at that, would you."

At first, I think she's referencing the result of my stupidity, but then I hear Bob say, "Son of a gun," under his breath and I look at him, intend-

ing to plead forgiveness and blame my clumsiness
on my exhaustion. Except he isn't looking at me
or the picture. He's staring at the wall where the
picture was hung. So are the women. I look there,
too, and mutter an "Oh, my," in surprise.

There on the wall is a safe. Or at least the door
to a safe. It is set into the wall so that its face is
flush with the plaster and it has a number pad lock
on it.

Rebecca looks over at her sister. "Did you know
Dad had a safe?"

Ruth shakes her head.

"I wonder what's in it," Rebecca says, her voice
blooming with hopeful expectation. "There might
be cash in there, lots of it. If he was selling marijuana, he might have kept some money aside and
not put it in the bank."

"Ooh, do you think so?" Ruth says, her eyes growing big.

It's obvious from their tones that the women are
assuming any cash we find inside the safe would be
theirs to keep. I glance at Bob and he gives me a
subtle shake of his head.

"I don't suppose either of you knows the combination?" Bob says.

"Heck no, we didn't even know he had a safe,"
Rebecca says. But then she and Ruth exchange a
look, one that tells me they have an idea about it.

"What?" I say. "You've thought of something.
Was there something your father used regularly
for a passcode or PIN?"

Rebecca looks down at her feet. Ruth looks over
at the window.

Bob doesn't miss their evasive behaviors. "You know," he says, "now that we've discovered the safe, the feds are going to want to take it, and who knows how long it will be before they can get it open. And anything they find in there will get tied up as evidence for months, maybe years."

Faced with the loss of a potential windfall that hasn't yet been realized, Ruth caves. "Try the serial number," she says, pointing to the framed ten-dollar bill on the wall by the window. "That ten dollars is from the first bundle of tobacco my father ever sold from this farm, back in the early eighties. Most people frame a dollar bill, but Dad said he wasn't like most people and using the bigger bill was a sign of the prosperity to come."

Bob walks over to the framed money and lifts it from the wall.

Ruth says, "In later years, when Dad needed a password for computer stuff, he started using the serial number on that bill. He had it memorized, but if he ever forgot it, or if one of us ever needed his password because something happened to him, we knew it was there."

Bob stands in front of the wall safe, holding the framed bill in one hand. "There are eight numbers here," he says. "And a letter at the beginning and the end. Not sure how that works on this keypad."

"Ignore the letters since there aren't any on the keypad," I say.

Bob does as I suggest but punching the numbers in doesn't work. "Try it backwards," I suggest. He does and six numbers into the combination there is a click and a green light comes on. Rebecca claps her hands excitedly while Ruth starts chewing at her thumbnail. Bob grabs the small handle and pulls the door open.

There is cash in the safe, all right. Lots of it. Bundles of fifty-dollar bills are stacked in there, along with several stacks of hundreds. It seems my fortune cookie fortune was right when it predicted lots of money coming into my life. Unfortunately, it failed to mention that none of it would be mine.

Rebecca tries to push past Bob and grab some of the money, but he stops her with his arm. "Sorry, but no one touches this money until we can process it as evidence," he says. "There might be fingerprints on it, or even DNA. Some of these bills look new, which means they may not have circulated yet."

"But you said—" Rebecca starts.

We've reached the point where the sisters are going to learn that the money won't be theirs, either.

"I know what I said," Bob grumbles. "Perhaps I misled you. None of this money is going to come to you. It's going to be taken in as evidence and then, by law, it's going to be confiscated by the DEA."

"What?" Rebecca screeches. For a moment I think she's going to smack Bob, she looks so pent up with anger. But she reins herself in at the last minute and lets forth with a string of cuss words instead.

Ruth just stands there and smiles.

"You people are rotten to the core," Rebecca

says, and then she spins on her heel and storms out of the room, down the hall, and out the front door.

Ruth looks at Bob and sighs. "She won't go too far since I have the keys to the rental car. But I suppose we should go. There isn't much point in trying to scavenge the remains here until the cop agencies are done with what they need to do."

Ruth is clearly the voice of reason when it comes to these two. And in my own moment of clarity, I decide I'm done with this mess for now. I need my bed and some sleep. After Ruth follows her sister out of the house, I look at Bob and say, "It's a shame, isn't it?"

"What?" he asks irritably. "That one of his kids couldn't care less that her father is dead? That no one will get any of the money he hid away? Or that Fletcher's secret garden might be part of a bigger, scarier plan?"

"All of it," I say with a tired smile. "So many lives ruined."

"Yeah," he agrees in a sad, tired voice. He looks at me and smiles. "I don't want to ruin your life, so go home and get some sleep. Thanks for sticking with me as long as you did."

"You're welcome." I whip off a snappy salute for reasons I don't understand and then head for my car.

I'm glad the drive home is a short one because my eyelids feel like they weigh a ton. When I enter the house, Roscoe greets me with his usual tail-wagging enthusiasm and then looks disappointed when I make a beeline for my bedroom, shutting the door behind me. I strip out of my clothes, tossing them toward the hamper, though all the items fall short. When I toss my slacks, something falls out of the pocket onto the floor. It's a Werther's hard candy.

I pick it up, toss it in the trash can, and curse to myself. Then I slip between my sheets totally naked, replacing the real world with a mindless, dreamless one mere moments later.

Chapter 21

When I awaken at a few minutes past five, I roll out of bed surprised to see that I have no clothes on. I head for the bathroom to pee, and then grab my robe off the hook on the back of the door. Seeing it there brings to mind the sight of that worn coat hanging on a hook in Arthur Fletcher's office and that whole scene replays in my head.

I go to the sink to brush my teeth and I'm taken aback when I look in the mirror. Mascara and eyeliner are smeared around my eyes and on my upper cheeks, making me look like a ghoul. I grab a washcloth and some face cream and remove the stuff, then I brush my teeth. Feeling a bit more human, I head back to my bedroom, where I see that remnants of the makeup P.J. so artfully applied last evening is also smeared all over my pillowcase. Note to self: remember to take makeup off before dropping dead into bed.

I stumble out to the kitchen and fix myself a cup

of coffee. There is no sign of Roscoe in the house, so I assume he's out with P.J. That means he, and she, could arrive back at any minute. A reminder pops up on my cell phone, which is almost dead because I forgot to plug it in again when I got home this morning, regarding Tamela's visit. I'd momentarily forgotten about it, and I curse under my breath when I realize I have less than an hour before she's due to arrive.

I plug my phone in, grab my cup of coffee, and head for the shower. I scrub, dry off, dress, blow my hair into some semblance of docility as fast as I can, and then return to the kitchen. To my surprise, I find P.J. and Tamela sitting at my kitchen island counter, Roscoe stretched out on the floor behind them.

"Hildy!" Tamela says, hopping off her stool and coming to give me a hug. I embrace her, delighted, as always, to see her. "You're looking good," she says when we finally pull apart. She eyes me from head to toe and back again.

"Yeah, right," I say. "Remember, I, unlike most other people, can tell when you're lying." Tamela smiles guiltily. "I take it you two have met," I say, looking over at P.J.

"We have," Tamela says.

"She says she's your sister," P.J. says, a scowl on her face.

"Yes, she is."

I'm about to explain further when P.J. says, "How come she's black and you're white? Did your mother adopt her before she died?"

Tamela arches her eyebrows at me, a wry grin on her face.

"No, it's nothing like that," I tell P.J. "I told you that I grew up in the foster system after my mother died. Some of the other kids who were in the system became good friends with me. And some, like Tamela, became like a sister to me. Tamela and I lived in the same group home for three years when we were in high school, and we got to be very close to one another. I could talk to her about anything and she understood me and where I came from. So, I refer to her as my sister because she's the closest thing to family that I have."

P.J. digests this for a few seconds as Tamela and I wait. Then P.J. says, "Can I be your sister, too?"

Tamela gives me an "Aw," look replete with puppy-dog eyes.

"I don't know, P.J.," I say. "Tamela, what do you think? Should we make P.J. an honorary sister? She doesn't have any siblings at home."

Tamela looks at P.J., puts a finger to the side of her chin, and takes on a contemplative expression. The eager anticipation I see on P.J.'s face nearly breaks my heart.

"Yeah, okay," Tamela says and P.J.'s face breaks into a huge smile. It's the most emotion I think I've ever seen from her.

"I think we should celebrate the addition of our new family member over breakfast," I suggest. Both Tamela and P.J. look at me like I'm crazy. "Oh, right. It's not breakfast time for you guys. Still, I can whip up some hellacious ham and cheese omelets. How does that sound for dinner?"

"You know me; I'm not a picky eater," Tamela says with a shrug.

With perfect mimicry, P.J. says, "You know me; I'm not a picky eater," and she shrugs.

I try to hold it back, but laughter bursts out of me. Fortunately, P.J. takes it in stride.

The three of us spend a pleasant three hours eating our omelets and toast, and chatting about all manner of things. Tamela brings me up to date on the status of our other "sister," Sarah, whose picture sits on my fireplace mantel, while we watch the self-professed non-picky eater P.J. sort out every single piece of ham in her omelet. She pushes them to one side and, when she thinks we aren't watching, she feeds them to Roscoe. I'm not sure if she does this because she doesn't like ham, or just because she wants to give Roscoe some treats.

When we're done eating, I try on all the clothing items Tamela has brought along with her, items I bought a week or so ago and had her take for alterations. The girl is a whiz with needle and thread, and everything fits me perfectly. I opt to wear the last pair of slacks I try on to work for the night.

I make P.J. go home knowing she has to be up early in the morning for school. P.J. tries to stall by claiming she needs to take Roscoe for one more walk, but I insist that she go, and tell her I'll walk Roscoe on my own. "I need the exercise," I say, tugging at the waist of my newly altered slacks.

Once P.J. is gone, I invite Tamela to come with me and Roscoe, and she happily tags along. It's a walk down memory lane as the two of us recall some of our times together—both good and bad—in the group home. When she finally gets into her car to head home, I feel a sense of loss. I wish she lived closer.

My loneliness sparks a reminder that I need to call Dr. Maggie Baldwin. Her advice and counsel will aid me in figuring out my role and responsibilities regarding both Danny Hildebrand and Marla Riley. I get her voice mail and leave a message, letting her know that I'll be up all night should she decide to call back later, and that no hour tonight would be too late. With that done, I decide to go into the station a little early, hoping I might catch Bob Richmond there and get an update on the Fletcher case. I'm dying to know if he had any more interactions with the Fletcher women.

I park in the gated back lot, badge myself into the station, and send Roscoe over to his doggie bed, telling him to stay. Then I make my way to Bob's office to see if he's in. He is, sort of. I find him sitting in his chair, arms folded on top of his desk, head resting on his arms. He is sound asleep, snoring lightly. I turn to leave him as he is, not wanting to wake him as I suspect he's been up all day. But before I take two steps, Brenda Joiner pokes her head into the office and says, "There you are. I knew you were here somewhere because I saw Roscoe in his bed."

Bob sits bolt upright, blinking his eyes several times.

"Oh, sorry," Brenda says, grimacing. "I didn't know you were sleeping."

"I wasn't sleeping. Just resting my eyes for a few minutes," Bob says.

I snort a laugh. "You were snoring." He scowls at that. "Not a bad snore," I add. "Very light, in fact."

Giving up any pretense of not sleeping, Bob rubs his eyes and asks, "What time is it?"

"Quarter to eleven," Brenda says. "I'll go put on a pot of coffee." She heads back toward the break room, leaving me with Bob.

"Anything happen today on the Fletcher case?" I ask him.

"Yeah, those two harridans got into a hair-pulling match after you left and a couple of unis had to go break things up."

"No kidding," I say. "Geez, I'm kind of sorry I missed that."

"Don't be," Bob says. "They've gone back home and good riddance."

"Were the federal guys excited about the stuff in the safe?"

"They were. But they were even more excited to hear about the ten-dollar bill serial number clue. It got them into some password protected files on Arthur Fletcher's laptop. He had a whole other email account, and software to encrypt the stuff he sent and to decipher the stuff he got. It's some very sophisticated software. It's unlikely he would have been able to come up with it on his own. Arthur Fletcher dropped out of school in the ninth grade."

"What did the emails reveal?"

"Sadly, not much. The software has an auto-matic destruct built into it that turns the emails and the ISP they came from into gibberish thirty minutes after it's opened. There was one email that hadn't been opened yet, but when the feds tried to trace the ISP it came from, they realized that whoever was sending the stuff was using a worldwide series of servers to bounce off at random. All they were able to get out of it was the username of the sender and the text of the email, both of which turned to gibberish half an hour after they opened the email."

"What was the username? Maybe it's a clue."

Bob shakes his head. "It was the letters WMC followed by a string of numbers. WMC might stand for Wisconsin Manufacturers and Commerce, one of the biggest organizations in the state. Unfortunately, there are thousands of people using those letters as an email address. A check with the email provider didn't offer anything useful, either. It's a phony name and a phony address somewhere in Uzbekistan."

"Well, that's depressing. I was hoping for some good news."

Bob makes a face and says, "I have more news, though I'm not sure you'll see it as good."

"Lay it on me."

"We were able to obtain security video from the Quik-E-Mart Danny went to the other night and it verifies that he was there, though I don't think it matters given the time of death. I heard back from Doc Morton this evening and he said they tested Fletcher's body for the presence of all the poisons represented by the plants growing in the barn basement. Lo and behold, he tested positive for strychnine."

"He was poisoned?" I say, looking confused. "But the gun . . ."

"Doc said the strychnine causes the muscles in the body to go rigid and what he originally thought was rigor mortis was likely this muscle rigidity instead. That means the time of death was sometime that same evening you and Devo found him. And there is no way Fletcher could have shot himself even if he was still alive at the time. Doc Morton said the guy wouldn't have been able to pull the trigger on the gun or even raise it to his chin due to the muscle rigidity. But that's a moot point because the livor mortis proves he was already dead by the time he was shot. Though he did say he's confused as to how anyone managed to get Fletcher into the chair because his body would have been stiff as a board."

"So, the official time of death is . . ."

"Probably between the hours of eight and ten on the night you found him."

"And Danny left work at what time?"

"No one saw him after noon."

"Allie said she saw him for a brief period that evening, but it was around eight if I remember right. She said he called her and told her he was working late. Has he ever said where he was the rest of the time?"

"He has not," Bob says pointedly.

"So, he has no alibi." I say this with sad dawning, knowing that Danny's life is going to get a lot more complicated.

"There's more," Bob says, giving me an apologetic look. I brace myself. "When you told me that Danny worked at the food processing plant, I assumed he worked the assembly lines."

I nod. "That's what he told me."

"Did he? Are you sure?"

I think back to conversations I've had with Danny in the past in the ER and elsewhere, talks about his medications, his illness, the side effects he had to deal with, and how they affected his life and his job. "He told me once that he didn't like one of his medications because it made it hard for him to focus and he couldn't do his job properly. He said his work required coordination, focus, and fast thinking and all of those were affected by the medication. I assumed from that that he worked one of the assembly or production lines. That's what nearly everyone who works there does."

"Nearly everyone, but not everyone. Did you know that Danny has a college degree?"

"I know he went to college, but he said he had to drop out because that's when his schizophrenia began to manifest itself."

"He did drop out, but it was in grad school while he was going for his master's. He already had a bachelor's degree, in biochemistry. His work at the food processing plant is as a biochemist, exploring different ways to grow, package, and preserve the foods they process there."

Dread washes over me. "A biochemist? I had no idea."

I mentally review the facts: Danny is a biochemist and the Fletcher barn has a chemistry lab in the cellar, a lab most likely intended to extract the deadly poisons growing in that basement. Danny clearly has a connection of some sort to Arthur Fletcher and that death scene in the kitchen. Danny also has no alibi for the time of death.

This leads me to a depressing but inevitable conclusion: the most likely suspect in Arthur Fletcher's murder is Danny Hildebrand.

Chapter 22

The shock of the revelations Bob has just dumped on me make me temporarily forget about the call I made to Maggie Baldwin earlier. When my cell phone rings and her name pops up, I'm momentarily puzzled by it before memory kicks in.

"Maggie," I say when I answer. Though she has a medical degree and is referred to as Dr. Baldwin by some of her patients and associates, she has always insisted that I call her by her first name. "Thanks for calling me back." I wave at Bob and make a quick exit from his office, heading for the break room. The oncoming cops will be getting their shift report from the outgoing group, so the break room should be empty.

"No problem," Maggie says. "I would have called sooner but I had to drive up to Columbia Correctional for an emergency psych evaluation on a prisoner there."

As I push open the break room door, I'm relieved to see that it is, indeed, empty except for Roscoe, who wags his tail when he sees me. I settle in at the table and spend the next few minutes filling Maggie in on the situation with Marla Riley.

"Sounds like an interesting case," Maggie says. "You think the police will be pressing charges against her?"

"I'm afraid so."

"And you're one of them now, aren't you?"

"Well, sort of," I say. "I'm discovering there are some fine lines when it comes to my duty toward the patients I've seen at the hospital before and then encounter in my work with the police."

"Okay. I'll try to see her tomorrow. What else can I help you with?"

"Well, a couple of things. For one, I have a dilemma regarding my eleven-year-old neighbor, P.J. I've told you about her."

"Yes, the one who walks your dog. You believe she has Asperger's, correct?"

"That's the one. So, her parents aren't very involved with her and she's recently overheard some things said by other girls at her school, things of a sexual nature. She's asking questions, and I'm not sure how to answer her, or even if I should. Any advice?"

"Hm, well, if you're right about the Asperger's, she likely won't be very adept at interpreting social cues when it comes to romantic or sexual innuendo and relationships. In my experience, these kids tend to be all about the facts. They don't embarrass easily, they're often highly intelligent, and since they tend not to socialize much, they don't get a lot of exposure to this stuff. But that also makes them vulnerable. The best thing you can do for her is give her some basic facts about anatomy and physiology, and then give her some warnings about the psychological games that both boys and girls can play. Make her understand that her body is hers and not to be touched or used by anyone else in any way unless she says okay. Let her know what to do if someone tries to push that issue. And then try to tell her why it's a good idea to wait until she's much older before allowing anyone permission to touch her. Most often, these kids don't like to be touched anyway, so that part of it might be easy."

"So, you think I should be the one to have this conversation with her? Not her parents?"

"It doesn't sound like her parents will do it, though I suppose you could go and talk to one of them about it and see what they say. If they seem eager to have that talk with the kid, then let them. But if they're dismissive about it, you should wear the mantle."

I sigh, knowing that no matter which way things go on the matter, it will be awkward.

"The kid is lucky to have you, and the relationship she shares with you," Maggie says, sensing my doubts and reluctance. "Don't leave her in the cold."

"You're just full of metaphorical advice tonight," I say.

"I've always loved a good metaphor," she admits. "What else can I help you with?"

"I have another client, or patient, that I've cared for before at the hospital and I'm now dealing with through the police department. He's someone I like a lot and I fear he's in a great deal of trouble. He has schizophrenia and there have been issues in the past with him not taking his meds, changing his meds, that sort of thing. Currently, he's a suspect in a murder case, and I'm beginning to think he might have done it. At the very least, he's involved somehow. But he's having all sorts of hallucinatory episodes suddenly, despite claiming that he's taking his meds as prescribed. He's been on the same meds for several months now and they've been working well for him up until recently."

"What meds is he on?"

I rattle off the names from memory.

"Hm . . . patients can sometimes build up tolerances to certain medications to the point where they don't work well anymore, but the meds he's on don't typically have that problem. Plus, you say he hasn't been on them all that long. Just a few months?"

"That's right."

"And they were working well for him until recently?"

"Yep."

"Are these recent hallucinations similar to his past ones?"

"Actually, they're not. In the past, his breakdowns have followed a pattern. He has auditory hallucinations, voices that tell him to do things like take his clothes off or run away from home. He'll get paranoid and say he thinks he's being watched. He stops showering. And he withdraws from life. That's been his pattern. The voices have never urged violent behavior before, and he's never acted out against anyone."

"Are you thinking his voices told him to kill someone this time?"

"No, at least I don't think they have."

"So, what's different then?"

"He's having visual hallucinations, one in particular." My voice drifts off with the last word as I recall that Danny's specific hallucination is one that I saw myself. "At least I think that's what it is."

"Explain."

I tell her about the call to Allie's house the other night, what Danny was saying, and how he was behaving. "At first, I thought he was having one of his usual episodes, though it was different than his others with this ghost he kept claiming he saw, and the stuff he was saying about a purple and pink polka-dotted dinosaur. But then we ended up at a murder scene and, lo and behold, there was this old-fashioned cookie jar sitting on a shelf behind the victim that was a cartoonish-looking, purple and pink polka-dotted triceratops. Later, when I talked to Danny again, he claimed that the ghost he saw was that of the victim, that it was at the cemetery when he went by there and it came flying out of a tree toward him."

"A manifestation of his guilt, perhaps?" Maggie suggests. I don't answer her immediately and she prompts me with, "What aren't you telling me, Hildy?"

I hesitate, unwilling to say what I need to. Finally, I blurt it out. "I think the ghost might be real, because I saw it, too."

Now it's Maggie's turn to be silent. After an interminable amount of time she says, "A trick of the light in conjunction with your own imagination, maybe a bit of mist or fog?"

"I really don't think so," I tell her. "I mean, I know ghosts don't exist, at least I don't think they do. But there was something there, Maggie. His sister claims she saw it, too, on a different occasion."

There is a moment of contemplative silence before Maggie says, "How have you been doing otherwise? Finding any odd food items in your pockets?"

I feel myself blush. "I have, but only a couple of times," I say. "I've just started this new job and that adds a lot of stress to my life. I'm still trying to figure out my new sleep schedule and my body isn't in sync with what my brain says I should do."

The door to the break room opens then and Brenda and Devo walk in, ready to start their shifts.

"Ready to go, Hildy?" Brenda says.

"One sec," I tell her. Then to Maggie, I say, "I have to go. My shift is starting."

"Do you have time for an appointment tomorrow?" Maggie asks. "I can try to squeeze you in after my regular appointments for the day."

Brenda points to Roscoe and says in a low voice, "I'll load him up if that's okay?"

I nod and she walks over to his bed and hooks up his leash to his collar. "Come on, Roscoe," she urges. "Another working night for you, boy."

As I watch Brenda walk Roscoe out, I tell Maggie, "I'll be working all night tonight and then I have to report for duty at the hospital when I get done here. I won't be getting to bed until I get off work at three-thirty tomorrow, and by then I'll be too exhausted."

"Hm . . . I suppose you're right. It won't help if you're too tired. So, let's do this. I'll plan on coming by the hospital tomorrow to see Marla Riley at noon. Let's try to hook up then, just to touch base. In the meantime, I'll think about what you've told me and see if I can come up with any great witticisms between now and then."

"That should work. Thanks, Maggie. I'll see you then." I disconnect the call and hurry out to the back lot where Brenda Joiner and Roscoe are both loaded into the car waiting for me.

"Here's hoping we'll have a quiet night tonight," Brenda says as we pull out of the lot.

My cell phone rings then, and I'm surprised to see Bob's name come up as the caller. "Hey, Bob. What's up?"

"Have you talked to Danny Hildebrand today?"

"No, why?" A cold feeling of dread spreads through my gut.

"The feds want to have a chat with him, and they went to his house this evening to get him, but he isn't there. His sister said he went out for a walk around noon and never came back. He didn't take his cell phone with him and his car is sitting in the street out in front of the house. Any idea where he might be?"

I think a moment. "No," I tell him. "Have you checked the hospital to make sure he isn't there?"

"No, good idea. I'll give them a call."

"Let me know what they tell you, will you?"

Bob agrees and I disconnect the call. "Danny

Hildebrand is missing," I tell Brenda. "And the feds want to question him. It isn't looking very good for him."

"Do you think he killed that farmer guy?"

"I don't. I can't say why, it's just a gut feeling."

"Ah, your gut again," she says in a teasing tone. "Why don't you use that gut to figure out where Hildebrand might be?"

We fall silent for a minute or so and then I say, "You know, I do have some ideas. I think he might go to either the cemetery or the farm. Fletcher's death is weighing heavy on his soul. Whether or not he was the one who killed the man, he feels responsible for his death. I think he wants to apologize to the guy."

"A bit late for that," Brenda scoffs.

"Not if he apologizes to his ghost." Brenda shoots me a look that says she thinks I'm off my rocker. "The cemetery," I say. "He thinks he saw Fletcher's ghost there. Maybe he went back hoping to see it again and make amends somehow."

"You want to go and search through the cemetery in the dead of night?" Brenda says. She doesn't sound leery of this idea. In fact, she sounds excited.

"Depends," I say. "Bob is checking at the hospital to make sure he isn't there. I suppose we could go out to the farm and see if they've had any suspicious activity. There is still a guard of some sort out there, right?"

"There is," Brenda says.

"Except Bob said Danny's car is at the house. I doubt he would have gone that far on foot."

"Good point," Brenda says.

Bob calls back then and informs us that the hospital hasn't seen Danny, and I tell him about my idea with the cemetery. He agrees it's worth a check and, the second he says this, Brenda turns the cruiser around and heads for the land of the dead.

Chapter 23

The city cemetery is in a part of town that is reasonably well lit at night, but most of the lights are on the streets. The bulk of the cemetery is shielded from these lights by the big old trees that cover the land. I've often wondered at the wisdom of planting that many trees in an area where frequent digging takes place as the root systems must be extensive. But it seems to work.

Brenda parks the cruiser at the entrance gates, which are never locked, and I get out and fetch Roscoe from the back. At first, I hook him up to his leash, but then I decide to let him run free and explore, figuring if there are any ghosts or live persons in the area, he will find them and alert us.

Brenda hands me a flashlight and gets one for herself, too, so we can illuminate the meandering paths well enough to keep us on the trail and avoid tripping over any gravestones. Some of the older ones are half buried in the earth, with just enough sticking up to make wandering off the path hazardous. We spend fifteen minutes slowly exploring the area closest to the gates, our flashlights creating long, creeping shadows as the light tries to eke its way around the large tree trunks and the more upright stones. The big tree where I thought I saw the ghost the other night is about fifty yards in, and I steer us that way with some trepidation, my heart pounding in my chest. I half expect to see an ephemeral wisp of something come looming out at us, but there is nothing. Roscoe wanders about, nose to the ground, weaving a serpentine path among the headstones. At one point he lifts a leg and pees on the side of someone's headstone, and I admonish him and make a silent apology to whoever is buried there as well as any loved ones who might come to visit.

Once we have searched the area near the gates, we venture down the hill toward where we found Danny the other day and start searching in and around the trees, even up some of those that have lower-hanging branches and are, therefore, easily climbable. There is no sign of anyone, living or dead, and half an hour later we are back at the top of the hill and venturing out toward the back area of the cemetery, which is bordered by the river that meanders its way through town.

I become fascinated with the engravings on the headstones, some of them marking entire families buried together in an area, others lone burials. There are a frightening and sad number of young children in this older part of the cemetery, which dates back to the late 1800s. Childhood deaths back then were relatively common, both from disease and injuries, and I wonder at the grief and sorrow that must have permeated families in those times. My grief support group that I run at the hospital has a core group of regulars who attend, but judging from the dates and ages on the headstones, had I been doing something like that back at the turn of the twentieth century, the group would have been huge. Or perhaps not. People might have become inured to the tragedy of death, given how common it was.

There is no moon to help us navigate our way, but there are fewer trees in the back section, so we make quick work of it and easily determine that Danny isn't hiding there.

It takes us a little over an hour to search the entire cemetery, and we come up empty. Brenda has been mostly silent the entire time, and her earlier excitement at the prospect of searching here seems to have abated. As we head back to the main gate, there is a rustle and some movement up ahead on the far side of a huge old oak tree, and for a moment I think we might have finally found Danny. But it turns out to be a deer, who stands frozen in the beam of my flashlight for nearly a full minute—living up to the deer-in-the-headlights cliché. When I finally lower the light toward the ground, it bounds off, leaping over several headstones and heading toward the river. With the fence back there it's going to be trapped. Its only exit will be through the gate because the fence is six feet high and made of wrought iron with spaces too narrow between the spindles for the deer to fit through. Hopefully, it will eventually find its way out.

Back in the car, Brenda calls in to the station to let Miranda, the weekend night shift dispatcher, know that we are done with our search and that it didn't produce anything. Miranda lets us know that Allie has called in twice asking to speak to me but was told I was otherwise occupied.

"She wouldn't tell me what it was about," Miranda says, "but I asked her if her brother had shown up and she said no."

I call Allie and get her voice mail, but after I leave a brief message and hang up, she calls me back a few minutes later.

"Hildy, any chance you can come by my house? Joel and I found something, and I want to show it to you before anyone else sees it."

"Is it something related to Danny?"

"It is," she says, weariness in her voice.

I look at Brenda, who nods. "We'll be there in a few minutes," I say.

When we arrive at Allie's house, the porch light is on to welcome us, though I suppose it might also be on to welcome Danny back home. Allie must have been watching for us because she opens the front door before we have a chance to knock.

"Please, come in," she says, and Brenda and I both enter. "I hope you don't think I'm being a nosy busybody, but I thought I should look at Danny's computer to see if it might offer up any suggestions as to his whereabouts. His bedroom is upstairs and normally I don't go in there, but tonight I made an exception."

"And you found something on his laptop?" Brenda says.

Allie shakes her head. "No, it's gone, just like

Danny. His cell phone is here in the house—it's downstairs in the living room—and I tried to check it for emails and such, but the thing has been wiped clean. There are no messages, no email access . . . nothing. Even his call history has been wiped. It's like he restored the phone to the factory settings." Her brow is creased with worry and her voice is tremulous, as if she's about to burst into tears.

Joel comes out of the kitchen and walks down the hall toward us, a grim expression on his face. He drapes what I'm sure is meant to be a reassuring arm over Allie's shoulders, but this small show of affection is all it takes to make Allie's fragile wall of strength crumble. Tears well in her eyes and she says, "I'm worried. Everything feels so . . . so final with him right now. I think he may be doing something stupid."

"You think he's suicidal?"

She doesn't answer but the fear on her face says all I need to know.

"If Danny's laptop is gone, what is it you wanted to show me?" I ask her.

"This." She reaches into her pants pocket and pulls out a folded slip of paper, handing it to me with a trembling hand.

I take it and carefully unfold it. It's a plain piece of standard copy paper, the kind used in printers and copiers everywhere. Written on it in block letters in black ink are the words: DO AS YOU ARE TOLD OR YOUR SISTER WILL DIE.

I hand the paper to Brenda, who takes it gingerly by the edge, and ask Allie, "Where exactly did you find this?"

"It was on his dresser inside a little box he keeps there that has some cuff links and a ring in it that he wears from time to time. I don't know what made me look in it. I was just standing in the middle of his bedroom, trying to connect with him somehow, and I thought I would look through his dresser drawers to see if . . . I don't know what I was hoping to see. I was desperate and grasping at straws."

Brenda says, "We can take this note as evidence and see if there are any fingerprints on it. Did both of you handle it?"

Allie nods, looking regretful. "Sorry," she says. "If I'd known what it was when I first found it. . . ."

"It's okay," Brenda reassures her. "We can always rule your prints out. It's not the best source for prints anyway so it may not produce anything. Have you got a paper bag I can put it in, like a lunch sack, or a grocery bag?"

Joel says, "Of course," removes his arm from Allie's shoulders and disappears back into the kitchen. He returns a moment later carrying a folded, lunch-size paper bag and hands it to Brenda.

She hands the note back to me, instructing me to hold it along the edge the same way she did, though this is shutting the barn door a little too late considering that I unfolded and held the thing just moments ago. Then she unfolds the bag, opens it, and instructs me to drop the note into it. I do so, and she closes the top, folding it over a few times. With that done, she takes a pen from her pocket and writes on the outside upper fold of the bag, putting down the day, the time, and her initials.

"I don't think there's much more we can do here," she says when she's done. "Unless you have anything else?"

Allie shakes her head woefully, one tear sliding down her cheek. Joel affectionately pushes a lock of hair back off her face and says, "Come on, babe. You need to get some rest." He twines one of his arms around hers and makes as if to steer her toward the stairs, but Allie resists. She wipes a sleeve across her nose, and this gives me an idea.

"Allie, can you get me a piece of clothing that Danny has worn recently, something that hasn't been laundered since he wore it?"

She gives me a puzzled look. So does Brenda.

"Roscoe is very good at sniffing things out. He helped me solve that college student case by tracking a scent. Maybe we can use him to try to find Danny instead of searching through a cemetery in the dark."

"Good idea," Brenda says.

Allie sighs and looks up at Joel. "Would you mind running upstairs and grabbing something out of the laundry hamper? I'm not sure I'd know his clothes from yours."

"Sure," Joel says. He gives her a quick kiss on top of her head and then goes upstairs, taking them two at a time.

Allie looks at me with pleading eyes. "Hildy, that note is proof that whatever Danny may have done, he did it out of love for me, and because he was being blackmailed, right? Won't that help if they find him?"

"It might," I say, though I have no idea if it will.

"I didn't want to give it to the federal guys. I don't trust them like I trust you."

Her words are like a stab in my heart. She's putting so much faith in me and I have no way to help her or Danny much at this point. "Joel is right. You need to get some rest," I tell her. "Keep your cell phone by you and if we hear anything at all, we'll let you know."

"We need you to do the same," Brenda says in a cautionary tone. "You won't be doing your brother any good if you try to hide him or keep him away from us. Okay?"

Allie squeezes her eyes closed, forcing two more tears down her cheeks. She nods reluctantly, stifling back a sob. "Please . . . f . . . find him," she hiccups.

Joel returns carrying a white men's undershirt. "Will this work?" he asks.

"It should, if we look in the right place."

Joel hands me the shirt and on that heartbreaking, parting note, we take our leave. Brenda drives straight back to the police station and we take our bag with the note downstairs to the basement level of the building where the evidence lab is located. No one is on duty down here tonight. Laura Kingston works a lot of night shifts, but she splits her shifts between our office and the medical examiner's office. As it happens, tonight is one of her nights off.

"Are you going to call someone in to process that?" I ask Brenda as she seals the bag closed with evidence tape and then enters the bagged note into the logbook.

"No. It can wait until morning. Let's take a drive out to the farm and have a chat with the guards out there. I want to make sure they haven't seen anything suspicious or unusual, make sure Danny didn't hitch a ride out there somehow. And let's see if Roscoe can sniff out anything while we're there."

Chapter 24

Brenda checks in with Devo and Al, the other officer on duty this shift, before we head out to the farm to make sure they don't need us for anything and to let them know where we'll be. Though the farm is outside of town, it's not far beyond the city limits and we can be back within a matter of minutes if need be.

There is a county sheriff's car parked at the entrance to the driveway and sitting behind the wheel is a uniformed guy who is sound asleep. He has his car parked in such a way that no other vehicles can get past him to go up the drive thanks to ditches on either side, but that also means we can't get by him.

"Great," Brenda says with a doleful shake of her head. "If Danny did get out here somehow, he could have walked right past this idiot." She punches the horn, sending out one, long, loud blast. The cop behind the wheel of the other cruiser startles, sitting up fast enough to give himself whiplash. His eyes dart about frantically for a second before seeing us. His posture relaxes then, and he climbs out of his car and walks over to Brenda's window. I note that his complexion has turned the color of ripe watermelon.

"Sorry about that," he says when Brenda lowers her window. "They've got us working so much overtime because we're short and I'm afraid it's starting to catch up to me."

"Have you been parked across the drive like that for a while?" Brenda asks.

"Since eight this evening. And the guy I relieved was the same way. He said there hadn't been anyone out here all day."

"Is there someone up at the farm keeping an eye out?" Brenda asks. "There is another access road that runs off County D."

"I don't think there's anyone at the farm itself, but there's another car posted by the end of that access road, so no one is getting in that way."

"We need to take a look at some things relative to our murder investigation," Brenda says. "Do you mind moving long enough to let us through?"

"Sure." He goes back to his cruiser, starts it up, and maneuvers it out onto the road so we can pull into the drive. Brenda drives past him and waves.

When we reach the part of the drive where it splits off, Brenda stops and looks over at me, eyebrows raised in question.

"Go left, to the house," I tell her. We can start there and work our way toward the barn. Based on Danny's psychopathy and the things he's been ranting about, if he came here, I think he'd be drawn to the house and the site of the murder more than anything else."

Brenda drives toward the house, pulling around by the front door.

"Is it locked?" I ask.

"I don't think so, but I guess we'll find out."

We get out of the car and I go around to the back, raise the hatch, and open Roscoe's crate. I have Danny's undershirt in hand, and I push it under his nose and let him sniff it all over for a minute. Then I tell him to go find. He jumps out of the car and wanders around in an ever-widening circle for a minute or so, nose to the ground. Then he takes off around the house toward the back. Brenda and I follow and find him on the back stoop, wagging his tail, looking at the closed door.

"We can't let him go in there and traipse through the crime scene," I say. "But given that he's followed the scent to here, I think it's safe to say that Danny was in this house at some point. But then, we kind of knew that already."

Brenda says, "Let's go around to the front and enter the house that way. We should look inside to make sure Danny isn't there."

We do so after I hook Roscoe up to his leash, tell him he's a good boy, and give him a pat on the head. I put him back in the car for now and then follow Brenda to the front door. She tries the knob and the door opens easily; the tape Bob sliced through earlier in the day hasn't been replaced. I let Brenda lead the way and secure the area, not because I'm afraid of Danny but because that's the way I was taught in my brief training and orientation to this new job. She checks the entire first floor, though we don't go past the crime scene tape across the kitchen entryway. One look tells us no one is in there. When we enter the room that Arthur Fletcher used as his office, I recite for Brenda the events of that morning with the two Fletcher women. This lightens both our moods and gives us a chance to laugh.

Having cleared the first floor, we do a quick search of the second floor, but find no evidence of Danny. I'm both relieved and disappointed.

"I don't know if I want Roscoe sniffing around in that barn basement," I say. "I heard that all of the plants were removed, but still . . ."

Brenda acknowledges my concerns and we decide to simply search the barn and the other outbuildings to make sure Danny isn't in any of them. This takes us the better part of an hour, particularly on the upper level of the barn with all its hay bales, stalls, farm machinery, and loft.

By the time we head back down the driveway, I expect to find our sheriff asleep at the wheel again, but apparently embarrassment from being caught the first time and the knowledge that we would be coming back by him again was enough to keep him up and going. He has parked his car on the shoulder just past the driveway entrance, so we are able to leave without waiting for him to move. Brenda gives him a salute as we go by, but we don't stop to talk to him.

As we head back to town, a feeling of foreboding settles over me. "I'm worried that Allie might be right about her brother," I tell Brenda. "In his current state, I wonder if he might not do something drastic."

"Suicide, you mean?"

I nod. "I'm not sure how else to explain his disappearance."

"There is another explanation," Brenda says, looking over at me with a troubled expression. "Clearly Danny wasn't working alone out at that farm, and whoever was working with him, whoever was in charge, might be concerned about him talking."

This idea sends a chill down my back. "Do the cops have any leads at all about who else was out there at the farm? Any fingerprints they found in that basement?"

"There were lots of prints collected," Brenda says. "But the only ones that have been identified for sure are Danny's and Arthur Fletcher's. The lack of any others suggests that the others involved are professionals who know what they're doing. And to them, Danny is going to be a loose end."

This angers me. Danny is a vulnerable person as it is, and the idea of someone threatening and blackmailing him into doing things he wouldn't otherwise do infuriates me. Yet no matter how much of the evidence points to him, I can't reconcile the idea of Danny as a killer. I don't have any hard evidence to back this feeling; it's simply a gut reaction. But over the years I've learned to trust my gut.

I hope Danny is safe somewhere, but I can't think of anywhere else to look for him. Instead, I fret over his whereabouts for the rest of the shift, which is blissfully quiet.

"Sunday nights are typically slow," Brenda says.

"People are done with their weekend partying and they're gearing back up for work on Monday."

Brenda's prediction holds true and the only other call we get for the night is from a lady named Agnes Silver who lives in a ramshackle house on the edge of town. She's well known to the police because she's paranoid as all get out and calls them constantly to report imagined interlopers and crimes.

"This is a perfect case for you, Hildy," Brenda says. "Agnes is a hoarder, in part because of whatever mental illness she suffers from, and in part because she piles up stuff in her house to create barricades so her imagined attackers can't get in. Her house is a fire hazard, and the city has tried to get it condemned, but so far Agnes has managed to skirt their efforts. She doesn't take well to strangers, so I'm not sure she'll like that you're here, but we'll do our best. She likes and trusts me for the most part, so hopefully I can get you a ticket in."

Since Agnes isn't someone who goes to the hospital or even sees a doctor, I don't know her. The screen door on the front of her house has oven racks and cookie sheets wired to it, and the window in the main door behind the screen has a piece of plywood nailed over it. A woman's voice hollers through the door when Brenda knocks, asking who it is.

"It's Officer Brenda, Agnes. You know me. Can you open up the door?"

"How do I know it's really you?" Agnes hollers back. "What's the password?"

Brenda looks back at me and rolls her eyes. "Spaghetti," she says.

The inside door opens a crack and a pale, jowly face framed with wild, gray hair peeks out. "Who is that other person?" Agnes asks, her voice rife with suspicion.

"It's Hildy Schneider.," Brenda says, and I smile at the face peering out the door. "She's a social worker who's going to be riding around with us. It's part of a new program to help us better connect with folks in the community, folks like you."

"How do I know she can be trusted?" Agnes asks.

"You have my word," Brenda says. "And I have my gun and my Taser, so if she doesn't behave, I can take care of her."

"Say what?" I whisper, maintaining my smile.

Brenda looks back again and winks at me. "But that won't be necessary," she says to Agnes. "Hildy is one of the good guys. I promise."

There is another minute of silence and then the inner door slowly opens, creaking on rusted hinges. Agnes, dressed in a ratty, stained, chenille bathrobe that is covered with bald spots where the chenille is missing, unlocks the screen door. "Come on," she says, and then she disappears into the darkness behind her. It's as if her house has just swallowed her up.

Brenda opens the screen door and motions for me to follow her in. Despite the preparation she gave me, I'm a little stunned when I step through the door and see what lies beyond. There is a ceiling light fixture with three bulbs in it, two of which are blown. The meager bit of light coming from

the third one barely illuminates the cave that is
this house. There is a path through the canyon of
junk that is about two feet wide. Agnes is easily that
wide, so I imagine it can't be easy for her to get
around, and I wonder how she gets her food. Judging from her physique she isn't missing many
meals. Creating the canyon walls are stacks of
boxes, bags, tied up newspaper bundles, various
linens and clothing items, kitchen pots and pans,
and God knows what else. Items are stacked to the
ceiling over by the walls, obscuring furniture, windows, and what appears to be a fireplace based on
the mantel I can see on the wall by peeking through
piles of junk.

Brenda and I follow Agnes along the path deeper
into the house and I hear something scurry in the
pile to my left. The path leads us into the kitchen,
where another ceiling light, this one with two of
the three bulbs working, sheds light on the most
disgusting mess I've ever seen. The sink is filled
with crusted, dirty dishes, some with mold growing
on them. The stove is likewise covered, though in
this case it's more pots and pans rather than dishes,
and the rest of the room is jam-packed with junk:
cups, plates, more bundled newspapers, stuffed
toys, and boxes of cake mix, mac and cheese, cookies, crackers, and pudding mix. There is a table in
the room, but the area beneath it is filled with
junk and its surface is piled high with items reaching almost to the ceiling. There is a refrigerator,
but it isn't working. The door hangs open revealing shelves crammed with rotting cheeses, sour
milk, and some other things that are unidentifi-
able. I see a cockroach scurry across the counter

and disappear into the fridge and suppress a shudder.

Brenda has clearly seen all this before because there is no evidence of surprise, shock, or disgust on her face. "Your call said something about acid in your yard?" she says to Agnes.

"It's out here," Agnes says, and she continues along the path into a small mudroom and then opens a back door after undoing the three dead bolts on it. "Look at my grass," she says. "See that shining liquid, the way it glistens? It's acid, I know it is."

The yard is as filled with junk as the rest of the house—an old washing machine, some car parts, rain-soaked, soggy boxes of who knows what, old and broken lawn furniture, several broken barbecue grills—and I'm surprised there is any grass growing out here at all. But there is, one stubborn little patch about six feet square that doesn't have anything resting on it. The sun is rising, and golden rays eke their way through the spaces between the junk.

"Agnes, that's not acid," Brenda says. "It's dew. Morning dew."

"No, it's not. It's acid," Agnes insists.

Brenda walks over and runs her hand across the blades of grass, then she rubs the moisture on her hand onto her cheek. "See, not acid. Just dew, Agnes. Nothing to worry about."

Agnes looks suspicious, but she doesn't argue the point again. She heads back inside, and we follow her. She makes her way to the front door, clearly ready to see us out, but Brenda stops and calls her back.

"Agnes, Hildy might like to come out and visit again. Would that be okay?"

Agnes eyes me with suspicion, and I think she's about to say no. But she surprises me and says, "I suppose. Do you have a card?"

I do have business cards that the police department made for me, and I take one out of my pocket and give it to her. "You can call me if you need anything," I tell her.

"What would I be needing?" Agnes says, looking at me like I'm stupid. "I got everything I need right here."

Well, she certainly has that right.

By the time we leave it's ten to seven, so Brenda drives us back to the station. I tell her I'll ponder the enigma that is Agnes and see if I can come up with a plan for her, but right now I need to go home, change clothes, and head to my job at the hospital. I don't even go inside the station. I just unload Roscoe from the back of the cruiser and put him in my car. Then I drive myself home, thinking I need another cup of coffee to give me energy to get through the day. My shift at the hospital won't be done until three-thirty, and that means bedtime is a long ways away yet. I suspect I'll probably sleep through the entire evening and most of the night, since I don't have to do my police shifts again until Thursday night.

P.J. is on her way to school when I pull in, and I roll my window down and tell her I'll walk Roscoe this morning, but could she come and get him after school and maybe a couple of times this evening? She happily agrees.

Once inside, I turn on the coffee pot, glad I had

the insight to set it up the night before, knowing I'd probably need a pick-me-up before going into the hospital this morning.

It promises to be a busy day. On top of all my usual hospital business, I want to search for some resources I can employ to help Agnes, and I need to check in on Marla to see how she's doing. I should probably call Stewart, too, to make sure he's managing okay. His commitment to Marla's commitment might be wavering.

Feeling exhausted just thinking about it all, I change my clothes, splash some water on my face, and then fix a cup of coffee to go. Then it's off to the races. I'm starting to think these two jobs might be the death of me.

Chapter 25

The ER is calm when I arrive at the hospital. That's typical for early in the morning, though it's likely to get crazy in an hour or so. Mondays are always busy for ERs for some reason. It's been that way at every hospital I've worked.

I decide to check on Marla Riley first thing and log into the hospital computer system to see what room she's been admitted to. I search for her by her name first, then I pull up all the floors and look for her that way, checking the names in each room. Fortunately, the hospital isn't that full, or that big, so it doesn't take me very long.

I come up empty. There is no sign of Marla. I track down the day shift charge nurse, a fellow named Mark, and ask him if he knows anything about her case. He doesn't, and neither do any of the other people on duty today. The weekend staffers are all off now and the crew on this morning have no idea what went down over the weekend.

Resigned to having to search through her chart, I find it and open it. Technically, she isn't my patient any longer once she gets admitted upstairs because my boss, Crystal, handles most of the inpatient needs. But since I was involved in Marla's care here in the ER, at least peripherally, I figure I won't get into trouble for perusing her chart. My history with Marla should help justify my involvement with her care on an ongoing basis.

I skim through the ER notes and see that she slept for several hours on Saturday night and was then admitted upstairs to the medical-surgical unit. After a largely uneventful day yesterday, plans were made to transfer her today to a VA hospital in Milwaukee for psychiatric and substance abuse treatment. This worries me because I know from experience that Marla hates the VA system and won't stay there. I make a mental note to look into the possibility of finding her placement elsewhere, but what I read next makes me realize this won't be necessary. It also shocks me to my core.

A note from last night says that a nurse went into Marla's room around midnight to take her vital signs and found her unresponsive. A quick check revealed that she had no pulse and wasn't breathing, so CPR was started immediately, and a medical emergency was paged. The physician on the floor ran a code on Marla for a full forty minutes but was never able to get more than a pulseless rhythm back on her. At twelve-forty-eight this morning, Marla was pronounced dead and the resuscitation efforts were stopped. The doctor's after-care note mentioned the presence of severe tetany, which led him to believe that Marla had had an unwitnessed seizure triggered by her alcohol withdrawal, despite meds that were given to prevent this. The seizure resulted in a respiratory arrest, which then led to a cardiac arrest.

I'm shocked and heartbroken that Marla is dead. After taking a few minutes to digest this turn of events, I wonder how Stewart is doing. That man adored his wife, and I suspect he's going to have a lot of trouble dealing with her death. Then again, maybe it will come as something of a relief to him after all the abuse and angst the two of them have been through. And Marla's future was looking grimly complicated, at best.

I make a mental note to try to convince Stewart to come to my grief support group at a later date. I think it will benefit him greatly and the group is always more dynamic when fresh blood is introduced. For now, I look up Stewart's number and give him a call to touch base with him and see how he's doing. His phone rings and then flips to voice mail. While listening to his outgoing message I mentally debate whether to leave one of my own and decide not to, but rather to try to call again a little later.

I decide to go the cafeteria to grab a cup of coffee. In the hallway on the way there, I run into Dr. Rollins, the physician who handled Marla's arrest, who, judging from the hour, the jacket he's wearing, and the briefcase he's carrying, is heading home for the day.

"Morning, Dr. Rollins," I say.

"Good morning, Hildy. What problems are you going to solve for us today?"

"None that I know of yet. Do you have a second? I'd like to talk to you about Marla Riley."

"Oh, yes. Sad case, that one." He shakes his head woefully.

"Was her husband here when she died? I've been working with him and his wife for a while now and I've gotten to know him quite well. Their marriage had some strange dynamics and I'm worried about how he's going to cope."

Dr. Rollins shakes his head. "No, he wasn't here. The nurse taking care of Mrs. Riley said that she had no visitors, unless you count the policeman sitting outside her room. Her husband didn't visit her at all. I thought perhaps their relationship was strained to breaking the way so many of these couples affected by addiction are, but when I called him to let him know that she had passed, he was quite distraught and upset. I imagine he'll be a good candidate for your grief support group."

"Yes, I've already made myself a note to contact him," I say.

"You might want to do that sooner rather than later. He kind of went off the deep end. He kept saying that *they* had killed her. At first, I though he meant we had killed her, but he kept saying *they*. And then he just hung up on me." Dr. Rollins shrugs.

"Wow," I say. "Sounds like he's going to need more help than I initially thought."

"Yeah, good luck with that," Dr. Rollins says. And with that, he's gone.

I stand in the hallway for a minute or two, replaying the conversation in my head. Stewart Riley's reaction to his wife's death certainly seems over the top but, given all the events of the past few days, I'm not sure they're as outrageous as I might have found them a week ago. If it wasn't for the fact that there was a policeman stationed outside Marla's room during her stay, I might be inclined to think that whoever is behind the bioterrorist potential out at the farm had tried to get rid of Marla to make sure she didn't say anything or give anyone away. But if she had no visitors, it doesn't seem likely.

I'm starting to feel as paranoid as Danny gets when he's in one of his full-blown episodes. Maybe I'm turning into Agnes Silver. Then that adage comes to me, the one about how being paranoid doesn't mean someone isn't out to get you. I decide I should gather as many facts as I can so that, when I do talk to Stewart, I can convince him that his paranoia and suspicions are unwarranted. Plus, there is something nagging at my brain, a worm of a thought that hasn't emerged far enough yet for me to grasp it.

After grabbing my coffee, I head upstairs to the nurse's station on the unit Marla was admitted to, find the charge nurse, a woman named Linda, and ask her if she can look up some information for me. "I'm curious to know if the woman who died last night, Marla Riley, was a coroner's case."

"It was," she says. "The night nurse told me they came and picked her body up for an autopsy. I think it's automatic when a patient dies within twenty-four hours of admission."

I thank her and start to go, but then turn back, needing to address that niggle in my brain. "Can you tell me what tetany is?" I ask her. "I know I've heard the term before, but I can't recall what it means."

"It's a term for muscle rigidity, or spasm," she says.

Alarms go off in my head, and after thinking things through for a moment, I head for my office and make a call.

"Hello. Medical Examiner's office. This is Cass. How can I help you?"

"Hi, Cass, this is Hildy Schneider. I'm a social worker over at the hospital and I'm calling to inquire about an autopsy on a patient that was here. Is there someone I can talk to about it?"

"Hold on and I'll let you talk to Doc Morton."

Perfect, I think, since Doc Morton was the one at the scene of Arthur Fletcher's murder. I'm put on hold and forced to listen to bad eighties music that sounds tinny and scratchy. After thirty seconds or so of this torture, Doc Morton finally comes on.

"Hi, Dr. Morton, this is Hildy Schneider. I'm the social worker who was with the police out at the Fletcher farm the other night."

"Yes, I know who you are, Ms. Schneider. What can I do for you?"

"You can call me Hildy for starters. And then you can tell me if you're doing an autopsy on Marla Riley. She was a patient who died here at the hospital yesterday."

"We have the body, but I haven't done the autopsy yet. Not sure I need to, given the circumstances. My understanding is that she was an alcoholic and had a withdrawal seizure that caused respiratory and then cardiac arrest. Sad, but not all that unusual."

"Are you aware of the police's interest in her?" I ask. "There is some indication that she might have been involved in that mess out at the Fletcher farm. She has a military background as a weapon's specialist."

"I wasn't aware of that, but I'm not sure how that changes the circumstances of her death."

"I understand from Bob Richmond that Mr. Fletcher's time of death was changed because you found strychnine in his system and that could have caused muscle rigidity that mimicked rigor mortis."

"That is correct."

"If Marla Riley was involved with whatever group oversaw those poisons out at the farm, the fact that she was hospitalized and having what appeared to be a mental breakdown might have been perceived as a threat. According to the doctor's note, the reason they think she had a seizure is because she had tetany."

There is silence on the other end, and I wait. It doesn't take Doc Morton long to connect the dots. "You're thinking she might have been poisoned with strychnine as well?" he says.

"It seems possible."

"I'll look into it, and thanks for calling me, Hildy."

"You're welcome." I disconnect the call and then make one to Bob Richmond.

"Hey, Hildy. What's up?"

"Did you know that Marla Riley died?"

"Yeah, I heard. Had a seizure. Sad thing, but that can happen when you withdraw from alcohol."

"Yes, it can. But it can also happen when you're poisoned with strychnine because the members of a certain militia group want you eliminated since you know too much, and they consider you a liability now."

There is a very long silence on the other end and I finally say, "Bob, are you still there?"

"I'm here," he grumbles. "What are you saying, Hildy. That you think Marla was murdered?"

"The doctor's note said that they found her with severe tetany, and I've been told that means her muscles were in a state of spasm and rigidity."

"Isn't that what happens if you have a seizure?"

"It is, but remember that the time of death on Mr. Fletcher had to be amended because of—"

"Because of the muscle rigidity caused by strychnine poisoning," Bob finishes for me, his tone suggesting that a light bulb just turned on in his brain. "But there was an officer outside her room the entire time she was in the hospital. He said she never had any visitors, not even her husband. Only hospital staffers entered the room."

"Did that guard outside her room ever leave his station, like to go to the bathroom?" I hear him take a breath in and continue before he can get defensive. "I'm not implying that he or she did anything wrong, but I've seen other patients who were on police holds and had a guard, and they were rarely there every minute. And since Marla was heavily sedated, they might have felt it was okay to

step away for a brief break. They were there to
make sure she didn't leave, right? Not to make
sure no one else went in the room."

"True," Bob says.

"And maybe I'm being paranoid, but with
Danny missing and Marla dead, it's sure starting to
feel like someone is trying to clean house."

Bob sighs wearily. "I'll call the ME's office and
have them check for the strychnine."

"I already did. I spoke to Doc Morton. He said
he'd test for it."

Bob chuckles. "Why am I not surprised? Good
work, Hildy. I'll talk to you later."

Before I can utter another word, I realize he has
disconnected the call. Just like that my floating
balloon of euphoria crashes to earth. "Okay then,"
I say to myself with a shrug. "Back to work."

My next call is to Dr. Maggie Baldwin. Since
there was no official consult request for her to see
Marla Riley, no one from the hospital would have
known to call her about Marla's death. I'm hoping
she'll answer my call because I wouldn't mind
bouncing some thoughts off her, but I get her
voice mail. I leave a message stating only the facts
and letting her know she doesn't need to come
and see Marla. I debate sharing my thoughts on
the matter but, in the end, I decide to stick to the
basic facts for now and update her later if necessary.

I tend to some routine paperwork and then give
Stewart Riley another call. I plan to leave a message this time if he doesn't answer and if I don't
hear back from him in a timely manner, I'll send
someone out to his place to do a welfare check.

Stewart's situation, personality, and history with Marla make him a high risk for suicide. But my worries are for naught because this time he answers my call.

"Stewart, it's Hildy Schneider."

"Hildy." He sounds exhausted, drained.

"I'm so sorry to hear about Marla," I say. "It must be quite a shock for you. Do you have family with you? Or friends?"

Stewart sighs. "Most of our friends disappeared around the time Marla started drinking heavily. And our families are out of state. My parents are coming up from Florida, but they won't get here until the day after tomorrow."

"So, you're alone?"

"I am, but that's okay. I'm fine. Really. And I need to stay here at the house to make sure no one else tries to break in."

It takes a few seconds for what he said to sink in. "Break in? Someone tried to break into your house?"

"They did. It must have happened yesterday. I was out running errands, grocery shopping, poking my head in at work to let them know I'd be out on Monday, picking up the dry cleaning . . . that kind of stuff. It was probably some neighborhood kids high on pot or something."

"You said they tried to get in. Does that mean they were unsuccessful?"

"No. They broke out a windowpane in the back door and I'm fairly certain they got in because the door was left wide open."

"Did you report it to the police?"

"Why bother? I've already boarded up the broken window and as far as I can tell there isn't anything missing other than what the police already took."

I hesitate with my response because I'm trying to decide how much to tell him, or even how much to hint at, but apparently Stewart's patience has reached its limits.

"Look, Hildy, I have to go. Thanks for calling."

Before I can utter so much as a syllable, he is gone. I frown at the phone a moment before placing another call to Bob Richmond.

"Hi, Hildy," he answers. "What have you thought of this time?"

There is no rancor or sarcasm I can detect in his tone even though his wording strikes me as a tad rude. I decide to treat like with like. "Stewart Riley's house was broken into sometime yesterday. Add that to your list of coincidences and tell me what you get."

After a brief pause, he says, "What did they take?"

"According to Stewart, nothing was missing. But perhaps that's because we got to it first."

"Did Stewart report it?"

"He did not." I hear Bob sigh again, the weariness evident. "I'm really worried about Danny," I tell him.

"I hear you. I'll have a chat with the feds and see if they can put some pressure on this militia group they know about. Maybe they'll know something about Danny."

"Can you put out a BOLO for him, both here and with the county guys?"

"What, you're no longer worried that we'll be too eager to hurt him?"

"I'm more worried about what someone else might do to him."

"I'll see what I can do." And then, just like Stewart, he abruptly ends the call.

All this rejection is starting to give me a complex.

Chapter 26

After giving recent events some thought, I make a call to Allie.

She answers with, "Have you found Danny?" She is breathless with hope and it makes my heart squeeze painfully.

"No, sorry. I guess that means you haven't either?"

"No, and I'm really worried, Hildy. He's never been gone this long before. What if something terrible has happened to him?"

Her voice borders on hysteria and I have no answer for her, so I ask a question designed to detour the conversation instead. "Allie, have there been any unusual happenings at your house lately?"

"Like what?"

"Any strange visitors, or any reason to think anyone has tried to break in?"

"No, not that I'm aware of. I'm at work now and I can call Joel at home and ask him, but I'm sure he would have told me if he'd noticed anything wonky. The only odd happenings have been Danny's behavior. Why?"

"You said his laptop was gone, didn't you?"

"Yeah, it disappeared when he did this last time."

"Is the laptop something he takes with him to work?"

There is a pause, and I assume she's thinking back to past days and Danny's routines. "No, not that I've ever seen, now that you mention it. Why?"

"Just wondering. Sometimes the most innocuous things can have meaning. I'm just trying to look at all the pieces and see if there's any way to put them together that makes sense. Do you know of any special places Danny likes to go to? Does he have a park, or a particular walking route he likes to take?"

"If he does, he hasn't shared them with me," she says. "And if he had, I would have checked them out already."

My boss, Crystal Hoffheimer, appears in my doorway and gives me a smile that tells me she has something she wants to discuss.

"Listen, Allie, I have to go but if I hear anything at all about Danny, I'll let you know. You do the same, okay?"

"I will."

I disconnect the call and wave Crystal into the room. "What's up?" I say with a smile.

"We need to talk." I feel my smile falter at the edges. Her tone tells me this isn't likely to be a friendly chat. She settles into the chair across the desk from me, her posture rigid.

"I heard about what happened with Marla Riley," she says. "A very sad ending to that story for her and her husband."

She has no idea just how sad yet, and I'm not about to tell her. I simply nod and look appropriately saddened.

"You've worked with the two of them a lot over the past few years," she goes on.

"Yes, I have. Definitely not the outcome I would have hoped for."

"No, I suppose not." She looks away from me then over toward the wall and I know from my past dealings with her that it's time to brace myself. I have no idea where this conversation is going, but I sense that it isn't going to make me happy.

"I heard that the police searched the Riley's house the other night, the same night that Marla was admitted through the ER. Is that right?"

"It is."

She starts picking at a cuticle, giving it an undue amount of attention. "Why did they do that?" she asks. "It seems over the top for a domestic abuse case. Were they hoping to find some weapons?" She looks at me now, pinning me with her eyes, watching me closely. I'm a decent liar, but I know Crystal will see right through any attempts I might make to pull the proverbial wool over her eyes.

"I can't talk about that," I say, thinking this is my safest reply. "Confidentiality, you know. I have to comply with it at the new job just like I do here."

"What about this job?" Crystal counters, eyebrows raised. "Don't you still have a professional obligation to maintain patient, and sometimes family, confidentiality?"

"Of course."

"And yet you participated in this search of the Riley house, didn't you?"

"I was with the police when it happened," I tell her. "But I don't see how that breached my duty of confidentiality. Stewart consented to the search. And the police are as familiar with the Rileys as we are. They already know their history. In fact, they've likely had more contact with them than we have since they've been called to the house on numerous occasions that didn't result in a trip to the hospital for anyone."

"And yet, they've never tried to get a search warrant for their house before."

I stare at her, wondering how she knows about the attempt to get a search warrant. "How do you know that?" I ask, figuring I might as well try to get everything out on the table.

"I have my ways and my sources," she says with a cryptic smile. "And I know that the search of their house had nothing to do with their usual domestic abuse situation."

I'm stymied and my mind races, trying to figure out how she knows all this. But my brain is running slow from a lack of sleep.

"I have some concerns about how these two jobs are going to mesh for you," she says. "I think you're going to run into some conflicts of interest that will impact one or both of these jobs."

"I think I can manage it," I say, angry with how feeble this response is.

"Can you?" Crystal counters, eyebrows raised in question. "What would you do if a patient here at the hospital told you something in confidence and you later encounter a situation with that patient when you are with the police, and the information that patient shared with you can impact what the police do, how they'll respond?"

"Simple," I say, realizing even as I utter the word that it will be anything but. "I wouldn't tell the cops anything. I'm under no obligation to do so."

"What if by not telling them you'd be risking the cops' safety? Or the patient's?"

My tiredness is making me cranky and I roll my eyes at Crystal and huff out a breath of irritation. "We can sit here all day and make up outlandish hypotheticals that may or may not ever happen. I will deal with each case individually as they occur and use my best professional judgment."

"Well, I have concerns about that," Crystal says. "And I intend to discuss them with Chief Hanson. I think you crossed a line with this Riley case and that may jeopardize the chief's trial of this new program, putting his grant at risk. I'm going to recommend that he replace you immediately."

I'm so stunned by what she has just said that I'm rendered momentarily speechless. And my sluggish brain is starting to comprehend Crystal's motive here. I stare at her in disbelief as she rises from her chair and turns to leave.

"You think they'll give the job to you, don't you?" I say.

Crystal pauses and turns back to me. "They'll need someone to step up quickly, and I'm more than qualified," she says.

"Yet they didn't offer the job to you when you interviewed for it."

Crystal's eyes narrow. "Yes, because I wasn't sleeping with a detective who had Hanson's ear," she says with a snide tone.

"Neither was I," I snap. "Nor am I now."

"Really?" She looks thoughtful for a moment and then smiles at me. It's a mean, predatory smile. "That's too bad for you, I imagine." And before I can get another word out, she's gone.

I sit there, still in shock, replaying what just happened in my mind, and trying to decide what to do. I'm surprised by Crystal's behavior. In the three years I've been working with her, we've always got on well and there has never been any real friction between us. This is a side of her I've never seen.

I decide to call Bob and run the whole thing by him. I punch in his number and he answers by stating my name in a wary, questioning tone.

"Hildy?"

I intend to explain the situation in a calm, professional manner, but my tiredness has removed the shackles I normally keep on my emotions and I blurt it all out in a frantic and rushed mess.

Bob listens, and then tries to calm me. "I wouldn't worry about it too much, Hildy. You have the job and, so far, you've performed in a stellar manner."

"I've only had three shifts," I say. "And Crystal has me over a barrel here. She's my boss at this job, so it's not like I can push her very far. She could fire me."

"Would that be the end of the world?" Bob asks. "It seems to me that you've got a lot on your plate trying to balance both jobs and maybe you should let go of your hospital position and just work for us."

"That's not a very economically secure suggestion," I say. "The job with you guys is a trial. There's no way to know how long it will last, or if it will continue. There isn't a lot of job security there." I sigh, feeling my frustration grow. "I don't know what's gotten into Crystal. This is so unlike her, or at least the her I've come to know. She's always been a rational, reasonable person, easy to work with and for."

"Well, I might have an idea about that," Bob says. "But if I share it with you, I need you to promise to keep it to yourself."

"You know you can trust me," I say without hesitation. Then I ruin it by adding, "Don't you?"

To my relief, Bob chuckles. "Yes, actually I do trust you. So here it is. The judge that I called about the search warrant on the Riley place? There's a rumor going around that he's having an affair with someone, and that someone happens to be Crystal. I'm pretty sure she was with him when I called about the warrant because I heard a female voice in the background while I was on the phone with him."

"Really?" I say, genuinely surprised. "I wonder if that means she's finally moving on from her fixation with Tom Reese."

"Who is Tom Reese?" Bob asks.

"He's Crystal's high school boyfriend. She's been carrying a torch for the guy for twenty-five years. Tom joined the military out of high school and Crystal saw him off thinking that the two of them would be engaged and married within the year. But while Tom was stationed in Germany, he met the true love of his life, married, and stayed there. Crystal didn't take it well and she's been fixated on the guy ever since. She stalks him on social media and knows everything about his life: where he lives, where he works, the name of his wife, the names of his three kids, the names of most of his in-laws, and who some of his best friends are. Crystal has always been convinced that she and Tom are meant to be together, and that it's only a matter of time before he comes to his senses, ditches the "frumpy Frau," and returns home to her."

"This has gone on for twenty-five years?" Bob says in disbelief.

"Yep."

"Sounds like she has a screw loose."

"To be honest, it's the only one. Or so I thought before today. In all other respects, Crystal is a reasonable, normal person. But her fixation with Tom Reese has led to her eschewing any other men in her life, up until now. Maybe she's finally seen the light, though if she's having an affair with a married man, it doesn't sound like she's made a smart choice for moving on."

"Look," Bob says, "I'll have a talk with the chief and see what I can find out. He's out of town right now, and I need to go home and take a nap. I've been up too long. I imagine you have, too."

"I am rather rummy," I admit. "But I've got to finish out my shift here. The last thing I want to do is give Crystal any ammunition."

"Don't let her get to you," Bob says. "Between you and me, Chief Hanson thought she was too bossy when he interviewed her for the position, so I don't think she'll have much of an in there."

"She can be pushy," I admit. "But you know, she has a point. I realized myself over the past four nights that there are going to be some delicate ethical situations that come up if I'm working both jobs. Maybe when you talk to Hanson you can mention to him that I think we need to iron out some guidelines for how to handle things when I run into situations that cause a conflict of interest."

"Will do. He's due back tomorrow, so I'll try to tackle it all with him then. I'll let you know how it goes."

I thank him and then disconnect the call, feeling mildly better about the situation. Then I head down to the ER, determined to hide out there for the rest of my shift in hopes of avoiding Crystal for the rest of the day.

Chapter 27

Fortunately, the rest of the day is busy. It keeps me moving and distracted, which helps me stay awake and keep my mind off the situation with Crystal. When the end of my shift rolls around, I can't leave fast enough. The thought of my bed is an irresistible lure.

When I arrive at home, I give Roscoe a few minutes of attention and then immediately head for my bedroom. I'm so tired I swear I could sleep standing up, but no sooner does my head hit the pillow than my mind starts whirling with thoughts about all the events of the past few days. I toss and turn fitfully for the next three hours. I hear P.J.'s arrival and her leashing Roscoe for a walk, hear their eventual return some time later, and I spend the in-between time pondering my future, questioning my decisions, and worrying about where it's all going to end up. Somewhere around seven,

I give up and get up, figuring I'll try again later when the hour is closer to my normal bedtime.

Feeling gritty from my lack of sleep, I make a pot of coffee. It's never kept me from sleeping before and I hope that's still the case. I need it to get through the next few hours. I pour a cup when it's done, and then get on my computer and start looking at furniture and design options with Bob's house in mind. The coffee table he has is a unique piece that I rather like, so I decide to keep it and try to find items that will work with it. Eventually I settle on a leather sofa and two chairs, some end tables, and lamps. They have a strong masculine feel to them that I think Bob will like, but I find some paint colors, an area rug, and some accessories that I think will soften and lighten things up just enough that it doesn't feel like a total man cave. I think about that large living room window for a few minutes and do some searching for drapery options. Then I get an idea I like much better: country-style slatted shutters.

It's nearly eight-thirty by the time I finish, and I let Roscoe out into the backyard to do his business. He's out there for less than a minute when he starts barking excitedly. There is a neighborhood cat, an orange tabby named Cisco, that likes to drop in for the occasional visit, and Roscoe isn't sure what to make of the creature. Typically, he just barks like crazy while Cisco sits back and stares at him with an air of disdain.

I look out the window, surprised to see Roscoe barking at the door to my utility shed, and no evidence of the cat that I can see, though the sun has set, and the yard is cast in shadow. Could Cisco be shut up in the shed somehow? I try to remember the last time I saw the cat and the last time I had the shed open. It would have been on Wednesday evening when I last mowed the lawn, a task I now see I need to do again. Surely Cisco hasn't been in there since then?

Roscoe's persistent barking makes me think otherwise, so I grab a flashlight and venture out into the backyard toward the shed. I open the door carefully, expecting a crazed and angry cat to come bolting out, but that doesn't happen. Instead, I realize that Roscoe's excitement is because he has completed his find command from last night. Sitting on the floor of my shed is Danny Hildebrand.

For one fleeting moment I'm certain that Danny is dead. He is sitting slumped, chin on chest, against the side wall.

"Oh, Danny," I say, and Roscoe hurries forth, sniffs at his face, and then gives him a lick. With this, Danny's head raises and his eyes open.

"Thank goodness," I say, sighing with relief. "Danny, are you okay?"

He nods and gives me a tentative smile. "I've been waiting for you to come home," he says. "Fell asleep." He punctuates this statement with a huge yawn.

"Are you okay? Can you get up?" I'm hoping he can because the chances of me being able to budge his six-foot-four frame with my five-foot, out-of-shape body are nil.

"I'm fine," he says, and to my relief he gets to his

feet, though he remains stooped to avoid hitting his head on the shed's ceiling.

"Come inside and let me get you some coffee or something."

I lead him into the house, noticing as I do so that he looks glassy-eyed. His hair is a ratty mess, he smells like he could use a shower, and his gait is stumbling. "How long have you been out there?"

"Don't know," he says, blinking slowly.

I steer him to one of the stools at my kitchen island and have him take a seat. "Coffee?" I offer. He nods. "How do you take it?"

He stares at me with that glassy-eyed gaze, brow furrowed, looking as if I just asked him to explain quantum mechanics.

"Cream? Sugar?" I prompt.

Danny doesn't answer. He just stares. I decide to give him black coffee for now and pour a cup, setting it in front of him. He's still staring but no longer at me. Now his eyes are aimed toward empty space, his head cocked to one side as if he's listening to something.

"Danny, why are you here? Why aren't you at home?" He doesn't acknowledge that he heard me; he just sits there staring off into space.

I take out my cell phone, thinking I should call Allie to let her know that Danny is okay and to have her come over and get him. Just as I'm about to punch in the number, Danny finally speaks.

"We need to get it done before sunrise." His expression turns anguished and his hands curl into fists. He starts pounding his fists against his temples. "I know, I know, I know. Don't hurt her. I'll do it." He is staring into space, his eyes unfocused.

"Danny, please, calm down. It's okay. Allie is okay. She's at home and she's worried about you."

"They are wrong. Wrong color, wrong size, wrong taste."

I stare at him, trying to make sense of what he's saying. "Danny, I think we need to get you your medication for today. Why don't we go to the hospital and get you checked out, see if we can get you back on track? Would that be okay?"

"No, it isn't right. But we must do it, or Allie will die." He pauses and takes on a pained expression. "Don't hurt Allie," he whines, and then he starts to sob. My heart breaks a little, but I also feel a surge of anger. That note Allie found must be part of the threats that were made to Danny to get him to cooperate. Who was making the threats? Was it the members of that militia that Bob mentioned?

I realize I'm going to need help, so I switch gears and decide to call Bob Richmond first instead. I'm reluctant to turn Danny in, but he clearly needs help, more help than I can give him here and now. Plus, I need to let the cops know he's been found. If I'm right in my suspicions about Marla, he may need protection.

As Danny sits at the counter, his face buried in his hands, his shoulders heaving with his sobs, I dial Bob's number. It rings four times and then I get his voice mail. Belatedly, I remember that he said he was going home to take a nap earlier. Hopefully he was luckier than I was and has been able to get some sleep.

I listen to Bob's message and then leave my own at the prompt. "Bob, it's Hildy. Danny Hildebrand is here at my house. He's in bad shape mentally. I think he's been here all night and day hiding in my backyard shed. I need to get him to the hospital but I'm not sure I can do it alone. I'll try to get him into my car when I hang up, but I'll probably call an ambulance if I can't." I disconnect the call and stand there a minute, thinking, trying to come up with a plan.

Roscoe, who has been sitting by the back door since we came in, gets up and walks over to Danny. He rests his chin on Danny's thigh, nuzzling him, and with the contact, Danny lifts his tearstained face and looks down at the dog.

"Hey, buddy," Danny says, and he reaches down to stroke Roscoe's head.

"Danny, we need to get you to the hospital," I say, seizing what seems to be a moment of clarity. "How about if Roscoe and I take you there, and then we can get you the medication you need?"

Danny looks at me with bemusement. "They are different now," he says. "The medicine is different. Wrong color. Wrong size. Wrong taste."

"I know you don't like the medications. I get that. But we need to get you something to help you feel better."

"They don't work," he says.

"Then we'll get you something that does work, okay? We'll figure it out."

"Allie," he says, looking miserable. "Where's Allie? I won't go without Allie. Make sure she's safe."

"If Allie comes with you, will you go to the hospital?"

He nods. "I need Allie."

I use my cell phone again, this time to call Allie. She answers on the first ring. "Hello?" There is an anticipatory, anxious note I can hear even in this one word.

"Allie, it's Hildy. I found Danny. He's here at my house. Can you come over and help me get him to the hospital?"

"Oh, thank God!" she says, relief flooding her voice. "I'll come right away. What's your address?"

I give it to her, but as I do it raises a question in my mind. As soon as I've disconnected the call, I go back to Danny. "Danny, how did you know where I live?"

Danny looks at me with that puzzled expression again.

"How did you know how to find my house?"

"Found it at sunrise," he says.

I have no idea what that means, so I let it go for now. "Allie is on her way," I tell him. "She should be here soon." Allie's house is only about eight blocks from mine, and I figure it won't take her more than five minutes to arrive. I just need to keep Danny calm and, if possible, focused in the meantime. "If you don't want the coffee, can I get you something else to drink?"

He looks at the coffee with a stunned expression, as if seeing it for the first time. "This is good," he says, and he wraps his hands around the mug and takes a sip. Roscoe, no longer being petted, drops to his belly beside Danny's stool.

I slide onto the stool next to Danny and gently touch his arm. "Danny, why did you come here? And why were you hiding out in my shed? Is someone threatening you?"

He doesn't answer me. He doesn't even acknowledge that he heard me.

"Danny, can you tell me anything more about Artie? Why were you out there at the farm? Were you working for Artie? Or for someone else?"

He shakes his head adamantly. "No, no, no, no, no!" he says, his voice growing more vociferous with each utterance of the word. He turns and looks at me, his eyes burning with some unknown torture he's feeling on the inside. I fear I've lost him, but then he looks me in the eye and, with sudden clarity, says, "Hildy, I need help."

"Okay, Danny. I'm going to get you some help. And I'll make sure that both you and Allie are safe, okay?"

"They're coming," he says, and the words make the hairs on my arms rise. "You're not safe. Allie isn't safe."

"I'll make sure we're all safe," I assure him, even though I have no idea if that's even possible. Not knowing exactly what the threat is, or if it's even real, makes this whole scene surreal. I decide to call the police station and see if they can have an officer come by, just as insurance. Not only will it provide help in case we need it with Danny, it will give me—and perhaps Danny and Allie—a sense of being safe and protected. I grab my cell phone to make the call but before I can, the doorbell rings.

"That's Allie," I say to Danny. I hurry over and open my door.

"Where is he?" Allie asks anxiously. She spots Danny then and pushes past me, hurrying over to her brother.

"Oh, Danny, I've been so worried." She wraps her arms around his neck and gives him a big hug, tears of relief coursing down her face. "Where the heck have you been?" she asks, a hint of chastisement in her voice.

"I found him in the shed in my backyard," I tell her. "I'm not sure how long he's been out there. He might have been there all night last night and all day today."

Allie releases her hold on her brother and gives me a puzzled look. "Why?"

I shrug. "I don't know how he knew where I lived. But when I found him, he made it clear that he was looking for me."

Allie reaches up and places her hands on either side of her brother's face, turning him to look at her. "Why, Danny?" she asks, staring into his eyes. They look blank. "Why did you come to Hildy? Why didn't you come home?"

He doesn't answer and I'm about to suggest that we try to coax him out to the car and take him to the ER to get checked out when my doorbell rings again. I go to answer it, thinking it might be Bob. But it's not. It's Joel, who's standing there, dressed in scrubs.

"Allie called and said you found Danny," he says. Then he looks past me, sees the two of them seated at the island, and hurries over to them. "I told work I had a family emergency," he says to Allie. He sidles up on the other side of Danny, who is still staring off into space.

Joel reaches over and lays a hand on Danny's arm. "Hey, bro," he says. "Where the heck have you been? You've had us worried to death." Not surprisingly, Danny doesn't answer him.

"I think we need to get Danny to the hospital as soon as possible," I tell them. "He's not right, and I think he needs to be evaluated."

Allie shakes her head, shifting back and forth from one foot to the other. "They'll call the cops and then they'll arrest him," she says, rubbing her brother's back as she does her nervous dance. "Let me take him home."

"I think we should call the police anyway," I tell her. "No one has said anything about arresting him. They'll want to talk to him, though, and make sure he's okay." I'm trying not to let on that I think Danny might be in danger and get across the need for police involvement without spooking Allie or Danny. In the back of my mind I see Crystal's accusing face from earlier today. Was I crossing that line she talked about?

"I want to take him home," Allie says, her voice pleading. "Please, Hildy." She gives me a beseeching look. I stall, unsure what to say next. Then Allie completely derails the conversation with her next question. "Man, I really have to pee. Can I use your bathroom, Hildy?"

That explains the nervous dance, I think. "Of course." I show her where the main floor powder room is and, after giving Danny a kiss on the cheek, she hurries off.

I look at Joel, thinking he might be the voice of reason in all this. I nod my head sideways, indicating that we should step away. He follows me off to a far corner, where I hope we will be out of earshot of Danny. "It's not safe to take him home," I say in a whisper. "You need to make Allie see that he'll be better off with the police."

Joel scoffs at my words. "You don't really believe that, do you?" he says. "Of course, they'll arrest him. They're going to want to know what he had to do with those poisons they were making out at the farm."

"But we don't want Danny to become a fugitive. They're going to talk to him sooner or later and it will look better if he does it sooner and voluntarily." I sigh, looking over at Danny's slumped form sitting at the island. "Though I doubt anyone will be able to get much out of him the way he is now, anyway."

Allie comes out of the bathroom then and joins us in our side conversation. "Do the cops think Danny killed that farmer?"

"I don't think so, Allie," I say honestly. "But they know Danny was somehow involved with what was going on at that farm. He knew things about the man who was murdered that put him out there at some point."

"Just what was going on at that farm?" Allie asks. "I'm so confused. Those people from Homeland Security showed up at the house with a search warrant and took a bunch of Danny's clothes. I tried to ask them what they were looking for, what they suspected, but they wouldn't say a thing."

"I can't go into the details," I say. As soon as I utter the words, a thought springs to mind, a disturbing, unsettling thought.

"Danny had an alibi for the time of the murder, didn't he?" Allie insists. "He was at work. His boss even said the cops came by and checked to verify that he was there."

"He was only there for part of the day," I tell her. "And I believe the timing of the death has changed." I don't want to give her false hope, but I also don't want to give too much away. I'm walking a tight-rope here, and that thought I had a moment ago is making my footing feel more precarious with each passing second.

"It had to look like it happened before sunrise," Danny says, startling us all, and we all move back to the island.

Danny's comment strikes me as odd, and I wonder if he's reiterating something he overheard. "Why?" I ask him.

"For the alibi," Danny says.

Before the sun came up, Danny would have been home in bed or getting up for work. His sister, if she was home, would be his alibi for that hour. I look at Allie. "Did you see Danny on Friday morning before he went to work?"

Allie thinks a moment, and then says, "Yes, I did. I woke him up because I heard his alarm go off at six-thirty, but he didn't get out of bed. That happens sometimes because his meds make him so sleepy."

"And what time did he leave for work?"

She shrugs. "The usual time, I suppose. I was already at work by then." She looks questioningly at Joel.

"That sounds right. I think he left around eight-thirty."

"Have to do it at sunrise," Danny says.

I frown at this. His words don't make sense, unless he's talking about stuff he did at the farm. "Did you have work out at the farm that you had to finish before the sun came up in the morning?" I ask him.

"No sun," Danny says irritably. "At sunrise. Right?" He cocks his head to one side as if listening, as if there is a voice he hears right now.

Joel sighs and says, "This isn't getting us anywhere. I think Hildy is right. He needs to go to the hospital, get his medications changed or something."

"We could take him home and make sure he takes his regular meds first," Allie suggests. "He hasn't taken them today and maybe that's why he's in this state." Clearly, she is desperate to get him home where she can better protect him. I know she doesn't want to face what's coming.

"Yeah, okay," Joel says. He tugs on Danny's arm. "Come on, bro. Want to go home?"

"I really don't think you should take him home," I say. "He's not well. He could be dehydrated and that might be contributing to his current state. He spent hours in my shed out back."

"Did he?" Joel says. He smiles and shakes his head.

"If it hadn't been for Roscoe, he might still be out there. Though I don't know why he came here, or how he knew where I live."

"We found it," Danny says. "Didn't we?" He cocks his head again as if listening to someone. "We found it at sunrise."

His last words mesh with that simmering idea in my brain and something clicks into place.

We found it at sunrise.

My mind scrambles back in time, recalling that Friday night incident that started it all when Danny said he saw the ghost. I replay what Danny did and said, what Allie did and said. What Joel did and said. That was it. Joel! He told us he'd just gotten home and that he worked at Sunrise Nursing Home. They would have my phone number on file there. In fact, they have my address on file, because I am the court-designated guardian for two patients there who don't have any other family to make care decisions for them.

We found it at sunrise.

I try to recall all the other things Danny said about sunrise, and instead of considering it as a time of day, I think of them in terms of the nursing home. Joel is a nurse, someone who knows a lot about medications, someone who presumably has access to a lot of medications. Someone who could mess with Danny's medications if he wanted to. And Joel wears scrubs for his job, scrubs that would make him look like any other staffer at the hospital if he wanted to slip into Marla Riley's room without the cop on duty being any the wiser. And what had Joel said just a few minutes ago about the cops wanting to know what Danny had to do with the poisons they were making out at the farm? Those details were kept under wraps. How did Joel know what was going on out at the farm?

I mentally curse at myself for not calling the police earlier. My gut tells me I need to do it now. When I see how Joel is looking at me, I feel a twinge of fear. I need to do it *now*! I take out my cell phone, hoping I'm wrong, and hoping I have enough time to call for help.

Joel purses his lips and lets out an irritated sigh. "Put it away," he says, looking at me.

"What?" I say, trying to smile, hoping to look innocently confused to give me more time. I swipe at the screen and start to jab at the appropriate icon when the phone is smacked out of my hand. "Hey!" I say, a mix of irritation and confusion. I start to bend down and pick up my phone, but Joel stomps his foot on it. "What are you doing?" I ask, trying not to sound too confrontational. But deep down I know the jig is up.

"Joel?" Allie says, sounding genuinely confused. "What *are* you doing?"

Apparently, Joel's stomp wasn't enough to ruin my phone because it starts to play a ring tone, indicating an incoming call. I glance at the shattered screen and can still see enough of the display to read that the caller is Bob Richmond. Joel sees it, too.

And then he lifts the hem of his scrub top and reaches behind him, pulling something out of the waist of his pants. "Don't answer that," he says, pointing a gun at my face.

Chapter 28

"Joel, what are you doing?" Allie says again, staring incredulously at him.

Danny says, "I'll do the work. Don't hurt Allie."

"Oh, shut up, you moron," Joel grumbles. "You've said far too much already."

"Joel, put that gun down," Allie says, her voice tremulous. "You're scaring me."

"You shut up, too," he snaps. "All of you, on the seats." He waves the gun in the general direction of Danny, indicating that he wants us to sit at the bar. I climb up on the stool on one side of Danny and, Allie, looking both irritated and confused, takes the one on his other side.

Joel glares at me. "You just couldn't mind your own business for one more day, could you? My final payment comes today, and then I would have been out of here and everything could have gone back to normal. But no, you had to go sticking your damned nose into things, trying to get Danny to talk."

"Don't say anything," Danny says. "Or Allie dies."

Allie gapes at Joel. "Are you involved in this thing out at that farm?" she asks.

He doesn't answer her. Instead he starts pacing on the other side of the island, wearing a path on my kitchen floor. Roscoe, who is still at Danny's feet, senses there is something amiss and he whines.

"It's okay, boy," I say. Roscoe thumps his tail a couple of times, but his body language tells me he's still not comfortable with the air in the room. He's not the only one.

"I think it's safe to say that Joel is very involved with the business at the farm," I say to Allie. "Are you a member of a local militia?" I ask him.

Before he can answer, Danny says, "W . . . M . . . C . . . go badgers! M . . . M . . . C . . . go wolverines!"

"Does this have something to do with sports?" Allie asks, still hopelessly confused and befuddled by everything. "What is going on?"

"No sports," Danny says. "Michigan militia corps . . . Wisconsin militia corp. We are brothers." He says this as if he's reciting something he has heard elsewhere.

Things start to click in to place. "They tracked your ISP," I tell Joel. "They thought the email address with WMC in it stood for Wisconsin Manufacturers and Commerce. But it stands for what Danny said, doesn't it? You're part of a militia group."

Joel keeps pacing, his brow furrowed. He shoots me a perturbed look but says nothing.

"What is your group planning to do with all that poison?" I ask Joel. "Are you planning a terrorist event?"

"What poison?" Allie says, clearly confused and frightened.

"We aren't terrorists," Joel snaps. "We believe in personal liberties and the right to choose how we live. We support national sovereignty and a new world order that doesn't include inferiors. We oppose the burden of government control and taxes. They want to limit our rights, take away our guns, take away our right to live the way we want to."

"Yeah, yeah," I say. "Standard white supremacist stuff. I've heard it all before."

"We are not white supremacists," Joel says angrily. "It's a simple fact that some people are inferior to others."

"Well, I imagine your plans are on hold for now, since all of your plants were confiscated and your little lab out there at the farm has been shut down."

A decidedly creepy smile spreads slowly across Joel's face. "You don't seriously think that's the only farm we have, do you?"

"Oh my God," Allie says, staring disbelievingly at Joel. "Who are you? And what the hell is going on?"

Joel looks at her with a mix of pity and disgust. "Sorry, sweetheart, but I needed your brother's talents and your knowledge."

"*My* knowledge," Allie says, sounding confused. "What are you talking about?"

My phone rings again, and Joel's lips thin to a

narrow white line. "You," he says, reaching into his pocket and tossing a set of keys at me. "Drive. We'll take my car. Allie, you ride in front with her. Danny, you're in the back with me. Let's go."

I slide down off my stool and head for the front door. I hear the others following along behind me, but don't look back at them. My mind is scrambling, trying to think of a way to stop this, to alert someone, to get that gun away from Joel. But it's too dangerous. Opening the front door, I see Allie's SUV parked at the curb, and another car, a sedan, that I assume is Joel's. A quick look around doesn't offer any solutions to my dilemma. It's late in the evening and everyone is tucked inside their houses, prepping for the day to come. My closest neighbors other than P.J. and her parents are a young couple who both have jobs entailing evening hours—he's a bartender and she's a waitress—and they'll both be at work. No way do I want to get P.J. involved in this.

Unable to see any reasonable route of escape, I walk around Joel's car and get in behind the wheel. Allie gets in beside me, her color ashen, her expression one of shock. I reach down to find the button to move the driver's seat up to a position appropriate for my height, watching in the rearview mirror as Danny and Joel slide into the back seat.

Once I manage to get the seat where I want it, I stick the key in the ignition and start the engine. "Where to?" I ask Joel.

"The cemetery," he says.

That surprises me, but then I start to think that if he plans to kill us, the cemetery is probably a great place to hide the bodies. I pull out, driving slowly.

Allie, in a weak, ponderous voice, says, "Was everything fake? Was any of it real? Did you plan to marry me?"

Joel says nothing.

"I think it's safe to say he was using you," I tell Allie. "Sorry. He needed your brother's chemistry knowledge and abilities to process the stuff they were making out at the farm."

"You used my brother to process marijuana?" she says, looking over her shoulder at him.

"Oh, it was more than marijuana," I tell her. "They were growing the kind of plants that are used to create poisons, bioterrorism kind of stuff. Things like ricin and strychnine."

"Danny wouldn't do something like that," Allie says. She turns to look at her brother. "You didn't do that, Danny, did you?"

"Do it or we'll kill Allie," Danny says.

Allie turns back to the front and stares out the window, her mouth hanging open. I feel sorry for her. Her world as she knew it has just imploded. Suddenly she whirls around and slaps Joel on the leg, making me duck. "You bastard!" she seethes. "I can't believe you used my brother to do that."

"Back off, bitch!" Joel sneers. I half expect him to shoot her, but thankfully he restrains himself.

"Allie, please," I say.

She seems to sense that it isn't smart to provoke Joel and she turns back to face front, her arms folded over her chest, her lower lip stuck out in petulant anger.

I pull up near the entrance to the cemetery and

park the car in the closest spot, which is only a half block away. I give Joel a questioning glance in the rearview mirror and the coldness I see in his eyes fills me with dread.

"Get out and walk into the cemetery," Joel says. "And remember that I have the gun trained on all of you. One funny move and I shoot Danny in the head."

One thing I'll say for Joel; he's no dummy. He picked the one person that would control the group the best since both Allie and I would do almost anything to protect Danny. Threatening to shoot Allie would give Joel control over Danny, but Danny is an automaton right now, malleable and pliable. And threatening to shoot me risks either Danny or Allie trying something, though Danny's frame of mind is so fuzzy I'm not sure he fully understands what's going on. It's an odd state for him, not a typical schizophrenic presentation. I'm certain now that Joel has been messing with Danny's meds.

We dutifully follow Joel's instructions and walk single file into the cemetery. The lack of any moon makes it hard going as most of the interior of the cemetery is a dark, eerie abyss. Many of the headstones are faintly visible, but after the warmth of the sun heated the ground all day, the cool night air has created a faint cloud of fog hovering just above the ground. The overall effect is spine-chillingly creepy.

"Head over the hill to the back area," Joel says.

I follow the path, which I can barely see between the dark and the fog, walking slowly. My mind is racing, hoping to figure a way out of this. I could scream, but I doubt anyone would hear it, and if they did, who's going to come running into a dark, foggy cemetery at night because of some screaming. To stall for time, I decide to try to get Joel talking. If I survive this night, maybe I can find out some tidbit of information that will prove useful in shutting down the militia group he's involved with, or maybe I can find out the location of their other "farms." Even better, maybe I can find out how they plan to use their cache of poisons.

"You've been changing up Danny's meds, haven't you?" I say to Joel. "He said something earlier about the pills being wrong, and I thought he was complaining about them not being the right medications to handle his symptoms, but it was a lot more than that, wasn't it? You've managed to get him into a highly suggestive state, not so doped up that he can't function because you needed him to be able to do his chemistry stuff, but docile, cooperative, and highly suggestible."

I pause, but there is no comment from Joel, so I decide to add a little praise and ego-stroking to the mix. "Whatever you've been giving him, it has worked extremely well. I'm honestly impressed. He's aware enough to know that he can't say anything that might give the game away, and to know what's at risk if he does. And presumably he has been able to function for you in the lab. Yet he acts like he's really stoned and confused all the time. Was it just marijuana that you used? Or were you smart enough to figure out what drugs you could swap for his regular ones that would give you what you need? I imagine you had access to plenty of drugs there at the Sunrise Nursing Home. That put you in the driver's seat, didn't it? Clever fellow."

A glance at Joel's face reveals the start of a smile at the edges of his mouth, so I continue with the flattery.

"I have to say, you've played your part really well in this, Joel. I imagine a lot of people underestimate you and your intelligence."

"Yes, they do," he says, finally biting at my bait. "A little bit of research, some experimentation, and it was relatively easy to come up with the right mix of drugs for Danny, though it was a close call back a few months ago when you had to stick your nose into things and get Danny hospitalized so his doctor could change his medications. You nearly messed up the whole operation. We should have found a way to put a stop to you back then."

"You've been messing with Danny's medications?" Allie says. She sounds appalled, angry, hurt, and bewildered.

"I've simply made some substitutions," Joel says. "You made it easy when you started using that medication planner box. All I had to do was open the slot for each day and swap the pills you put in there for the ones I needed him to take."

"I can't believe you did this," Allie says, her voice catching in her throat as she fights back tears. "I hate you!"

"Yeah, well, it's all for the greater good. You'll see. In the end the world will be a better place because of our efforts. And you can be proud of the fact that you had a part in it."

Allie gives in to her sobs now, and the sound of them carries over the night air.

"I also came up with the idea of using the cemetery for our exchanges, and thanks to Allie here, it's gone off without a hitch, at least until dufus here claimed he saw a ghost."

"Thanks to me?" Allie says. "How?"

"You know those conversations we've had about the people who are buried in this cemetery who have no family? No one to come and visit their graves?"

"Yes," Allie says, sounding puzzled. "What does that have to do with anything?"

"It's quite easy to give those names to the people who want to pick up the items we made for them and then they can leave cash in return. Since no one goes to those graves, it's a simple matter of disguising the items in vases and memento boxes. Your brother has done an excellent job of handling the exchanges." Joel pauses and sighs wearily. "If only that Fletcher guy hadn't developed a conscience, we'd still be raking in the dough."

I have led our sad little group deep into the cemetery and the back fence is only fifty feet away when Joel says, "Take that path to the left."

I do as I'm told and after a few feet I see something up ahead that makes my gut go cold. There is a large mound covered in green cloth and beside it there is a dark void.

"Stop here," Joel says.

I stop a few feet from the edge of an open grave, one I fear is about to become my own.

Chapter 29

"It's handy to have this here ready to go," Joel says, eyeing the open grave. "I figure I can fit all three of you in there without too much trouble. If I cover you up with a layer of dirt, maybe no one will notice. Then all three of you can spend eternity together with Mrs. Culpeper. I do believe that's whose funeral and burial you told me is scheduled for tomorrow, isn't it dear?" He looks at Allie when he says this, and she fires flaming arrows at him with the look she gives back.

"You're going to shoot all three of us?" I say. "That's going to make a lot of noise. It's bound to attract some attention. There are a lot of homes around this cemetery."

"I suppose it's a good thing I brought the silencer then," Joel says, pulling something from his jacket pocket and screwing it onto the end of the gun he has. "You said it yourself, Hildy. Don't underestimate me."

With the silencer firmly in place, he aims the gun at me, and I brace myself for what's coming. I've run out of ideas at this point, but I grasp at one thought, one I'm not sure is even true, but I saw it on a forensic show on TV once. "You know, the silencer only works on the first shot," I tell him. "After that the shots will be just as loud as if you didn't have the silencer."

Joel frowns at this, his brow furrowed. I can tell he's trying to decide if I'm lying to him. "Tell you what," he says finally. "All three of you can save me some time and trouble by getting down into that hole before I shoot you. It will speed up my get-away and it will help muffle the sound of the shots."

Dang. I hadn't thought of that. My heart is al-ready pounding in my chest and the thought of climbing down into that grave to be shot makes it pound faster and harder. I can see my bosom bouncing with each beat.

"Joel, you don't have to kill anyone," I say, grasp-ing at straws now. "You didn't kill Fletcher, did you?" I'm thoroughly convinced that he did, but I figure if I instill the idea of doubt in him here, it might make him think he can convince others of the same. "The militia will take the fall for Fletcher's death, so why make things more difficult for your-self by killing us now? Just leave. Run while you have the chance."

He appears to be considering this idea for a few seconds and my hopes soar. But then he says, "Right, and what's going to stop you three from running for help the second I'm gone?"

"Put us in that grave," I say. "It's a deep hole and

we won't be able to climb out of it. We'll have to wait until the funeral tomorrow for someone to come along and find us."

Joel looks at me with disgust. "You must think I'm stupid," he sneers. "Danny boy here is well over six feet tall and it would be a piece of cake for him to put one of you on his shoulders so you could climb out of there. Plus, you could all start yelling and that would draw attention the same way the gunshots would."

I was sort of hoping he was stupid enough not to see the solution. Had to try though.

"Although," Joel says with a new ring of hope in his voice that I don't like at all. He is looking over at the mound of dirt. Just beyond it is a shovel and parked down by the back fence is a backhoe. "If I put all three of you in that hole and cover you up with enough of that dirt there, I won't have to fire any shots, and you won't be able to yell."

"You'd bury us alive?" Allie says with horror.

Joel shrugs. "It's all for the greater good." He shifts his attention to Danny. "You get down in the hole first and lie down."

I watch Danny closely, half expecting him to leap at Joel, or try to run . . . anything but what he finally does. He dutifully walks over, steps in between the protective sawhorses surrounding the grave, and then sits down on the edge of it. Just as he's about to push himself down into the hole, he hesitates, his face turned upward.

"He's here," Danny says. "Arthur Fletcher is here and he's mad as hell."

"Oh, shut up with that ghostly gobbledygook,"

Joel snaps. "Get in the—" Joel stops what he's saying and gapes in the same direction as Danny.

When I hear Allie whisper, "Oh my God," I look that way, too. Not far beyond the grave there is a stately old oak tree, its trunk as big around as two Dannys. And materializing from the trunk right before our very eyes is the ghostly figure of an old man. It's thin and wispy to start, though the shape is unmistakable, and over the next few seconds the figure grows more visible, more formed, yet still ephemeral in nature, shape without real substance.

All of us stand mesmerized, staring as the shape grows more solid and then swoops toward us, seeming to fly right over our heads. Joel ducks and lets out a girlish-sounding scream, then he aims his gun at the apparition, pulling the trigger. There is a *phht* sound and then he pulls the trigger again, and again, each one a little louder. The smell of gun smoke fills the air, and I'm afraid Joel's wild firing might hit me, or Allie, or Danny.

"Get down!" I say to Allie and, to my surprise, she runs forward, dodges around the sawhorses, and then jumps into the grave.

The apparition has disappeared, but then a second later it reappears in the tree trunk, once again taking shape and form. Seconds later it starts to swoop toward us, and Joel starts firing again. I run toward the hole after Allie, get to the edge, drop to my butt beside Danny, and slide down the eight-foot wall. For a second, I'm in free fall and then I land with a bone-jarring thud.

I hear bullets whizzing overhead and I grab

Danny's leg and tug as hard as I can. "Get down here!" I tell him. To my surprise, he drops into the grave. We're momentarily safe from the bullets whizzing by overhead, but I realize that now Joel has us right where he wants us.

Then I hear voices, several of them, very human in nature.

"Drop the gun!" I recognize this voice. It's Devo. "Hands over your head," he says next.

"It's the police," I say to Allie, and she squeezes her eyes closed with relief. There is a flurry of activity above with muffled voices and pounding feet. Danny is sitting on the floor of the hole, staring at the dirt wall. I decide to risk a holler to let people know we are down here.

"Hello up there. Can someone help us out of here?"

The first thing I hear is Joel in a high-pitched, girly voice squealing, "What is that? Make him go away!"

There are more muffled sounds and finally a head peeks over the edge of the grave above me. "Hildy, is that you?" Brenda Joiner says.

"It is," I answer. "Me, Allie, and Danny. Can you get us out of here?"

"Yeah, hang on. Let me find a ladder of some sort."

It takes an interminable amount of time for anyone to return and for a moment I fear that we've been forgotten with all the hubbub going on above. Finally, someone comes back with a metal extension ladder that is lowered down into the grave. I let Allie climb up first and then she and I manage to coax Danny into climbing out. I'm the last one up, and when I reach the top, I'm surprised at the number of people there are. In addition to several police officers, there are firemen, and at least three other adults milling about. There are also two teenage boys off to one side chatting with Devo and Bob Richmond.

"We weren't trying to hurt anyone with it," one of the boys says. "We were just looking to have some fun. But when we got here tonight, we heard that guy over there threatening to kill a bunch of people. We called you guys and then used it to try to distract him. It worked," he says with a wicked grin. "I think we scared the crap out of him."

"I'll say," the other boy says with a chuckle. "That dude screamed like crazy."

Brenda has taken Allie and Danny off toward her car, and I approach Bob and the boys. "Hildy, are you okay?" Bob says.

"I am. My ankle is a little sore from dropping down into that grave, but I don't think it's anything serious." I look at the two boys, putting the pieces together. "I take it you two are somehow responsible for the ghost?"

The boys smile sheepishly. "It's not against the law, is it?" one of them asks Devo.

"I don't think we'll find a specific law to address this issue," he says, scratching his head.

"Exactly what is the issue?" I ask.

One of the boys steps aside, revealing a small device that looks like a movie projector. "We're making a movie for a school project. We've been experimenting with this gizmo to try and create a holographic image that appears to be moving through space," he says. "Over there we've suspended a small screen between two trees so that the image that we display on it appears to be coming out of the tree that's behind the screen. We projected one on a headstone, too, and it looked like a ghost coming up from the grave. We have a Halloween CD with several images on it that we can project."

"I've seen something like that at someone's house," I say, recalling the very spooky Henderson house one block over from my house. The Hendersons are known for their love of Halloween and they always go all out on the decorations, sound effects, and such. The kids, and many adults, love it. "Were you two here on Saturday night playing with this?" I ask, realizing with relief that the ghost I thought I saw that night did exist and it meant I wasn't crazy or hallucinating.

The boys look guiltily at Bob. "Yeah, we were," one of them says. "But other people come out here, too. That big guy who just climbed out of the hole over there, we've seen him out here before a couple of times."

Bob looks puzzled by this and I tell him, "I think I can explain that." I roll my eyes toward the boys. "But I best do it in private."

Bob nods his understanding and he tells the boys to go home, take their ghost-making machine with them, and to stay out of the cemetery. Relieved that they aren't in any serious trouble, they gather up their projector and head toward the tree where the ghost image emanated from earlier. I gather they need to take down whatever it was they were using as a screen.

Bob looks at me and smiles. "This isn't your usual shift, is it?"

"No, it isn't. But this is what happens when gun-wielding maniacs show up at your house."

"I think you're going to have to come down to the station and explain some things for me," he says. "I need to question Joel, but there are a lot of holes in this story. Can you help me with that?"

"I think I can fill in most of them for you. Let me go and talk to Allie and Danny first, and make sure they get the care they need."

And just like that, I'm back on duty.

Chapter 30

Late in the afternoon on Wednesday, I leave the hospital and drive over to the police station, where I let myself in through the back door and head for Bob Richmond's office. I'm happy to see that the break room isn't a pig sty already after my cleaning efforts over the weekend, and I hope that maybe the other folks who use this room are taking the hint and doing a better job of keeping it halfway neat.

"Hildy!" Bob says when I enter his office. It's by far the most exuberant greeting I've ever gotten from him and I smile broadly, feeling oddly pleased about it.

"Are we still on for our shopping spree?" I ask him.

"We are. I just need to wrap up this report. Give me two minutes."

I stand by quietly as he types away on his keyboard. He's a two-fingered typist, but he's quite adept and fast at it. When he's done, he saves what he was working on, shuts down the program, and then spins around in his chair to look at me.

"Are you caught up on your sleep finally?" he asks me.

"I think so. I slept for twelve hours straight last night. I'm revved up and raring to go. How about you?"

"I'm a little behind you, but I did get a decent bit of sleep last night, so I'm okay. Can't deny that I'm looking forward to climbing in the sack tonight, though."

As he utters these words, I hear a noise behind us and turn to see Detective Steve Hurley enter the office. "Someone is impatient," he says with a grin. "If you two are that eager, I can back out and return later."

Realizing what his words implied, Bob blushes to the tips of his ears. "No, no," he says, a little too fast. "I was simply referring to sleep." He glances my way and then quickly looks at his feet, his face beaming red.

"So, I hear you are the hero of the day, Hildy," Detective Hurley says. "I heard you nabbed a ringleader involved in a local militia, thwarted a bioterrorism plot, solved two murders, and cleared the name of Danny Hildebrand. Not bad for your first week of work."

Now it's my turn to blush. "I think the militia fellow found me rather than the other way around and I got lucky on the rest of it," I tell him.

"She's minimalizing it," Bob says, looking happy at the change of subject. "She did some stellar work. She and that dog of hers."

"Roscoe is a hero, too," I agree. "What's happening with Joel?"

"The feds have taken over the case, now that all the heavy lifting has been done by us peons," Bob says with a roll of his eyes. "They threatened Joel with the death penalty unless he agreed to talk, and he sang like a bird. He's given up the names of twenty-two other members of the militia group, most of them high-tier operatives. It turns out they were planning a multi-level assault using ricin and the other poisons. They had one plan that targeted several government buildings where they intended to poison the water cooler bottles and the water supplies. The last time I talked to someone at Homeland Security, they weren't sure what the hoped-for outcome was supposed to be, though most of the buildings they had listed as targets do house judges and district attorneys. A different group was going to create ricin bullets and randomly fire them at people who attend anti-gun rallies, creating panic and supposedly proving their favorite pro-gun statement that it isn't guns that kill people, it's people who kill people. And there was a third plan, one that had a much larger scale and longer timeline that involved the mass murdering of several targeted groups primarily represented by people of color." Bob pauses and shakes his head, a look of disgust on his face. "There are some sick and twisted people in this world," he says.

"Yes, there are," I agree.

"How's Danny doing?" he asks.

"Much better. I spent a lot of time with him in the hospital today because Allie couldn't be there.

The feds are questioning her today, trying to get some background info on Joel and how she came to be hooked up with him. Turns out the guy targeted Allie and her brother and came up with the whole plan regarding the cemetery exchanges and the manipulation of Danny. That guy is scary smart.

"As for Danny, now that he's back on his normal meds, he's calm, alert, and talking sensibly. No more hallucinations. Joel was very clever in the way he manipulated things, stealing the drugs he needed from the nursing home and then substituting those pills for the ones that Allie was carefully putting into Danny's medication box each day. As soon as Allie left for work, Joel would make the changes and Danny had no idea. Though he did notice that his pills looked and tasted different. But I think by then his head was too fogged up to get the significance of it. Or maybe he did, and he just checked out, knowing he couldn't do much about it since Joel made it clear that if Danny said anything or didn't do what they asked of him, that Allie would be killed. Joel really did a number on Danny, both mentally and physically, giving him drugs that not only didn't control his schizophrenia, they exacerbated it. And some of them put Danny in a hypnotic-like state that made him highly controllable and suggestible."

Bob nods. "Yeah, the fed I talked to said Joel told them it took some time and experimentation to get the right combination of stuff to make Danny pliable, but still leave him intact enough on a cognitive level to be able to do the stuff they needed him to do in the lab to extract the poisons.

And apparently you got involved a few months ago and messed everything up for them."

"If only I'd known that was what I was doing," I say, shaking my head. "I should have realized something was wrong sooner. The way Danny was behaving, lucid one second and blabbering gibberish the next, that's not the way he's ever presented before."

"Hey, don't beat yourself up over any of this," Detective Hurley says. "From everything I've heard, you did a fantastic job."

"Thanks," I say with a meager smile. I want to glow and bask in his praise but lurking at the back of my thoughts is the knowledge that Crystal seems to be out to get me, or my job. Maybe both. "Those kids at the cemetery deserve some credit, too," I say. "However incidental. It's ironic that the CD they were using had an image on it that bore such a strong resemblance to Arthur Fletcher. That thing had several people wondering if ghosts were real."

Detective Hurley chuckles and then says, "I have to run. Keep up the good work, Hildy."

"Thanks. Say hi to Mattie for me, will you?"

"Will do."

Once he's gone, Bob says, "By the way, before I forget, Brenda wanted me to let you know that the deer you saw in the cemetery the other night made it out okay. She said she knew you were going to worry about it. Apparently, it fell into the same open grave you guys ended up in, though luckily it wasn't injured. The cemetery workers found it in the morning and were able to lift it out and transport it to a safe area."

"Oh, good. I'm glad to hear that." I then ask the first of many questions that have been burning in my mind for the past two days. "Have they figured out yet who killed Arthur Fletcher and why?"

"According to Joel, it was one of the other militia members who administered the strychnine to Arthur earlier in the day. They decided Arthur was too much of a risk because he was starting to balk at what they were doing with the poisonous plants. He was okay with the marijuana and he initially thought the lab they constructed was to extract THC from those plants. When he realized what they were doing with the other plants, he told them he didn't want to play anymore. So, they eliminated him. It took about two hours for him to start seizing after he ingested the strychnine and he died quickly after that."

"That mug of milk in the microwave?" I ask.

"Joel claims he doesn't know how the strychnine was given to Arthur, but he knows who gave it to him and that it kicked in when Arthur was in the kitchen prepping for bed. He started to feel ill, sat down in one of the chairs, and then seized shortly after that, making the chair fall over backward. That explains how they were able to get his stiff body into a sitting position later, and why there was livor mortis on Arthur's back. His muscles seized up while he was still in the chair in a sitting position, but with the chair on its back on the floor."

"And the gunshot?"

"Joel had a front row seat for that part, and he dragged Danny along because he was also starting to have reservations about what was going on.

Danny overheard an argument between Arthur and someone in the militia about Arthur wanting to stop what they were doing, and it bit at Danny's conscience. Joel needed Danny's chemistry expertise and his continued cooperation, so he decided to ramp up the threats he'd been making with a little demonstration, to show Danny how serious things were. Joel propped Arthur up on the kitchen chair—basically just sitting the chair back up. Arthur was already dead, but Danny didn't know that and Joel had him so doped up by then, he didn't know what was real and what wasn't. Joel brought Danny into the kitchen and stood by him, talking into his ear about what they would do to Allie if Danny didn't continue to cooperate. While he was saying this, another militia member put the gun under Arthur's chin and fired. That was to make sure Danny knew they weren't kidding."

I squeeze my eyes closed, imagining the mental and emotional horror of what Danny went through. "That poor guy," I say. "Though ironically, I think that watching them shoot Arthur like that was what did the militia in. It pushed Danny over an edge that left him so mentally unhinged that he became unstable. I think he's going to need some heavy-duty counseling once we get his meds right to be able to cope with what he did and what he saw. Are the feds going to prosecute him for his role in all of this?"

"I doubt it," Bob says. "Based on what they've told me so far, they have the masterminds and they don't feel Danny would be prosecutable given his mental health issues. And while Joel didn't kill

Arthur Fletcher, he did kill Marla Riley. You were right when you guessed that one. The cop who was on duty outside of Marla's room remembers him because he was wearing a surgical cap and mask and he kind of wondered why at the time since Marla wasn't having surgery of any kind. No one else wore that kind of gear into the room, but Joel had a legitimate hospital ID badge, one he stole off someone else's lab coat, so the cop just figured it was something he didn't understand and let him by without a second thought."

"Did he admit to breaking into the Riley home?"

Bob shakes his head. "No, that was likely other members of the militia, but they came away empty-handed because we got there first, thanks to you."

"And what about Danny's laptop? Did that ever turn up?"

"It did. Joel took it and turned it over to the militia when Danny started acting so crazy. He was afraid of what might be on it and didn't want it to fall into the wrong hands."

"I have to give Joel credit for being clever and devious."

"You're lucky he wasn't being more devious that first night out at the farm. It was him you heard running in the barn and, later, driving off. He thought he had time before anyone would find Arthur's body and he was in the process of trying to remove some of the plants when you and Devo showed up. Fortunately for you, he thought if he just took off, no one would find the plants. Unfortunately for him, he left the lights on downstairs and didn't know the glow would show through those floorboards. It's a good thing he decided to run. Otherwise, you might have . . . bought the farm that night."

He looks at me expectantly, his expression like that of a little boy who can't wait for someone to see what he's done. I make a face and groan, making him laugh.

"Sorry, I can never resist a dorky pun," he says.

"I'm just jealous I didn't think of it first," I tell him. Then, on a more sobering note, I say, "Boy, when you think about what this militia group was doing and how close they came to pulling it off, it makes me scared for the future."

"I hear you. You don't expect to find that kind of thing in a small town like ours, but that's why they targeted us. They figured a sleepy little town like Sorenson with its surrounding farms was the perfect hideaway for their project. And targeting farmers was particularly brilliant on their part. So many of them are hurting financially right now and vulnerable to this sort of bribery. And a lot of the farmers are in sync with the anarchist's anti-government beliefs because they feel let down by the government. Who knows how many more of these poison farms there are out there?"

"The farmers feel that way because they *have* been let down by the government," I say. "The future of our farms is very unpredictable these days."

"Speaking of futures, did you talk with Crystal today?"

I shake my head, suppressing a shudder. "No. I spent the day trying to avoid her and it was easy, too easy, though I was able to escape from the hospital for part of the day to do some stuff for Agnes Silver."

"The hoarder lady?" Bob says.

I nod. "She remains a work in progress," I say with a roll of my eyes. "As for Crystal, I think she's prepping to have me fired, but I can't figure out which job she thinks I'm going to lose. I just hope it's not both."

"Well, I can't speak to the hospital job, but I'll share a little insider information with you about this one."

"It won't get you in trouble, will it?" I ask, hoping that even if it will he'll want to tell me anyway.

"And that, right there, is what's going to save you in this job," Bob says with an appreciative smile. "People come first with you and it's obvious that you care. That came through loud and clear during this case and Chief Hanson is aware of it."

"That's all well and good, and it might get me a pat on the shoulder at a cocktail party, but I've heard that Crystal's new paramour, this judge, is eager to try to please her by putting pressure on the chief to replace me with her. And I imagine the chief isn't too keen on ticking off a judge."

"That may have been true initially, but I think Judge McCallister has changed his point of view ever since it was pointed out to him that you were largely responsible for capturing the culprits who had formulated a plan to murder him. You saved his life, Hildy. And I have it on good authority that the chief and the judge hashed this issue out and resolved it in your favor. That outcome might have been helped by a small threat to reveal a certain affair to the judge's wife."

"I'm not sure how I feel about that," I say. "On the one hand, I'm glad for the outcome, but I'm not happy that it's because of blackmail."

"Are you happy that the judge is cheating on his wife? Or that your boss is having an affair with a married man?"

"No," I admit with a frown. "But it seems there are a lot of ethical gray areas here. And a lot of them with my jobs."

Bob nods, looking somber. "I know, and Chief Hanson has agreed to address the issue. In fact, he has invited members of the hospital's ethics committee to a luncheon with him and a rep from the sheriff's department to discuss and formulate some guidelines for you on the matter."

"Really?" I say, surprised and pleased. "I think that will help. And speaking of the sheriff's department, why didn't you tell me that my job was going to include ride-alongs with them?"

"Didn't know it," he says. "The chief opted to keep that little tidbit to himself and then sort of leaked it out." He chuckles. "He had to do it in order to please the decision makers who gave him the grant. To be honest, I think he was afraid you'd back out of the job if he told you up front and he's been committed to you from day one, Hildy. As have some other folks around here. I don't think you'll have to worry about having a job."

"Thanks, Bob. I appreciate that, given that I have a mortgage and a car payment to keep up with. And speaking of money, can we go spend some of yours? I not only have some furniture I want you to look at, I picked out some paint colors for your walls, and some window treatments that will let some sun in but keep nosy people out. I'm excited about it."

"I am, too, oddly enough."

"Why does that surprise you?"

"Because I'm an old fuddy-duddy, stuck in my ways. I'm not one who embraces change most of the time."

"I beg to differ," I tell him with a smile. "Look at the changes you've made with your health and your body. And with your social life. You've made some huge changes recently and you've not only embraced them, you've rocked them."

Bob smiles a bit bashfully. "Were you ever a cheerleader, Hildy? Because you certainly are good at boosting people's spirits."

"A cheerleader?" I scoff. "Lord, no. I was one of the bad girls hanging out behind the bleachers smoking cigarettes and making fun of the cheer-leaders."

Bob gives me a crooked smile. "I kind of wish I'd known you back then."

"No, you don't," I scoff, eyes wide. "Trust me. I was a hellion. But you know me now and that's something, isn't it?"

"I don't know that I do know you yet," he says with a curious look. "Something tells me I've only scratched the surface with you and there are more delights to be found."

"You do flatter me," I say with an aw-shucks wave

of my hand. "And I think you need to dig below the surface. What do you say you try to peel away another layer tonight?" I wiggle my eyebrows suggestively.

Bob blushes and doesn't answer. But he gets out of his chair, offers me his arm, and leads me on to our next adventure.

Acknowledgments

So many people are involved in the writing of my books. There are the friends, coworkers, and fellow writers who brainstorm with me and let me steal their witty bon mots; family members who provide love, support, and understanding when I beg off of social engagements because I need to write; and the endless parade of humanity I observe on a daily basis, always taking mental notes and stealing traits, characteristics, and bits of dialogue from them like a vampire.

There is my agent, Adam Chromy, who believes in me more than I believe in myself at times. And there are all the folks at Kensington Books whose hard work goes into making my books a success. It is a pleasure and an honor to work with all of you. Thank you.

Of course, the most important people are the readers. Without you, none of this would be possible. So thank you from the bottom of my heart and happy reading!

Did you miss the first book in the Helping Hands Mystery Series? No worries! Here's a sample excerpt from NEEDLED TO DEATH. Keep reading to share the excitement.

Chapter One

I can still see the shadows of death on some of their faces, evident in the droop of their eyes, the taut, thin line of their lips, and the pale, pasty coloring of their skin from spending too much time indoors hiding away from society and life. It's evident, too, in the tentative and wary way they walk, their shoulders hunched over defensively, as if they're expecting another grievous blow to descend upon them at any second.

Some people wear their cloak of grief for a long time. Others shrug it off in good time and good order, eager and able to get on with their lives, even if it's only a few small steps at a time. The people who are with me tonight tend more toward the former group, and it's my job to try to help them become members of the latter group.

I'm about to start the session when a new face enters the room—a woman who looks to be in her mid-to-late forties—and I'm tempted to clap my hands with delight. This would be both inappropriate and unprofessional, so I quickly rein in the impulse and focus on forming a smile that looks warm and welcoming, and hopefully doesn't show the excitement I feel. I hurry over to her, aware of the curious stares coming from the others in the room.

"Hello," I say. "Are you here for the bereavement group?" The question is rhetorical, since this woman is wearing her mantle of grief like a heavy shawl. Her face is expressionless, her shoulders are slumped, and her movements are sluggish and zombielike. She looks down at me—nearly everyone I meet looks down at me in the strictly physical sense, since I'm barely five feet tall—and nods mechanically.

"Well, welcome," I tell her, touching her arm with my hand. "I'm Hildy Schneider. I'm a social worker here at the hospital, and I run this group."

She nods again but says nothing. I suspect her loss is a recent one, very recent. *Who was it?* I wonder. Based on her age, a parent is a good guess if one assumes the natural order of things. But I've learned that death doesn't care much for order.

"What's your name?" I ask, hoping to ease her out of the frozen, deer-in-the-headlights stance she currently has. She looks at me, but I get a strong sense that she doesn't see me. I've encountered this before and suspect she's mentally viewing some memory reel as it plays repeatedly. I tighten my touch on her arm slightly, hoping the physical connection will ground her. It does.

She blinks several times, flashes an awkward, pained attempt at a smile, and says, "Sorry. I'm

Sharon Cochran." Her voice is mechanical, rote, with no lilt or feeling behind it.

"I'm glad you're here, Sharon," I say. "Can I get you something to drink? A water, or some coffee?"

She looks at me with brown eyes that are stone-cold and dull, and then shakes her head.

"There are some cookies, too," I say. "Can I get you one?"

Again, she shakes her head, her gaze drifting away from mine. The others in the room have lowered the tenor of their conversations to soft, whispered murmurs, no doubt so the newcomer won't hear them talking about her.

"Sharon?" I say firmly, wanting to bring her attention back to me. "Have you ever been to a support group before?"

"No."

"Okay. Let me give you a brief overview of how the group works. We meet every week on Thursday evenings unless there is a holiday that falls on that day. In that case, we often meet the evening before. Attendance is totally voluntary. Come as little or as often as you want and come as many times and for as long as you want. Typically, I pick a topic for us to focus on each week, and I talk a little about that topic before opening things up to the group." She is looking down at the purse she is clutching, fidgeting with its clasp, making it hard for me to tell if she's hearing me or not. I continue anyway.

"The members of the group have the option of discussing something relative to their individual grief issues and experiences, and if it happens to be related to the topic at hand, that's great. But it doesn't have to be. Anyone who wants to talk may do so, but there is also no obligation to do so. The others who are here tonight have all been coming for some time, and they do plenty of talking. You might feel like an outsider because of that, but I promise you that if you commit the time and effort to attending several sessions, that will dissipate. It's a very friendly and supportive group of people, and all of them share one thing in common with you. They've all lost someone close to them."

She looks at me then, and I see the first spark of life in those mud brown eyes. "How?" she asks.

I'm confused by the question. "How what?"

"How did the others die?"

"Oh. Well, there's a mix. And rather than my trying to give you any background on the others, I think it will work better if you let them tell you their stories." I again ponder who it is Sharon has lost. Maybe it was a spouse?

"Any suicides?" she asks. Her eyes are scanning the others in the room.

"Yes," I say. "Did you lose someone to suicide?"

She nods slowly, frowning and surveying the other attendees.

"There is someone here who lost her husband to suicide," I say. "She hasn't had anyone else who shares her situation up until now. I can introduce you to her, if you like."

"No." Flat, dead, robotic. "What about homicide?" she says, eyes still roving, though I get the sense that she isn't focusing on anything or anyone.

"What about it?" I reply, unsure where she's going.

"Has anyone here lost someone to murder?"

"No." Something in the back of my brain connects with something in my gut, and instinct makes me qualify my answer. "Well, none of the group members have lost anyone to murder," I clarify, "but I have. My mother was murdered when I was little."

I see a spark of interest soften her face, and she looks me in the eye for the first time. "Did they catch who did it?" she asks, which strikes me as an odd thing to ask before expressing some token condolence or inquiring about the circumstances. Though most people merely make an awkward attempt at changing the subject whenever I bring it up.

"No, they never did," I tell her, feeling a familiar ache at the thought. I glance at the clock on the wall and see that it reads two minutes past seven. "I need to get things started," I say. "But I'd like to talk with you some more after the group ends, if you can stay for a bit."

"Sure," she says, and she gifts me with a tentative smile.

I give her shoulder a reassuring squeeze and then address the room at large, speaking loudly. "Okay, everyone, let's get started."

This command is typically followed by one last dash to the snack table to get another cookie, or to top off a cup of coffee. Generally, I allow a minute or so for people to heed my request, and then I start regardless of what's going on or who might be still hovering over the cookies. Tonight, however, the presence of a newcomer has intrigued everyone enough that things get changed up. The music of the various conversations stops as if on cue and everyone quickly claims a seat as if we are playing a game of musical chairs. I suspect they are eager to rubberneck on someone else's misery for a change.

The dynamics always change when someone new joins a group. Most of the time it's a good thing, if knowing that someone is struggling with grief can ever be considered a good thing. I've been spearheading this group for nearly two years now, and its composition and size has ebbed and flowed, fluctuating with some regularity. This is good because when all the players stay the same, things can get stagnant. A little fresh blood always invigorates the group.

I've had people who came only once, some who came for a handful of sessions, and two regulars who have been here since the group's inception. The average stay is about ten to twelve weeks for most. Some come alone, others with friends or relatives. The size of the group varies, too, having reached twenty-two people at its peak, though for the past two months it's been a core group of nine. We are in Wisconsin, so in the winter months the weather sometimes forces cancellations or keeps the group smaller. Now that it's springtime, I've been hoping the group would see some new blood.

I always arrange the chairs in a circle, and while this configuration is designed to create a feeling of community and equality, people tend to form smaller niches within the larger circle, mini groups where they feel the most comfortable.

My two die-hard attendees (though I should probably try to come up with a less offensive descriptor, under the circumstances), the ones who

have been coming since I started the group, are
Charlie Matheson and Betty Cronk.

Charlie is in his fifties, a widower, with a full
head of gray hair that typically stands like a rooster
comb by the end of a session, thanks to his habit of
running his hands through it. Charlie works here
at the hospital in the maintenance department and
fancies himself as some sort of soothsayer or prog-
nosticator. He swears he can "read" people and
predict their futures after chatting with them for a
few minutes. While I don't deny that the man has
accurately predicted the behaviors of some of the
group members in the past, it has less to do with
any special powers he has than it does his ability to
recognize when he has annoyed someone to the
point of action. It didn't take a wizard to figure out
that Hailey Crane, a teenager who came to the
group with her mother when her father died, would
decide to leave the group after one session as
Charlie predicted. The fact that, despite my attempts
to rein him in, Charlie badgered the girl a couple
of times to "open up" and "express yourself " when
she clearly didn't want to be there helped with that
prediction.

I had a stern talk with Charlie after that, and
I've had to do so on other occasions as well, since
his actions often necessitate a cease-and-desist warning. If I let him, Charlie would take over the group.
I've come to realize that he sees himself as my assistant, a coleader or facilitator of sorts, a percep-
tion I try hard to extinguish every week. I should
probably ban him from the group, but he has a
reputation around the hospital of being some-

thing of a tattletale. Whenever someone does something he doesn't like, he's quick to run to the human resources department and file a complaint. He knows how to play the system and isn't afraid to do so.

Since I can't steer clear of Charlie, I do my best to control him instead. I don't want to be on Charlie's bad side, so I struggle to balance my occasional desire to kill or maim him with my best professional façade. I don't have the luxury of picking and choosing my clients or patients in this hospital setting, and it's a simple fact of my professional life that I won't like some of them, and some of them won't like me.

Betty, my other long-term attendee, is a widow in her fifties, a stern, hard woman with a sharp-edged face, a tall, lean body, and a no-nonsense attitude. She wears her hair in a tight bun and dresses in drab, sack-like dresses, holey cardigans, heavy stockings, and utilitarian shoes. Betty's husband, Ned, was a quintessential Caspar Milquetoast kind of guy who not only let his wife lead him around by the nose, but seemed to like it. Theirs was a match made in heaven, but when heaven came calling for Ned, Betty found she didn't know what to do with her bossy personality. She and Ned never had any children. Just as well, I think, as I imagine little Bettys running around like creepy Addams Family Wednesdays—and not surprisingly, Betty doesn't have many friends. She came to the grief group because she felt befuddled and confused, a rudderless ship adrift on a foreign sea. And she found the perfect home for her acerbic style.

Unfortunately for me, her style is often at odds

with what my group is about, and like Charlie, she can be a disruptive influence. The two of them keep me on my toes, I'll give them that. Tonight, with a newcomer in the mix, I know I will need to be extra vigilant and stay on top of them both lest things get out of control. They're like sharks smelling fresh blood in the water.

Charlie and Betty don't like each other, and they often seat themselves on either side of me—a subtle way, I suspect, of declaring their perceived leadership status. This works in my favor, however, because it's much easier to shut them up if they are within a hand's reach.

Charlie swears I once pinched him hard enough to leave a bruise on his thigh, a mark he offered to show me after everyone else had left for the night.

"Charlie, that would be completely inappropriate!" I chastised as he started to undo his pants.

He paused in undoing his belt and blinked at me several times. Then he smiled and refastened the belt. "Yes, I suppose it would be," he said with a shrug and a smile.

After that incident, I kept expecting a call from human resources, but it never came. Charlie was on his best behavior for a few weeks, though Betty stepped in to make sure my duties as group leader remained challenging. While she tends to ignore the women in the group, she has this seemingly uncontrollable need to harangue the men who come, muttering comments like "Man up, you big sissy" or "Warning, man cry ahead."

Betty would have made a great drill sergeant.

I steer Sharon to a chair and then settle in beside her, earning myself angry stares from both

Betty and Charlie, who are seated in their usual places. I tend to sit in the same seat each week, and clearly neither of them anticipated me doing anything different tonight, since they are situated on either side of that chair. I resist the urge to smile, because I have to admit, I enjoy rattling them a bit. It's good not to let them get too complacent.

"Welcome to this week's meeting of our bereavement support group," I begin. "I want to start by reviewing the ground rules first, both as a refresher for those of you who have been here before and to inform our new visitor."

Predictably, most of those who have been coming for a while roll their eyes or shift impatiently in their seats. But reciting the ground rules is a must.

"First and foremost, remember that anything said in this room is confidential and is not to be discussed or relayed to anyone outside of the group. Remember that we are here to share experiences, not advice. Be respectful and sensitive to one another by silencing your cell phones, avoiding side conversations, and listening to others without passing judgment. And finally, try to refrain from using offensive language."

I pause and scan the faces in the group. "Any questions about the rules?"

I'm answered with a sea of shaking heads and murmured declinations.

"Okay then. Since we have someone new here tonight, let's start by going around the group and stating your name and who it is you've lost." I turn and smile at Sharon Cochran. "Sharon, would you like to start?"

I'm pleased when she nods, even though it's an almost spastic motion. My pleasure then dissipates as she completely derails the evening's agenda.

"My name is Sharon Cochran, and I'm here because the cops think my son took his own life two weeks ago. But I know he was murdered and I'm hoping you can help me find his killer."

Connect with U(s)

Visit us online at
KensingtonBooks.com
to read more from your favorite authors, see books
by series, view reading group guides, and more.

Join us on social media

for sneak peeks, chances to win books and prize packs,
and to share your thoughts with other readers.

facebook.com/kensingtonpublishing
twitter.com/kensingtonbooks

Tell us what you think!

To share your thoughts, submit a review,
or sign up for our eNewsletters, please visit:
KensingtonBooks.com/TellUs.